Serpent Visions

Serpent Visions

Jinny Webber

BlueTide
BOOKS

BlueTide
BOOKS

CONTENTS

Glossary of Characters

Divinities in Myth and Literature

Ananke: goddess of Necessity whose net enmeshes humanity. Mother of the Fates. The only shrine to her worship was on the Acrocorinth.

Aphrodite: beautiful laughing goddess of love, bounty, fertility, and joy. Born of the seafoam off the coast of Cyprus near Paphos. Another tradition has her the daughter of Dione and Zeus, born on Cythera. Wife to Hephaestus, paramour of Ares, who fathers her daughter Harmonia. According to some sources, the mother of Eros. (In others, he predates her.) Lover of mortals Adonis, Butes, and later, Anchises.

Apollo: god of prophecy, music, archery, healing, and sometimes, the sun. Twin brother of Artemis, born of Leto and Zeus. Kills the Python, a serpent of the deep, and so takes over the oracular shrine at Delphi, originally belonging to Gaia, the Great Mother. Apollo pursues the nymph Daphne and other maidens.

Ares: god of war; son of Zeus and Hera. Paramour of Aphrodite and father of her daughter Harmonia, as well as of Deimus [Fear] and Phobus [Panic].

Artemis: virgin goddess of the waxing moon; lady of wild animals, the hunt, and childbirth. Born before her twin, Apollo, she matures immediately in order to help her mother deliver him. Like Apollo, known for skill in archery.

Asclepius: god of healing: born of Apollo and the mortal Coronis. The healing shrine of Epidaurus dedicated to him; previously to the Great Mother and Apollo.

Athena: goddess of wisdom; born full-grown from Zeus' head according to Olympian religion where she's a virgin who favors all things male.

Baubo: trickster; exposes her vulva to Demeter when she's grieving her daughter Persephone, which makes the goddess laugh. Also called Iambe.

Bia: goddess of force. Shares the shrine of Ananke on the slopes of the Acrocorinth.

Circe: goddess and sorceress dwelling on Aiaia island. Daughter of Hecate and Helios. An early sun-goddess.

Delphyne: serpent mate and brother of the Python, sacred to the Great Mother. Though Apollo slew Python, Delphyne still coils beneath the omphalos, navel stone of the earth at the oracular shrine of Delphi.

Demeter: goddess of fertility and harvest; ancient mother goddess. Mother of Kore [Maiden], who's called Persephone after Hades abducts her. Her sacred Mysteries at Eleusis concern death and rebirth.

Dionysus: god of wine and ecstasy. Son of Zeus and the mortal Semele.

Eileithyia: goddess of childbirth, daughter of Hera.

The Erinyes or **Furies:** agents of justice of the Mother, especially in crimes against kin and hospitality. Named **Alecto, Tisiphone,** and **Megaera.**

The Fates or **Morae:** Three spinning sisters who allot mortals' portion in life and determine their death:

Clotho, **Lachesis**, and **Atropos**, who cuts the thread of life.

Eros: son of Aphrodite and a love god in his own right.

Gaia or Ge: Mother Earth, generally called the Mother or the Great One in this story. Original holder of the oracular shrine of Delphi; went deep underground, embodied in her serpent Delphyne.

Hades: brother of Zeus and king of the underworld, also called Hades. Abducts Persephone when she is gathering flowers and makes her his queen, though she remains with him only a third of the year before returning to sunny earth to assuage the grief of her mother Demeter.

Hecate: a Titan, allowed by Zeus to keep her share of the triple realms of earth, sky, and underworld. Goddess of the waning moon and sorcery. Presides where the three roads meet, stirring her cauldron.

Helios: god of the sun.

Hephaestus: god of fire and artisans, the lame smith. Husband of Aphrodite. Son of Hera.

Hera: queen of the gods; wife of Zeus and patron of marriage in Homer and after. Her shrine in Argos suggests that she, like other goddesses of the pantheon (Aphrodite, Artemis, Athena, Demeter, Hecate, Hestia, and Themis) was a powerful independent goddess in earlier times, a fertility goddess and daughter of the Great Mother. Argos is her favored city and Thebes, like Troy later, she detests.

Hermes: messenger god between Olympus and earth. Trickster and god of thieves and travelers.

Hestia: goddess of the hearth. Eldest sister of Zeus in Olympian religion who gives up her seat on Olympus in favor of Dionysus; remains virgin, worshiped at every hearth. Honored with the first drops of wine poured as libations.

Iambe: early name of **Baubo**. Brings laughter to Demeter, grieving over the loss of her daughter Persephone. Her ribald joking represents the energy of female sexuality and fecundity; her limp gives the lilt to the iambic meter.

Leto: Titan, mother of Artemis and Apollo by Zeus.

Metis: Titan whose name means wisdom. When pregnant by Zeus, her child is prophesied to become greater than its father, so Zeus swallows her. The infant is Athena, who springs full grown from Zeus' head at term. This myth is further evidence of the father-god religion subsuming goddess power and taking unto himself the power of giving birth, as he does with Dionysus.

Persephone: daughter of Demeter, whose ravishment by Hades throws her mother into such deep sorrow that she makes earth barren. Zeus decrees she can return to her mother if she's eaten nothing in the Underworld. Tricked into eating a pomegranate seed, Persephone may remain above ground only part of the year, returning to Hades to reign as Queen of the Dead for the remaining time.

Poseidon: brother of Zeus, god of the sea and earthquakes.

Python or **Pytho:** the serpent Apollo slays to capture Delphi as his oracle. Mate and brother of Delphyne.

Snake Goddess or Snake Mother: Mother goddess worshiped in ancient Crete. Minoan religion influenced the later Mycenaean.

Selene: goddess of the moon in its fullness.

Sphinx: monster daughter of Echidne, with the body of a lion, a serpent tail, eagle wings, and the breasts and face of a beautiful woman. Sent to Thebes as a curse by Hera because of Laius' abduction of the boy Chrysippus.

Zeus: ruler of the gods on Mount Olympus who supplants his father the Titan Cronos. Married to Hera and has a predilection for raping Titans and mortal women.

II. Mortals in Myth and Literature

Adonis: beautiful youth beloved of Aphrodite and killed by a wild boar. Anemones (or cyclamen) spring from his blood. Each spring he returns to the goddess for a week of loving. Their festival of joy and mourning is celebrated every spring, especially in Cyprus.

Adrastus: King of Argos, who marries his two daughters to foreigners who come to him for help in regaining their thrones: Polyneices of Thebes and Tydeus of Calydon. They organize an attack on Thebes which only Adrastus, of the seven captains, survives. His son Prince Aigialeos joins the Argive Epigoni in their revenge war against Thebes. Of the victorious Argive captains, only his son Aigialeos is slain. Adrastus dies of grief.

Alkmeon: son of Amphiaraus, who leads the Argive Epigoni in their revenge attack on Thebes in which all their fathers except Adrastus were killed.

Amphiaraus: seer beloved of Zeus and Apollo. Advises against the first war against Thebes, prophesying that only Adrastus will survive, but is forced to serve as one of its seven captains. Rather than dying in battle, he and his chariot are swallowed up by Earth.

Antigone: daughter of Oedipus and Jocasta who guides her father (and half-brother) Oedipus in his blindness. Against Creon's decree, she buries brother Polyneices after he's killed when leading the assault on Thebes, and is sentenced to death.

Ariadne: Cretan princess, daughter of King Minos who helps Theseus escape the labyrinth of the Minotaur and elopes with him to Naxos. When Theseus abandons her there (this novel offers two alternative explanations), the god Dionysus comes to her rescue.

Bellerophon: a hero who achieves many great deeds with the aid of the gods, including being given the winged horse Pegasus. The hoof of Pegasus strikes a rock on the Acrocorinth, bringing forth the eternal spring Peirene.

Biton: pious son of a priestess of Hera (in this novel called Polydora, as her name is not recorded); brother of Cleobis. Large archaic statues of the brothers stand at Delphi today.

Cadmus: founder of ancient Thebes, called Cadmeia, on the site prophesied by the oracle where a white heifer he has been following collapses in exhaustion. He kills a serpent (or dragon) of Ares and, as instructed, casts its teeth behind him in a tilled field. They spring to life as full-grown soldiers and battle each other until only five remain: the Sparti, or Sown Men, who become his faithful followers. Marries Harmonia, daughter of Aphrodite and Ares, whose wedding feast is attended by the gods. Famous for bringing the Phoenician alphabet to Greece.

Chyrisippus: son of King Pelops abducted by their houseguest, Prince Laius of Thebes, who teaches the boy the art of the chariot. After Laius sneaks him into his bed, Chrysippus dies in a riding accident—or by his own hand. Laius' violation of the youth arouses the wrath of Hera, who punishes Thebes by sending the Sphinx.

Cleobis: brother of Biton.

Creon: brother of Jocasta,. Rules as regent until Eteocles comes of age. Sentences Antigone to a traitor's death for burying her brother, Polyneices, after the war where he and his brother kill each other.

Daphne: dryad of the woods, turned into the laurel to escape Apollo, who is pursuing her. Also the name of Teiresias' daughter who becomes Pythia at Delphi. The idea that Manto and Historis are fathered by Teiresias and Daphne mothered by Teira is original in this story, but nothing in mythology contradicts it.

Epigoni: 'the born later', referring to the sons of the Theban and Argive captains in the war of the Seven. Eteocles' son Laodamas leads the Thebans; Alkmeon, son of Amphiaraus, leads the Argives, and Thersander, son of Polyneices, is also one of the captains. Of the Argives, only Adrastus' son Aigialeos is killed, as only his father survived the first war. After Thebans flee, the Epigoni raze their city.

Eteocles: son of Oedipus who rules Thebes when he comes of age. At the end of the year, when he is supposed to relinquish rule to his brother Polyneices, he refuses. Polyneices raises an army with seven captains, where the brothers, cursed by their father Oedipus, kill each other.

Haimon: last surviving son of Creon and Eurydice, betrothed to Antigone. When he cannot `convince his father to reverse Antigone's death sentence, Haimon goes to the cavern where she's been entombed alive. Discovering that she has hung herself, he threatens his father, then kills himself.

Harmonia: daughter of Aphrodite and Ares. The necklace Aphrodite gives her as a wedding gift when she marries Cadmus brings a curse to all future recipients, beginning with her daughter Semele. At the end of their long life together, she and Cadmus are turned into serpents.

Historis: daughter of Teiresias. Midwife who delivers the infant Heracles onto a shield.

Ismene: daughter of Oedipus, who fears joining her sister Antigone in burying Polyneices.

Jocasta: wife of Laius, King of Thebes, and mother of Oedipus who Laius exposes on Mount Cithairon as an infant because he's prophesied to kill his father. After Laius' death, she marries the man who solved the riddle of the Sphinx and saved Thebes. After they have four children together, she learns that her husband is her son Oedipus. In Sophocles' play, Jocasta kills herself when she realizes Oedipus' identity. In Euripides' *Phoenician Women*, she survives to try to reconcile her warring sons.

Labdacus: king of Thebes and father of Laius.

Laius: king of Thebes. Warned not to father a son because he will one day kill him. Dies at the hand of a stranger many years later where three roads meet.

Laodamas: son of Eteocles. Inherits the Theban crown when he comes of age. Killed in the battle of the Epigoni, where he's the Theban leader. His troops flee, leaving their city to be torched by their Argive enemies.

Manto: daughter of Teiresias and prophet in her own right. After her father's death, serves as a Pythia in Delphi. Marries King Rhacius and goes with him to Halcarnassus and founds the oracle of Claros, where her son Mopsus also serves as seer. Credited with inventing the epic poem, *The Thebiad.*

Menoeceus: two members of Creon's family have this name, the father of Creon and Jocasta, who throws himself from the high wall of Thebes in hopes of appeasing the Sphinx, and Creon's son, who does the same hoping to save Thebes from destruction by the Seven.

Merope: queen of Corinth. Childless in her marriage to King Polybus, they raise as their own a child found on Mount Cithairon with his ankles thonged together. Associated with the moon.

Oedipus: 'swollen-footed' child of chance adopted by King Polybus and Queen Merope of Corinth. According to the tradition Sophocles adheres to, Oedipus is cursed by Apollo and unknowingly fulfills the prophecy that he will kill his father and marry his mother. Unaware of his true parentage, he flees Corinth. As his reward for solving the riddle of the Sphinx, he marries the widowed queen Jocasta. They rule many happy years, until the plague comes and truth must out. A man he killed years before was his father King Laius. Oedipus blinds himself at the discovery. Like many stories, this one has other possible derivations and interpretations such as the ancient 'year king.'

Pandora: in Hesiod, the bringer of evils to humanity, with the one (possible) saving gift of hope. Earlier stories portray her as the bountiful one who brings gifts of domestic agriculture, community, and the art of pottery to humanity.

Polybus: King of Corinth, adoptive father of Oedipus. Descended from Sisyphus.

Polyneices: son of Oedipus and Jocasta, whose name means 'full of enmity'. When his brother Eteocles refuses to yield the throne to him in turn, he brings troops. In the war, the Seven Against Thebes, he and Eteocles kill each other. As he's the rebel, Creon forbids his burial, which precipitates the tragedy of Antigone.

Pythia: the sibyl at the oracle of Delphi, named for the Python Apollo slew. Stories vary, whether the sybil is one or several, young or old, intoxicated or otherwise entranced, speaks from her tripod in a cave or from the Sibyl's Rock. In time, a priest of Apollo translated her oracles.

Semele: daughter of Cadmus and Harmonia who Zeus falls in love with. When he agrees to do whatever she wishes to prove his love, she, asks that he reveal himself in his full glory. His heat and lightening of are too much for a mortal to bear, and Semele is destroyed. The son she carries, Dionysus, is saved by Hermes, who sews him into Zeus' thigh to finish gestation.

Sisyphus: ancient King of Corinth, some say its founder, descended from the sun god Helios. Known for his trickery which he practices even on the gods, making him one of the three shades punished in Hades.

Teiresias: advisor to King Labdacus and father of two tiny daughters, walks deep into the woods, sees two serpents mating, strikes his staff between them and is transformed into a woman. After seven years as Teira, strikes apart coupling serpents and becomes male again. Blinded by Hera for saying woman enjoys sex more than man, Zeus gives him the compensating gift of prophecy.

Ancient Greece
Aegean Sea
Mt. Ath[os]
Mt. Pelion
Iolcus
Ithaca
Mt. Parnassus
Delphi
Mt. Helicon
Thebes
Gulf of Corinth
Mt. Cithaeron
Eleusis
Elis
Corinth
Athens
Mt. Hymettos
Mt. Cyllene
Saronic Sea
Olympia
Mycenae
Argos
Epidauros
Tiryns
Nauplion
Troezen
Ionian Sea
Mt. Taygetos
Sparta
Pylos
Cythera
Cretan Sea
Miles
0
50
100
Crete

Part I: Grace Unveiled

My mind leads me to speak now of forms changed
into new bodies: O gods above, inspire
this undertaking (which you've changed so well)
and guide my poem in its epic sweep
from the world's beginning to the present day.
    Proem to Book I, Ovid's *Metamorphoses*,
        translated by Charles Martin

Everything changes and nothing can die, for the spirit
wanders wherever it wishes to, now here, now there
living in whatever body it chooses . . .
Nothing persists without changing its outward appearance
for Nature is always engaged in acts of renewal,
creating new forms everywhere out of old ones;
nothing in all of the cosmos can perish, believe me,
but takes on a different shape.
    Book XV, Teachings of Pythagoras,
        Ovid's *Metamorphoses*
            translated by Charles Martin

Unveil your grace before my eyes
    Sappho

Chapter One: Manto

Seven-gated Thebes emerges from a yellowish haze like a mirage. I can easily imagine it a cursed place. Not that I thought so as a girl, dwelling at the shrine of Artemis and roaming the woodlands, but from our wagon they are no more than a green blur.

A sense of adventure helped me ignore the rutted road from Eleusis. I knew the soothsayer Teiresias would answer my question. But now, exhausted, I wonder why I came. Eleusis was peaceful, and I was privileged to serve as Demeter's priestess there, guiding initiates through her Mysteries year after year. True, I had an ominous dream and heard the goddess speak to me from her well, but did I really need to leave? No priestess ever does, not for good.

I close my eyes, lulled by the rhythmic clip-clopping of the donkey under Alexios' guiding hands. *You were called, called, called*, they echo. *Destiny beckons.* When I open my eyes we're close to the city wall, with shacks of the old and poor scattered along its length.

A youth steps into the road and snatches the reins. His head is large under a fringe of black hair and his expression blank. Will he abscond with our donkey? I grab Alexios' arm.

The odd-looking lad leads us toward a cottage more tidy than most and hobbles the donkey in a patch of shade. An agèd man, unkempt white hair and beard, eyes milkily unseeing, sits on a pallet against the cottage wall.

Alexios asks if he's called Teiresias, and he croaks a welcome. I step down, examining his wrinkled face.

"You want to consult me, Priestess. Sit, and Cenchrias will bring you something to drink."

Alexios asks if the youth is mute.

"He is, nor can he hear us. Cenchrias is my eyes and I his ears."

"How do you understand each other?"

"We have our ways. The blind often possess heightened hearing, and so it is with me. I can read in his step whether Cenchrias brings food or a pilgrim. Who are you?"

"I'm Alexios, son of the farmer who oversees the crops below Eleusis and this is Manto, priestess of Demeter. I must return today."

"Not until you refresh yourself. You, Manto, may stay as long as you wish."

"Thank you, Seer. I have a simple question, and your answer will send me on my way."

As I sit on the pallet beside Teiresias, hunger and fatigue sweep over me. Cenchrias brings lemon water, goat cheese, and bread. I eat slowly, my exhaustion slipping into anxiety. Yes, I must discover who my father is so I can continue my journey, but this sanctuary seems a dead end.

I turn to Alexios. "Take me with you." But the words die in my throat. He's intent on refilling his water jug, and before I can stop him he's freed his donkey, jumped onto the wagon, waved goodbye, and is heading away with a confident grip on the reins.

Birds flutter in the shady trees, and the scent of late roses vanquishes traces of road dust. I sigh. I will remain for as short a time as possible. Surely I can make Cenchrias understand when I need a ride to continue my journey.

Teiresias' voice cuts into my thoughts. "I'm curious about your name. Manto. How did your parents choose it?"

"My parents? I never knew them. My sister and I were orphans, raised at a shrine of Artemis. The priestesses told us that after our mother died birthing Historis, our father disappeared. I hope, with your vision, you can tell me about him."

"Why now?"

"I had an ominous dream and an even more ominous message from Demeter. I must find my father. I know nothing about him, so I came seeking your wisdom. Can you tell me about my parentage?"

"Does it matter? You came here for other reasons."

My voice rises in irritation. "I came hoping you can help me find my father. That's my only reason. I cannot ignore my dream or Demeter's voice."

"Describe the dream."

"I was entangled with two serpents, crushed between them until I could scarcely breathe. As I struggled to break free, they hissed what sounded like 'follow your destiny.' A frightening vision, with serpents hissing prophetic words."

"What does destiny mean to you?"

"I don't see my life as destined—that's not how we think in Eleusis. The Mysteries are all-encompassing, deepening year after year. Our training has one purpose only, transcending ordinary life and developing spiritual depth."

"Yet you say Demeter sent you in another direction."

"She did, rare as it is for her voice to arise from that well."

"Your goddess gave you a prophecy because in Eleusis you were missing something essential."

Words I've never spoken burst out. "I possess a gift so unwelcome in Eleusis as to shame me."

"You couldn't hide it from your dream or your goddess. What is that gift?"

"You're the soothsayer. You tell me."

Teiresias speaks in a bardic tone. "You must honor your second sight and make best use of it. First, learn your place in the world."

"Demeter said I must find my father. But I don't understand. The Mysteries focus on the bond of mother and daughter. In the story of Persephone, gods are seducers who abduct virgins. And my earthly father, whoever he was, thought nothing of abandoning me."

"Your goddess sent you on this quest because your father can guide you. You have denied your insights, your doubts, your sadness. Only a profound emptiness would draw you away from Eleusis. You seek healing, Manto."

Perhaps it's true. By suppressing my second sight I suppressed my true self. The thought chokes my throat.

"Wipe your eyes and sip your water."

I empty my cup.

"Sit quietly. Still your mind and listen for a sound deeper than bird song or the rustle of leaves. Focus on Thebes."

"The city behind this wall means nothing to me."

"It shall. Sharpen your ears. Let your mind move beyond us. Just listen."

After long moments I murmur, "Thunder? Distant thunder?"

"I knew you would hear it. You have vision, even with your ears. Every sense is more than simply physical. You drank consecrated kekeon in Eleusis. You know the transcendent power of our senses."

"What's that sound? I feel it all through my body."

"The Epigoni gallop toward us."

"Epigoni?"

"Do you know nothing of the history of Thebes?"

"Only that Cadmus founded it on murder. In Eleusis we cared nothing about Ares and his war cries."

"You speak of being raised in a shrine of Artemis. Where?"

Something kept me from telling him. I can't pin down my hesitation, but from my first glimpse of the formidable city walls and the gate beyond Teiresias' cottage, Thebes felt alien.

"Right here, but the temple of Artemis was set apart from royal Cadmeia. The priestesses who raised us must be long dead, but I wonder if my sister Historis remains. Do you know? Is there still a shrine to the divine Huntress? Why do you live outside the city walls?"

Teiresias laughs. "You answer one question with three. You were a grown woman by the time I arrived here. I had no desire to live inside these walls. A priestess or two may still dwell at that temple, but I'm more familiar with shrines in the woodlands tended by a single priestess, descendant of the Minoan sisterhood of old."

"I've never seen such places. Alexios and I took the main road."

"Your sense of time differs from mine. In Eleusis, time was cyclical, Demeter's rituals circling, season after season. I, however, have known more than one lifetime."

"How can that be?"

"I shall tell you. That's why I speak of the Epigoni."

"I don't care about the Epigoni or why they are bent on destroying Thebes. I'm asking you about my father."

"Everything is connected. Be patient." My sigh is audible, but he takes it as acquiescence. "The Epigoni are descendants of King Labdacus who reigned here when you were a child. Hera's curse on Thebes began with Labdacus' son Laius."

"That's not a story to interest a priestess of Demeter."

"No, I suppose not. I myself never visited Eleusis, but for different reasons."

"You aren't tainted."

"I'm no murderer nor do I share the curse of this city, but I have my own meandering story. I trust you will remain long enough to hear it."

"Well—" That's so far from my intentions I say no more.

"From time to time we'll hear those savage warriors hurtling toward us, fueled by vengeance and bile. Soon they'll shatter the seven towers of Thebes, where death rained upon their fathers. Blood-drunk, they will breach our walls, flame our temples and gardens, and smash this cottage."

"Even outside the city walls?"

"My sanctuary will be a battleground."

"How can you be so certain?"

"That is the prophecy we must prepare for."

My ears are ringing, and I beg him to deafen me to the thundering hoofs.

"You opened your ears to this prescient sound. Now let it go."

I inhale and exhale, focusing inward, until my head stops throbbing.

"When the warriors are coming. we and all unarmed Thebans will flee. Before then, I have stories to tell."

"Please begin with my father. Why would he abandon two baby daughters? Demeter never gave up hers. When Persephone was half-grown, Hades stole her into the Underworld and her mother mourned her loss inconsolably. My father, whoever he was, left us to Fate." My ancient grief wells up.

"A profound loss," Teiresias says. "Did it haunt your childhood?"

"Historis and I had each other, and the priestesses raised us with love. We learned young that suffering is part of life so no, I wasn't haunted. We lived in a world of women and meant to always. No doubt Historis too has made her way as a priestess. We didn't cry over our lost parents. Yet being here with you saddens me."

"Why?"

I look at him long and hard, unable to find the words. Is he testing my vision?

"I have something shameful to tell you," he says at last.

A terrible suspicion is dawning. "Something about me?"

"Yes, about you and your sister."

"Perhaps I'm far off the mark."

"What would your guess?"

"Did you know my father? Or—" I stop— "are we related?"

"We are. Say the worst, Manto."

"Are you my father? Were you the one who—" I can't finish. Until now Father has been a mysterious presence rather then a real person, but the anguish on Teiresias' craggy face confirms the truth. "How could you leave us? How did my mother die? Why did she, a virgin serving Artemis, marry? Why did she become a mother?"

At the word mother, a memory comes to me, arms smelling of rosemary holding me close, a soft gown swishing, long hair tickling my cheek. Her image jolts me: how could I have forgotten her vivid presence? What happened?

He puts his hand on mine. "You have a right to be distressed. But, dear Manto, your life hasn't been misspent, orphaned though you were. You gained more from Artemis and Demeter than I could give you. I beg your forgiveness and hope for your love. If you grant me both, you will be able to fulfill your true purpose."

"Forgiveness? Love?" I lower my voice. "A lot to ask. Why did you desert us? How did you end up a soothsayer attended by a deaf mute?"

As Teiresias weighs his words, I glance at him, his profile sharpened with age. Who is this man who fathered and abandoned me? "Why didn't you remain to oversee our upbringing? No wonder Historis and I never imagined marrying, with you so faithless."

"I knew you would be in safe hands. That's not the answer to your question, but it's true."

"What comes next for me, Teiresias, now that I've found you?"

"After a lifetime of secrecy, I must entrust my story to the right listener before I die. You are that person, Manto. I cannot escape death, but you will find a new home far from here and carry this tale with you. In times to come you shall recount it to those who in turn will pass it on. You will live your life as Fate determines, but my story, Thebes' story, goes with you."

What can he mean, pass on his story? Any orphaned girl would want to know about her father, but why would it matter to anyone else? Yet I feel a quiver and cannot refuse him. His sightless eyes hold me, so I say, "However long it takes to explain why you left us, I shall attend your every word." My tone conveys the sense of this much and no more.

"I shouldn't have begun so abruptly. You need only listen. I long to describe my life in as much detail as time allows, a luxury for an old man who's shrouded his past in silence. Carry my story forth as opportunity grants."

"Who would want to listen?" I don't say the obvious: I'm a woman. Being female has brought me close to Artemis, Demeter, and the sisterhood of priestesses dating back time out of mind. But can I be a bard?

Teiresias follows my thought. "A woman has as much skill in storytelling as a man."

"Old crones, you mean."

But in Eleusis, the priestesses who tell the story of Demeter and Persephone during the Mysteries needn't have reached a venerable age. My turn would have come.

A sudden vision causes me to shudder. In my mind's eye I see, instead of a priestess, a hierophant lording over the ceremonies. Women have always guided initiates through the Mysteries, men humbling themselves to our rituals. A priest as leader? My heart says never in Eleusis, but the image mocks me, the priest's imperious bearing as clear in my imagination as my friend Lydia's grieving face when I left Eleusis. A man cannot speak for Demeter.

"An image of the future just struck you, didn't it?" he says. "Gaia has been losing power ever since her priestesses fled Crete. Whatever changes, Eleusis will continue its worship of Demeter far into the future and, through her, the Mother. By telling my timeless story you will help the sisterhood."

"You overrate my gifts. Why would a man like you value the Great Mother?"

"I possess expanded vision. So will you as we proceed. That is second sight, seeing more than others in the present and envisioning the future. I know I shall die after Thebe's destruction. Our time together is short."

I cannot read Teiresias' face as he gazes at me with rapt, unseeing eyes. "No one knows all I experienced in my long, rare life, entwined with the gods. After death, my wisdom will be pursued to the depths of Hades. Although I've not participated in Demeter's rituals, my initiations have been even more extraordinary."

I laugh. "Plural? More than one?"

"You'll find the word apt."

I shake my head. "Will I see Historis? Does she know about you?"

"That I am her father? No. Once she came here for a prophecy. That was easy: her talent for midwifery would take her far. Very far, as it turned out, but that story is for another day."

"You haven't told me why you left us."

Cenchrias stirs the coals to life and begins chopping vegetables. In the flickering firelight his face looks ghostly yet content, as if his inability to hear and speak means ethereal music plays in his head.

"After we dine," Teiresias replies.

Chapter Two: Transformation

Our meal seems the earthy equivalent of the gods' ambrosia. When I touch Cenchrias' hand as he clears our bowls, he gives me a shy smile.

"Do continue, Teiresias."

"My father Everes descended from one of the Sown Men of Cadmus. The Sparti, as they're known."

"I know Athena instructed Cadmus to sow the teeth of Ares' dragon. After he did so, warriors sprang from Earth. They drew their swords and killed each other, only a handful left standing—the Sparti. What a heritage!"

"Everes' grandfather was one of them, who then helped build the Cadmeia."

"So his origins were murder. And your own?"

He shrugs, and after a pause continues. "Everes took as wife a wood nymph named Chariclo, but I have no memory of her and little of him. Chariclo returned to the woods when I was young, and Everes died soon after. I was raised in the palace of King Labdacus in royal Cadmeia."

"You too were orphaned," I say quietly.

"I was, but besides Labdacus and the queen, I had Apollo, god who conceals with light, to guide me into manhood. When I came of age, King Labdacus appointed me master of revels and suggested the girl Chloris to be my bride. I took her unthinking, as I would have accepted any lovely bedmate. I found us a house with a shaded courtyard, provided a serving maid and all I supposed a wife required.

"In the palace of Labdacus, I arranged feasts and entertainments, sang old songs, and gave speeches on the theme, 'Know Thyself.' Little did I heed Dionysus, Theban-born deity, and even less Great Goddess Gaia or Demeter or Artemis."

"Tell me about Chloris."

"She—" Teiresias holds his head in his hands, thin white hair falling over his brow. "A painful subject." He exhales. "Chloris possessed more qualities of mind and spirit than I understood. She had a lithe grace, long runner's legs, and a woodland air such as my mother must have had before she fled to the woods. Yet when I heard Chloris had been votary of Artemis, vowing never to wed and sent unwilling to our marriage bed, I scoffed."

I don't interrupt him, though I can't help but see the similarity between my mother Chloris being a worshiper of virgin Artemis and Teiresias' mother a wood nymph. Two unwilling brides who belonged in the wildwood.

"Chloris' eyes have haunted me ever since, so like a hare's, timid yet shrewd. Back then I perceived nothing, finding our life together agreeable, and she never said otherwise. Chloris gave birth to you, a pretty girl child, though, Goddess forgive me, I regretted you weren't a son. Nor was I an obliging father, spending most of my time at the palace."

Worse and worse, even if this old man is no longer that self-centered young one.

"When our second child was due, I heard rumors that Chloris was keeping company with the serpent priest Mydon. A double offense, for I brought Mydon from Delphi when Labdacus sent me there for an oracle. *The Goddess seeks her own. Hera will avenge the lost youth.* I should have heard that as a fearsome oracle for Thebes but had no ear for Delphic riddles. Mydon insisted on accompanying me back to Thebes to deliver the oracle himself. Labdacus didn't understand it either and didn't try. Now it was whispered that this man betrayed me with Chloris. I raged at the thought.

"I'm glad I can't see your face as I tell the next, Manto. Never have I forgiven myself, much as I have paid. Crazed with anger, I confronted Chloris. She moved unsteadily away from me and somehow, in grabbing for her hand, I pushed her. To my horror, she fell against the hearth.

"That night she went into labor and delivered Historis. Chloris did not survive the birth. The midwife closed her eyes, smoothed the terror from her face, and fetched a wet nurse for the infant. Artemis had reclaimed her votary."

I feel the loss to the depths of my being. This blind old man killed my mother. His story is a confession. But a murderer! How can I forgive that? I hug myself, breathing harshly.

Teiresias gives me time to recover.

"I can't express my sorrow, Manto, my shock and despair. I spent that night holding Chloris in my arms, trying to warm her to life with my tears, my heartbeat. Who were you, Chloris? Can your spirit forgive me? Her lifeless body was mute proof of my failure. I feared meeting her reproachful eyes in the Underworld.

"No returning to my service at the palace, nor could I stay alone in our house under the scorn of the nurse. The wailing newborn and your toddling self had become unbearable, to my shame. I ask your forgiveness from the bottom of my heart, but please hear me out."

I nod in tearful agreement. I shall listen, but forgiving words are not in my power.

"At dawn, I stumbled out the door. A sleepwalkers' trance took me through a city gate. I must have cut through fields; there must have been birds, herdsmen with flocks of goats, scurrying mice and lizards in the bushes. I noticed nothing until I found myself walking on dry pine needles beyond all human paths. Sticky webs brushed my face and caught in my hair, and branches pushed against me. I swept them aside with my staff and walked on.

"Chill silence startled me. I caught a wild smell, a dread surrounding presence. Breath shallow, feet leaden, I saw nothing, shadow-blinded. The deep woods, its raw odor and whispering presence, overwhelmed my senses. At my feet gnarled roots came to life, a ripple of blue on copper. No! Two serpents writhed before me in a primal dance of love.

"Holding my staff above the snakes, I stood suspended. That eternal moment was the end of my certainties of self, of body, of Teiresias, man and knowing mind. The coupling serpents represented horrifying union and fathomless power. The coppery glint of their twisting bodies ignited a fire in me and: I struck.

"Driving my staff between them with all my might, my arm vibrated. The earth shook beneath me and I staggered forward. Around me, not a sound. My vision opened full circle, encompassing both serpents as they slithered away in opposite directions.

"A film covered my eyes and I fell to the ground, an unbearable tightness enveloping me. Compulsively I burrowed into pine needles and leaves, into the abrading soil and pebbles and roots beneath, out of my clothes, and still I pushed, as if through my very skin."

His words freeze me. To strike apart serpents of the deep forest! An offense to goddesses of the wilds. No man would dare such in fear of unimaginable consequences. My dream serpents pressed against me, but Teiresias attacked his!

"Exhausted as if I'd fallen into the depths of Hades, I slept. In my dream a fat old woman loomed over me. 'Trespasser! Man of Cadmus, how dare you stray into the Great One's garden?' She pulled her robe open and laughed, huge breasts and belly shaking. Then a wave went through her, serpent undulation, and she exposed her dark triangle. 'Look. Know.' She moved in an obscene dance. 'Worshiper of sun-bright Apollo fell into the womb cave!' Her cackling laughter echoed, wave upon wave. Then the voice of Artemis overpowered her, chiding my neglect of Chloris, of you and your sister and all my blind folly, until I fell into an agonized sleep.

"When I awoke beneath an innocent blue sky, I felt thrust into the world newborn and stifled an infant's wail. Something was terribly wrong. My body felt strangely light. My hair was longer and fuller. How soft my skin! I'd walked into the woods a man of three decades, and now everything about me was altered, younger. I pressed my eyes shut. Let this be a dream.

"My hand couldn't resist running over my chest. Breasts! And my waist, tapering down to a rounded mound soft with hair opening to woman's subtle organ. A secret. A terrifying transformation. I wanted to pound the earth and shout to the skies. Trespasser indeed! Step into the Mother's garden and *he* becomes *she?*

"I couldn't summon Teiresias' vigor. I sat, a nothing, a hollow. I spoke my name, 'Teiresias,' in a woman's voice. As Teiresias, I failed my wife and daughters. Now my mind dwelt in a woman's body. Could I call it *my* mind? So it seemed, yet I was no longer that man."

I'm speechless. This old man became a woman? Yet here he sits, male. All is beyond understanding. Many a man has failed as husband and father, but some divine whim picked Teiresias for a unique fate.

He seems overcome by his story, though surely his question has been answered one way or another over the intervening years.

Finally I'm able to respond. "In Eleusis, initiates are freed from the self they've known. They drink sacred kekeon to prepare for a spiritual transformation. Male initiates share Demeter's mourning for her lost daughter. In that sense they become women." I shake my head. "Never has one done so in reality. Your bawdy old Baubo appears in our preparation rites as well. Baubo shakes Demeter out of her grief over the loss of Persephone. She makes the goddess laugh, for unrelieved suffering cannot be borne. I hope she started you laughing."

"Oh she did, she did. After Baubo's taunts, as I sat in the mud among knotted roots and decayed leaves, I laughed aloud and threw the Great Goddess a kiss. 'You caught me. Your serpents caught me, the trespasser.'

"I had fallen into the void. Nothing to do but surrender. Dazed, I sat in the musky forest, unable to take a step."

His bewilderment becomes mine, as if I too hover between existences.

"A peculiar story for daughter to hear," I finally manage. "Sitting stunned in the forest was a moment between— between parts of your life, your self. Liminal time out of time. We're in such now, you and I. In telling your story, you're in neither past nor future, and I, having left Eleusis, find myself between that past and whatever future awaits. Fresh selves in this moment."

"My new self was unformed except in body. In Teiresias' cloak, I stumbled this way and that. Finding my way into the city by moonlight, I slipped through the gate, over familiar streets unobserved, and into my room in the quiet house where I fell into a dreamless sleep.

"Next morning I was still female. My metamorphosis was no dream." He laughs. "I hadn't drunk kekeon; I bathed in it! Everything was unfamiliar. All I could do was imitate what little I knew about being female.

"I used the privy squatting as Chloris had. I stared down at myself, at my neat triangle—no remnant of Priapus. Gazing into Chloris' small metal mirror, the eyes that looked back at me belonged to Teiresias, gold-flecked brown. My hair was matted above a familiar yet softer face. I ran her comb through the snarls and put on one of her gowns, skirt flapping above her sandals that now fit my foot.

"At the door of her empty chamber, I gazed at the bed where Chloris had lain, where I held her in desperate farewell. During my absence, her funeral rites had begun. And finished? I'd lost all sense of time. Bright Apollo had abandoned me. I could only move forward without divine aid.

"Chloris' shawl woven in a blue serpentine pattern caught my eye. I picked it up, stung by the memory that Mydon brought it from Delphi, serpent priest I'd heard called her lover. Beneath it something glittered. A golden girdle, as intricately designed as the one encircling Aphrodite's waist, the mythic girdle making her irresistible to god and man. I fastened it around myself, snug above my hips. Never did I see such a girdle on Chloris, even before pregnancy swelled her belly.

"Adorned in a girdle like Aphrodite's own, I heard a voice that could only be hers whispering. *Teira. Tears and laughter.*

Aphrodite's Teira. The voice of Artemis joined hers. *Rash man must learn what woman is.*

"Teira. The goddess named me. What would it mean to be Aphrodite's Teira? Kitchen noises reminded me I was an intruder. Concealing my girdle under the blue shawl, I slipped across the courtyard and around to the front door. When the servant girl responded to my knock, I presented myself as Historis, aunt to the newborn Historis her namesake. The girl looked at me strangely, but apparently took my disheveled appearance as evidence of mourning. I'd missed Chloris' funeral rites but could pay my respects at the shrine of Artemis. Teiresias fled in grief, she told me, and only the nurse, the infant, and you, Manto, remained at home."

Cenchrias bestirs himself, refilling our cups, then retires to his sleeping pallet in a bower beside the cottage. It's late, but Teiresias keeps talking. Even though my eyes burn with fatigue, I don't want him to stop here.

"As the servant girl led me to the guest chamber, I looked into the room of Teiresias. Never again would it be mine, nor his razor or gifts from King Labdacus: the finely-woven robe for state occasions, the embossed knife. They represented all that had been my life, pomp and show and superiority in the light of Apollo. Did I wish to be that man again, to claim his knife, his house? Something within me flared. What did *he* know? Teiresias could only be *him*, past. I was now Teira.

"Wherever I was going, I would need the knife, so I tucked it into the girdle. Do you see why I never told this story, Manto? Too strange to be believed."

"Many's the old tale of metamorphosis, all fantasies. Yours, you say, really happened." Startling as it sounds, I'm willing to believe him and urge him to continue.

"There on the guest bed, I ran my hands over my new body, its curves firm and soft. I let my curious fingers find their way between my female lips. Immediately warmth arose in response to my fingers' explorations. Could this mysterious organ mean anything like Teiresias' protruding maleness did? Was it a flower with smooth inner petals? Was it a labyrinth into the mystery of existence? What were its secrets? Teiresias' dim experience of Chloris provided no answers.

"Aphrodite enticed me to explore sensations rather than structure, but each time my touch built toward climax, my wondering mind intruded, or anxiety, or a sense of absurdity that put me on the verge of laughter. What was woman's climax? Finally, body tingling and yearning, I fell into a dead sleep."

He turns to me. "You are a virgin, are you not?"

I nod. He can't see me, but my silence is sufficient answer.

"Does my speaking frankly make you uneasy?"

"Don't worry about me, Father. How I would tell anyone else this story, though, I have no idea. Nor do I understand. If you became the woman Teira so long ago, why are you now a blind old man?"

"You called me Father." He smiles and looks at me with a smile of complicity. "Blame it on the serpents," he continues. "But you must wait. I have a request for you as well. You may think I want to tell you about my years as a woman."

"And how they ended."

"I shall satisfy your curiosity on both, but you will need more than my transformation to woman to hold your listeners. You must weave in the story of Thebes."

"The Epigoni?"

"Partially. Laodamas and Thersander, leaders of the opposing armies, both descend from the same doomed family. That story must be told, up to the present day. A tragic fate enmeshed the rulers of Thebes from King Labdacus onward. Betrayal, perfidy, error, dissension, and war."

"I never witnessed war nor understood the reasons for it. The worship of Artemis and Demeter is free of warfare. How can I describe battling armies?"

"Use your imagination to arouse the imaginations of your hearers. When I said the Epigoni will crush Thebes, did you picture them galloping here in chariots, horses sweating, shields, spears, and gleaming helmets ready? Did you feel their blood lust? You don't need to experience a fierce desire for revenge to feel it as a man does. You will sense the plight of warriors' wives and daughters more intensely than a male teller focused on the glory of a victorious army. You know war's cost.

"I ask that as you listen, imagine me after my transformation and what I learned as a woman. Your understanding of Demeter and the age-old sisterhood of priestesses will enhance your storytelling."

"You're asking me not only to recall your womanly life but connect it to Thebes' royal family. Isn't that the job of a male rhapsode?"

"We cannot tell about men while ignoring women; about fathers and sons while ignoring mothers and daughters; about gods while ignoring the Great Mother. You will recount a richer story than any man could."

The thought drains me. I cannot listen to another word.

Teiresias stretches out on his pallet. Cenchrias covers him for the night and points me to the cottage. Warm as the evening is, I'm relieved to sleep in its solitude.

Chapter Three: Serpent Priest

Next morning a breeze has chased away the previous day's heat. I slept soundly in Teiresias' cottage, the bed not too hard, the fragrance of sage through the open window conducive to rest. The fresh day brings back his bizarre story and my conflicting emotions. I'm curious, yet I would be happy to explore the garden and sit beneath the fig tree to reflect on it.

Teiresias sits on his pallet eating a pear, and Cenchrias offers me one. The bread is yesterday's, thickly spread with goat cheese. I have no choice but to sit beside him, eat breakfast, and listen.

"I needed to seek out the priest Mydon, wiser than any man in Thebes. As I was leaving, the servant girl asked if I would stay on, but I couldn't say. The empty streets that morning might as well be in Tyre across the sea, brilliant, foreign, unreal: a gleaming veneer over darkness. I tried to move gracefully, or at least with short steps, until I came to the temple of Artemis, blooming with white roses, asphodel, and lilies in honor of Chloris. I knelt and prayed for her soul."

I interrupt. "You stopped at the temple where the nurse Agathe took Historis and me after you deserted us? Why couldn't you pretend to be our aunt and remain with us in Thebes?"

"Teira's destiny couldn't be fulfilled in Thebes."

"You weren't brave enough to try. You didn't love Chloris, and you didn't love us. Perhaps your transformation was the doing of Artemis and Aphrodite, but you could have made amends for your wrongs by loving your daughters."

"I possessed neither the courage nor the imagination. Parents leave their children, and children survive."

"We survived because of priestesses."

"I might as well have been a child myself, newly born female. How could I play aunt? My womanly discoveries were guided by Aphrodite."

"I can see how the golden girdle would make you think so, but why turn to Mydon? What kind of man was he?"

"Ah, Mydon. He understood the oracle I could not, which may be why I believed gossip about him and Chloris."

"How would you describe him?" As soon as I ask, I realize Teiresias' wish that I tell his story provoked the question. I will need to understand all the people in his life—her life, I should say—if the story is to come alive.

"I want to tell it chronologically, Manto, but I can't do that with Mydon. What I knew of him then was less than what I experienced later. I won't jump forward; his traits I discovered were present all along. You recall he came to Thebes with me from Delphi because I didn't understand the oracle. *The Goddess seeks her own. Hera will avenge the lost youth.* Vengeance would be exacted upon Prince Laius, as Mydon understood. He possessed insight into the gods' ways but resisted the role of seer. 'Priest' was sufficient for him, and he served many gods: Apollo and Dionysus as well as Aphrodite and Artemis. Of all Thebans, he's the only one who might have been initiated in your Mysteries."

"How did he react to seeing the man he knew standing before him as a woman? Did he recognize you?"

"Mydon said he'd dreamt of a serpent shedding its skin, so he expected to witness a dramatic rebirth and asked what happened to Teiresias. When I said I was now Teira, he guessed Aphrodite named me, but she couldn't have changed my sex. Her transformations come from passion.

"Mydon didn't need to tell me how my life as Teiresias' was an affront to Artemis and Great Mother Gaia. No place disrespected goddesses more than Thebes. Priests of Apollo speak the oracles, but they originate with the sybil in the deep cave of Python's mate Delphyne. Of course Apollo-loving Thebans couldn't understand riddling prophecies."

"In Eleusis," I say, "we know Delphyne coiling deep beneath the omphalos is the source of Pythia's oracles. Apollo's victory over Python was a recent and partial triumph. As Teiresias, you must have thought only women and slaves worship the Goddess."

"I know better now. But when Labdacus sent me to Delphi, I couldn't understand. The Pythia spoke a prophecy for me as well. *You shall know yourself through excess.* I never joined Maenads frolicking in the hills with Dionysus, but I discovered what she meant."

"Did Mydon tell you what you wanted to know?"

"He didn't need to say he wasn't Historis' father. I understood that much. Now I was Teira, who needed to find a life to counteract Teiresias' fatal misjudgments. Mydon pointed the way to my female destiny beyond Thebes. He assured me you and Historis would be well cared for by Agathe and the priestesses of Artemis.

"I felt pangs of sorrow for Chloris, for you, for the infant I'd barely seen. If I left I couldn't atone for my failures, but I couldn't remain here as I was. I felt torn, and I regret that my choice hurt you."

My anger flares. Regret? What an inadequate word. "You don't sound torn. You never considered staying. Never considered us at all."

"But you and Historis were well raised, were you not? I would have enjoyed roaming the woods myself when young."

How blithely he dismisses his wrong. Our upbringing made Historis and me disdain marriage, though that's no harm for girls who will be priestesses. I could refuse to hear him out, let alone commit his tale to memory. But Teiresias is a puzzle, and I'm beginning to be pleased he wants to entrust this story to me. Without intending to, my mind is forming his words into poems I might recite. So much I don't yet know, but opening words pop into my head.

Sing of a complicated being, Muse, one who who discovered the realms of the male and the female like no mortal before or since.

I sigh. Inspiration is with me for the moment, but much is yet to learn.

"Mydon instructed me to go to the temple of Aphrodite in Corinth, where dwelt the most beautiful women in all of Argos, ruled by no man, god or mortal."

My voice is sharper than I intend. "Aphrodite is a goddess whose mysteries I know nothing of."

He laughs. "Neither did I."

"Even though you married my mother?"

"You must know that Aphrodite isn't goddess of marriage."

"I'm not curious about her rituals."

"What you disdain summoned me to Corinth: flutes and tambourines, musky perfumes, seductive laughter. Corinth was a distant walk from Thebes and I must travel alone.

"Alone? What a fearsome thought. Even with the serpent-embossed knife, would I be safe? Never did Teiresias have such a worry."

Chapter Four: The Sisterhood

I myself have traveled, but as on Alexios' wagon coming here, never alone. Lydia and I were conveyed from Thebes to Eleusis by a youth much like Alexios. Nor have I heard of a priestess or woman initiate to the Mysteries who traveled the open road unescorted. The rare men who walk alone are generally exiles, soldiers, or vagrants.

"Mydon told me I could go safely as a woman if I sought out priestesses at hidden shrines, members of an ancient sisterhood descended from votaries of the Snake Mother on blessed Crete who would welcome me for a night or two. The path between shrines was charged by the power of the earth serpent, he said, one of the secrets of eternal female power."

He turns to me. "You understand, Manto? Zeus and Apollo will not rule supreme forever."

"Certainly not!" I jump to my feet, nearly upsetting the table with our water jug. "Zeus stole his authority from the Great Mother. He even claimed woman's sovereignty in childbirth, birthing both Athena and Dionysus after he destroyed their intended mothers. I owe fealty to the Goddess above any male, human or divine, who denies her dominion."

"That I had to learn for myself. Only after becoming Teira could I lose Teiresias' confident beliefs. Apollo's creed, *Nothing in excess:* gone. Teiresias' noble heritage as descendent of a Sown Man: gone.

"Thebes' past was a bloody saga of murderers who failed to honor Earth from which they sprang, who scorned any power older or more mysterious than Zeus of the thunderbolt or blood-loving Ares. They believed divinity acted through them. Women counted for little more than bedmates and mothers. Now I'd become a woman who, with the goddess' agency, must be strong and independent. Mydon said I would travel forth as the equal of any man, belonging to no man."

I sit back down. "Yet you were to seek out hidden shrines."

"For more than safety. Those priestesses had much to teach me before I reached Corinth." He extends a gnarled hand to show a gold seal ring bearing the image of a goddess with a skirt of serpents. "Mydon's parting gift to grant me safe passage. When nearing Corinth's temple on the Acrocorinth, I should detour to the shrine of a priestess of Demeter named Carpho. She knew more about Corinth than he did."

"Did you find her?"

"Yes, but I won't jump forward in the story. After leaving Mydon, I saw Agathe carrying you and baby Historis to the temple of Artemis. That was my last sight of you."

A sense of my childhood comes on a wave of sorrow. Should I walk through Thebes to see the priestess' dwelling where I grew up? I imagine it little resembles the place I knew as a girl, but Teiresias' prophecy of Thebes' destruction by ravening horsemen grieves me. I suppose as long as he's telling his story, we're safe, but doom hangs over us. No wonder he wants to speak while he can.

"Say on, Father."

"In Chloris' room I found a serviceable cloak and chiton, folded in a string of gold wire loops and the knife, and departed the city, the gateman dozing at his station. No initiate at Eleusis could feel more separated from all that was familiar than I. What would become of me? I could only heed Mydon's advice and walk south toward Corinth."

I take a deep, relieved breath. Now that Teira has left Thebes, the story no longer relates to me. She wasn't the father who abandoned me.

The sun is reaching its peak as Cenchrias brings us a fat pomegranate and jugs of wine and water. I watch him break apart the fruit, red juice staining his fingers. What goes on in his silent realm? His serene expression makes it difficult to guess his thoughts, and I wish for a way to communicate with him.

Teiresias touches the wine jug. "Pour a few drops of this dark wine onto the rich earth to bring to life the ghosts who inhabit my story in their vibrant days. Drink with me to golden Corinth and the path I took to reach her." He lifts his cup. "To secret tales, and you to speak them."

"A big responsibility," I murmur.

"But not too much for you, Manto. More than anything besides your love and forgiveness, I value your listening ear. I hope you will hold my story in your mind's eye until it becomes a compulsion."

"A compulsion!" I laugh. He looks pained, and I take his hand in my own, both of us sticky with pomegranate juice. "You want me to care enough about your life to hear every detail and imagine speaking it." I don't tell him that I have the opening lines of his epic.

We wash our faces and fingers. I pat his beard dry with Cenchrias' towel, surprised at how natural the daughterly gesture feels.

"Early that late spring morning, I walked south to the rhythm, I should have stayed; I couldn't stay. I should have stayed; I couldn't stay. You were on my mind, Manto, and your baby sister. But I couldn't let doubts overpower me. I had to go."

"You left behind the man you had been: Teiresias, respected royal advisor. Was he still within you, or had you completely transformed? In mind, spirit—all that you were in your male body?"

He pauses. I don't know him well enough to read his expression, and his milky eyes reveal little. "My body was female after I returned from the deep woods, but I was yet to become a woman in mind and spirit, nor did I know the mysteries of that body."

"Women's feelings and views of ourselves in the world differ from men's. I can't see myself as a man!"

He laughs at the affront in my voice.

"You will see the kind of woman I became. At times I may shock you, spending your life until now in your protected temples. I matured from a boy into Teiresias, but as a woman, I had no girlhood to teach me."

"And much to undo of Teiresias."

"Priestesses became my teachers as they were for you. I expected to be a woman for the rest of my life. After my rebirth as Teira, I felt double within myself. And now this." he waves his hand over his body. "When one has changed sex twice, what remains of each in the other? Some people are flexible, changing with time and circumstance. You were raised in the domain of Artemis, then served Demeter, and are destined for further changes after we flee this place. Others follow one path, then another. Teiresias was a single-minded male, so my change was drastic. As I set out on my journey, confused emotions tore me.

"Have you been double ever since?"

"No, a time came when I knew myself fully female."

He looks so sad that I cannot ask how he feels now, a wrinkled old man. Some form of duality, I suspect. I could feel compelled to hear his story simply to know how it was to be each sex and then not. "Tell me what happened next. You went on a pilgrimage."

"You could call it that, though most pilgrims know better what they seek than I did on the road to Corinth. The serpent path beckoned me into shady woods, breezes fluttering the leaves and birds singing me on my way.

"Late the first afternoon, I knelt to drink from a stream and noticed a trail of crushed grass along its bank. I followed it to a simple sanctuary set in a circle of wooden columns. A woman stepped out to meet me, saying she was called Halia, priestess of Artemis of the new moon. Halia radiated ancient authority: tall, strong, and old enough to be my mother, wearing a heavy linen chiton and strong sandals.

"I told her my name and asked if she dwelt alone.

"'Just me, my goddess, and whoever chances this way. You are younger and more beautiful than most pilgrims, Teira. How did you find me?'

"I did my best to present myself as a pilgrim like any other, but this seemed a test, and my words sounded stilted. 'I come from Thebes and am journeying south. I never knew of a place like this until a priest described it.'

"'We woodland priestesses have a secret sisterhood. We find solace in the Mother and share with visitors our blessed solitude. What do you hope to find here?'

"'A place to sleep for the night and whatever wisdom you can offer.'

"Halia filled a bowl with berries and motioned me to follow her. Beyond the shrine was a spring, bubbling into a generous pool, and she offered me a cup of its cool water. She was the first person beyond Thebes who spoke to me as a woman, and I appreciated her gentle, welcoming manner. She offered me a handful of the berries, her dark eyes penetrating.

"In her loving presence, I was aware how starved Teiresias had been. Even with feasting at the palace, he was famished, never nourished by Chariclo, who fled to the forest, and starved by his father's military curtness and frequent departures."

Teiresias' sightless, questioning eyes rest on me.

"Historis and I had no mother," I say, "but we never went hungry. No lack of food or love, living with priestesses."

"Such a woman was Halia. Sitting on the damp bank of the pool, we dangled our bare feet in the water. She lifted mine one at a time into her lap and massaged them. Then she stood, dropped her chiton on the bank, and waded in. I glanced in wonder at my new body as I floundered after her. We splashed water back and forth until we fell together laughing. Halia held me like a mother, rocking and humming as the rosemary-fragranced water lapped around us. Never had I known such comfort.

"Then she left me alone in the pool. I lowered myself into its sloping center and floated on my back, idly kicking, which made my breasts bounce. My hair drifted over my shoulders, sweeping to the middle of my back. The snarled curls beneath that top layer I had smoothed with Chloris' comb now yielded to the water in sensuous waves, and my body grew soft and feminine as the last sense of maleness washed away. I belonged to the pool, the pines and beeches above, earth and mud beneath, setting sun and rising moon: Teira with the mind of Teiresias, subtly altered. Refreshed through and through, I climbed into the balmy evening air, shook off the water and dressed, warm drops running down my back.

"After our supper of creamy gruel, Halia directed me to a leafy bed beside the sanctuary where I fell into a peaceful sleep. In the depths of night I woke to see Python shining in an immortal starry arc from Mount Parnassus. Apollo hadn't destroyed the Mother's serpent, hadn't sealed its breathing place in the earth." Teiresias turns to me. "Perhaps you will see Python above these trees tonight, Manto. I can sense his brilliance through my blindness.

"There I lay suspended between heaven and earth, witness to the secrets of creation. What difference *woman* or *man*? I began to laugh, a weak gurgle in the vastness. I heard Artemis echoing Apollo's credo in a taunting voice: *Know Thyself, self, self.* In that moment I shed all that I was so certain of as Teiresias, seeing my vast ignorance, my wrongs and self-righteousness. My path was now Teira's, the Goddess path.

"Earth warm beneath me, I fell into images and sensations. A golden bracelet pressed into my upper arm and a gossamer gown grazed my nipples under a silken robe, striped in purple overlaid with bands of red and gold. I was as beautiful as the hetaera Potnia of Thebes, who came to royal banquets in a magnificent striped robe, eyes rimmed in kohl and a wreath of golden leaves crowning her hair, red-tinged in the lamplight. A sinuous line of mysterious women danced through my dreams, me stumbling after them."

Teiresias' dream becomes mine, his words floating toward me from a great distance, something about Halia giving him an herbal drink. I doze off, so what he says about a priestess' guidance bringing understanding beyond words spirals into the Eleusinian Mysteries.

"Your breathing told me you were dreaming," Teiresias says as I open my groggy eyes. "Do you know about the dream cure?"

"The dream that sent me here was hardly a cure!" As soon as I say that I realize it may turn out to be. In Eleusis I had no need to be healed, but Teiresias is right. I must learn to acknowledge my pain, release all that has compensated for my losses, and honor my second sight.

"I spent time in Epidaurus," he says, "sanctuary of Asclepius where suppliants dream themselves into health. Those practices have been useful in my blindness but caused my history to haunt me. You came here to free me of it. Once, thinking about Cadmus bringing the alphabet to Boeotia, I believed I could master writing for this, but I learned only how records of trade were kept before I was blinded. I would need to tell my story to a trusted listener."

"Blinded" strikes me. I assumed Teiresias was blind because age clouded his vision. How was he blinded? I lose track of what he's saying about writing, catching only that I can recount his story for future bards to sing and maybe one day someone would record in writing.

"But now I know that telling you gives me all I need."

I squeeze his hand. "Then carry on."

"First more wine." He drinks, then, setting his cup on the table, asks what I know about the sisterhood on ancient Crete.

"I know Crete was the Motherland where Demeter was born," I say. "Before her daughter disappeared, she kept it fruitful. Then Hades abducted Persephone to be queen of the underworld. Demeter searched everywhere for her, allowing Crete and all of Hellas to wither.

"Poseidon flexed his muscles and rumbled the mountains, striking the source of underground fire, spewing blazing liquid rock into the air. In tinder-dry Crete, every spark became a wildfire. Wind chased the flames down the hills to the coast. Poseidon rumbled again and again. Islanders ran toward the sea, stone columns falling on them, burning lava pursuing them. Some priestesses fled to the mountains, running up streambeds to high springs where they found refuge and could maintain their worship, but most sailed northward to the lands of Zeus and Apollo."

"You learned far more in Eleusis than I did in Thebes," Teiresias says. "When Halia saw how little I know of the Cretan sisterhood, she invited me to remain another day. She said the precincts and caves where Demeter came to rest in her search for Persephone became sanctuaries devoted to Demeter, Artemis, Selene. Halia's was one of those shrines."

"Are they still there?" I ask. "I've heard of remote shrines where Demeter is worshiped, but not a serpent path through the forests to such sanctuaries devoted to goddess daughters of the Mother."

"Originally these goddesses were powerful, and some still are. But Zeus subdued Hera and in varying ways diminished her sisters Hestia, Metis, Hecate, and Cybele as well. Nature is eternal. Skygods will not rule forever."

"Ever since Apollo seized the Mother's oracle at Delphi, priests have been gaining power. I can't see how the Goddess in her many manifestations will again prevail in my lifetime, even if I live as long as you. Your woodland priestesses hid their worship. Now priests and hierophants preside at Delphi and soon will at Eleusis and beyond."

"That's the anguish of second sight. But despite dire visions, we mustn't fear the worst for the distant future, Manto. Ares, Zeus, Apollo—no, we don't want to fear their power forever even though at this very moment Ares inspires the Epigoni to besiege our sanctuary. As Teira, I discovered other forces fueling our lives and ancient depths that still remain."

"The Mother?" I ask.

"Yes, the Great One. The knowledge I could have benefitted from as Teiresias I learned as Teira. Since then, I've gained a different sort of wisdom."

"You became a soothsayer whose prophecies are widely sought."

When will he explain how that came about? I know Teiresias wants me to tell his history, but why skip something so basic? He omits more than he says.

"Sometimes I heartily wish I weren't called upon to prophesy." He drinks a slow draught of wine. "Do you wear gold in your ears, Manto?"

"Gold?" I chuckle. "No gold. My homespun is newer than yours, of a paler shade, but otherwise I dress much like you."

"At one time I wore gold jewelry and spangled gowns and gossamer veils."

"I suppose fine raiment will add to the story. Even wealthy initiates leave all such clothing behind when they come to Eleusis. The only goddess who values pretty garments is Aphrodite."

This sets Teiresias laughing. I pat his back, and he calms down enough to take a drink.

"So. You were bound for Corinth to serve in Aphrodite's temple."

"Where I wore jewels and sandals of the finest leather studded with copper."

"And danced sinuously and enchanted men. Is it true? Priestesses dance their prayers to the goddess, and worshipers join in? Such rituals couldn't be more different from ours at Eleusis! Pilgrims come to Corinth seeking—what exactly? It can't be enlightenment." My voice rises with exasperation. "How can Aphrodite's rites grant a profound understanding of life, death, the perpetual cycles and blessed afterlife? Besides, her rites are for men only. Women priestesses, men suppliants: I don't like it. Who were these worshipers?"

"I hoped to linger over my story in every delicious detail, but I can't answer all your questions at once. I'll tell two more stories of my preparation as priestess in Corinth, and then we'll prepare for sleep. Is there a moon tonight?

"Waning. It was in the sky this morning."

"This next scene takes place under a full moon."

"Some say the best time for rituals."

"Perfect for this one. When I left Halia, I turned southward on the grassy trail, carried by currents beneath my feet to the sanctuary of Selene, goddess of the ripe moon. Unlike Halia's shrine with its circle of wooden columns, here the figure of the moon goddess stood on a base mounded with boughs abloom with tiny white flowers as if for a celebration.

"Behind the statue with her serene face was a sleeping porch under a vine-hung trellis. A priestess rose from her shaded cushion as I approached. Wearing a robe that matched her silvery hair, she said her name was Laothoë.

"When I inquired about the occasion, she smiled. It would be a private festival, the moon serpents entwining that very night. I know, I know. More entwining serpents. That thought threw me off balance as well. Laothoë assured me I had nothing to fear. It was an ancient rite of Selene at full moon, a night of sacrifice and worship, and I would know what to do.

"I must do something? That sounded ominous.

"Laothoë offered me a cup of honeyed wine, her voice trailing off as the moon appeared, a flame-orange egg on the horizon, rounding as it rose. Never had I heard of a special rite to Selene and stared at the moonrise uneasily. When whispery sounds arose from the pond, Laothoë told me to remain and await destiny.

She disappeared into the shadows.

"From the gleaming moon reflection on the still water arose a luminous figure: a Naiad, haloed in silver. She drew me into a moon shadow, her flowing garment enwrapping us."

Teiresias holds me in his sightless gaze, an unnerving practice I'm becoming accustomed to.

"Even in your Mystery rites, you never will have known such a ritual. I'll say what I can and when you tell it, allude to it as a mystery. This pale Naiad could have been a shaft of moonlight, so otherworldly was her touch.

"Her gown, a gauzy wisp, barely covered her nakedness as she showed me joys I could know as woman, beginning with the tender sensitivity of my skin under her fluttering fingers and my breasts in her hands. She kissed my nipples, gently and then with a sharp nip that made me dizzy. I opened to her as her mouth moved downward.

"How does a Naiad resemble a mortal woman? Her body was ethereal, watery yet substantial. She engulfed me in sensations, touching my female center tenderly, exploring and intensifying until I was aflame."

He stops abruptly, aroused by the memory.

On me, the effect is horror. In Eleusis, the worship of Demeter incorporates no such spirits, no arousing embraces. If I were seized by such a being, I would be deathly afraid.

Teiresias speaks softly, as if his words arise from the depths of that moon pool. "The way she caressed me, touching every sensitive spot gently, then with vigor, brought me to a climax that sent me soaring. I wanted the sensations to last and last—and so they did, until I wept. She covered us with her veils and we lay together, drifting between heaven and earth." He takes a slow, deep breath, exhaling in a long sigh. "I linger on the memory, for here began my true initiation."

Teiresias' voice sounds otherworldly. "Through the night my soul followed a moonlit labyrinth into the dark, my body merging with the cosmos. I awoke before dawn on dew-sodden grass, no sign of my Naiad. Did I dream her? I wrapped myself in the shawl and fell back to sleep.

"Aphrodite's laugh shimmered. 'By your worship of Selene of the moon, you have become mine.' In a serpentine vision, she taught me her dance, a circling ebbing and flowing that would become as natural to me as walking.

"At dawn when I found Laothoë, sweat filmed my body as if I had truly danced. She said the moon ritual allowed me to inhabit the ancient age of silver before human separation and suffering. I would ever grieve its loss in the depths of my being, beneath consciousness.

"When I told her the Naiad left without speaking a word, Laothoë smiled. 'She wasn't your truth, only its means. Now you know woman's passion and the sacred dance.'

"I longed to sit by the grassy pool through the day, reliving my moonstruck night. Laothoë gave me breakfast, and though she didn't rush me, I knew it was time to go. I followed the path away from her shrine, barely marked yet clear to me.

"The landscape began changing, but I sensed the path, so on I walked, reluctantly leaving the dense woods behind. Step by step the lushness slipped away. The trees were tamarisk, growing smaller and more gnarled with each step, as if fighting for their lives in a terrain where streams flowed deep underground. They gave a lacy kind of shade, sufficient on this late autumn day.

"The sound of distant travelers reminded me that I was near the road. My feet seemed to know where they were going, but I felt lost in that inhospitable landscape. When I looked behind me to see if I could simply repeat my steps, the path had vanished in knotted undergrowth. I discerned a pathway of sorts moving onward, so with trepidation continued. Surely I would soon encounter a hermit, if not a priestess, and stayed alert. But as I walked on and dusk approached, I feared for my life.

"Near exhaustion with only a few sips of water remaining, I spotted a hut surrounded by laurel bushes in a grove of healthy tamarisks. A girl came running from her scanty garden. 'My mistress expected a visitor would arrive today, and here you are. I'm Leuce. Come meet Dora, priestess of Gaia.'

"In such a bleak place, these women must live in Gaia's protection. But they had a well, and their cottage looked sturdy. Thus did I discover that hidden sanctuaries to Gaia are scattered everywhere. Was there one in Eleusis?"

"If there was one nearby, I never visited it." I know Gaia is the primal Earth goddess, grandmother of Demeter, but Demeter is the maternal focus of Eleusis. "Tell me about this priestess."

"Dora was the oldest woman I'd ever seen. She wasn't blind, but she relied on Leuce as I rely on Cenchrias. Yet despite moving slowly with the aid of a stick, Dora had a unique demeanor, combining age and youth. Her face was wrinkled, but her dark eyes sparkled, and a full set of teeth gleamed in her wide, smiling mouth. In the strong voice of a young woman, she welcomed me.

"When Leuce brought us water, I saw a large snake basking in a sunny spot, enclosed by a circle of sticks. Fear struck me dumb. Fine to speak of the serpent path, but this one was as real as those I broke apart in the deep woods. I jumped, splashing the water out of Leuce's hand. I'd not only trespassed in the Goddess' woods, I violated the intimacy of the serpent realm, committing a crime against primal forces.

"Dora and Leuce were laughing.

"'Surely you aren't afraid of snakes,' Dora said. 'She's harmless. You must know, in the earliest days of humanity, the Snake Goddess herself was a serpent. Perhaps that ancient divinity sent you here to confront your fears and understand her powers.'

"I couldn't smile with them nor explain my alarm."

I look at Teiresias. "Do you really believe you committed a crime in the deep woods?"

"That's what I felt then, but no, not directly after I struck. That was my last moment as a valiant man.

"Leuce refreshed my water cup from the meager spring, and I tried to calm myself.

"Dora spoke quietly about how the serpent was central to Crete's worship of Gaia. Her priestesses were devoted to serpents, her artisans depicted them in decorations and votive offerings. Dora added that I must know this, did I not?

"I struggled for words. Yes, I knew snakes were part of esoteric cults in times gone by, and because they shed their skins, they represent regeneration. But they transformed my very being! I could scarcely tell her that.

"She took my hand with the serpent-priestess ring. 'I know something profound shook you just now, Teira. But you wouldn't be here if you weren't guided by deep forces. Serpents embody cosmic and chthonic realms beyond our earthly one.'

"We sat quietly sipping water in the patchy shade until I collected myself. What's your thought, Manto? Serpents brought you here."

"My dream serpents must have arisen from the depths." As he was telling the story my body felt tense, and perhaps this was why. Serpents crushed me—and played a part in directing my destiny. "There are earthly snakes like Leuce's in its circle of sticks and there are primordial ones. Let's simply grant that, and keep them separate."

"So have I done since that encounter in the deep forest. With just one exception."

"Story for another day?"

He nods.

"Dora described Crete of earlier times, with temples painted in bright colors and decorated with art rich in flowers and sea creatures. No images of battle, for war was unknown. As she spoke I recalled an agèd priest in Thebes speaking of a Golden Age before strife and greed, where men and women were equal, working together in harmony, sharing and cooperative. It seemed like a precious dream, that harmony prevailed among our early ancestors.

"Dora's Crete in ancient days resembled that mythic Golden Age. No one went hungry; children and elders were cared for communally. Men were as beautifully garbed as women, and the sports pursued by both were for pleasure and to honor the Goddess rather than serving as preparation for warfare. No distinction was made between work and play, for both were equally embraced. She said we have evidence from refugees from Crete. Their handsome buildings weren't fortified. They possessed neither armaments nor weapons, only knives for preparing food."

"Sounds idyllic, especially here with the threatening horses of the Epigoni. Our life in Eleusis was peaceful, but nearby stands Athens, fully fortified."

"Thebes is much worse." He sighs.

"After I said I was traveling to Corinth, Dora invited me to stay the night. 'It's less than a day's walk from here on the open road. You came from the direction of the woods, but now you must gather your strength for the challenges ahead. Do you plan to go on alone?'

"When I replied that I made my way from Thebes by myself, she said, 'Women don't walk this road alone. Corinth is considered a benign city, but I hope you have a clear destination there when you arrive. As for the road to get there?' She shook her head.

"'You soothed my fright at your snake, and now you stir up worry,' Her expression remained severe. 'What do you suggest I do? I can't hire a mule and driver.'

"'You mustn't be seen as an attractive young woman.'

"Leuce brought me a shabby cloak. It could as well have belonged to a man as a woman, and was large enough to cover me head to toe.

"She prepared a simple meal of an odd fruit that grew on the stunted trees and gruel made from their large bag of barley. I hadn't noticed bee hives nor the goat grazing beyond their dwelling, but their honey and milk sweetened the gruel.

"Afterward I lay on the bed Leuce made for me, sleepless while they breathed quietly beside me. I prayed to Hermes, god of travelers, for protection. The words 'Rely on your strength. Rely on your strength,' finally let me drift to sleep.

"Next day I bid Dora and Leuce farewell and covered myself with the cloak, growing more and more dusty as I walked. The road was sunbaked, no more secret paths. Peddlers and pilgrims ignored me in their press toward Corinth. I walked firmly, like a man about important business, and so reached the city safely."

He stands, and Cenchrias comes to take his arm. "My dear Manto, I'm exhausted. I never talked so long, and memories tumble in my head. I trust my dreaming mind to guide me, so shall sleep now."

I watch Cenchrias walk Teiresias to the privy and make up his pallet. The old man appears to fall asleep immediately.

Soon I too shall, but Cenchrias returns and sits beside me, a companionable feeling between us even without conversation. I pay attention to his moving hands and understand that he's expressing friendship. Trust. A bond of affection.

Simple messages, but enough to make us both smile.

Chapter Five: Corinth

I awaken well rested, dream images from Teiresias' story lingering. Cenchrias is setting out our morning meal, looking cheerful, Teiresias too seems refreshed, though I see traces of tears on his cheeks. I sit beside him and help myself to bread and melon.

"Is Corinth as splendid as they say?"

"It was dazzling then. Now?" He shrugs. "Perhaps not, but when I first saw the temple on the Acrocorinth, its ocher walls shone more brilliantly in the afternoon sun than a palace. Instead of climbing there, my feet took me on a narrow path to a bluff with spindly windblown trees and a cave opening into the hillside where I was greeted by Carpho. She resembled a farmer more than a priestess with her sunburnt face, bare muscular arms, and sturdy legs under a rough tunic she'd hiked into her belt to better maneuver around her rocky domain. Did you ever know such a votary of Demeter?"

"Shrines to Demeter can be found many places, but I haven't heard of a priestess who resembles a farmer. Was Carpho of the secret sisterhood?"

"A sister, yes, but her shrine wasn't secret. Recognizing my girdle as a sign from Aphrodite, her eyes crinkled with laughter, reminding me of obscene Baubo in my dream. But her instructions were serious. Next day, I should go to Aphrodite's temple and join in the dance. When she told me that living there I would fulfill my female destiny, I wondered what she intuited.

"On my way, I should take a half-hidden path to the shrine of Ananke and Bia, goddesses I'd heard of only as dread powers. Ananke: Necessity. Bia: Force. Carpho told me to weave a wreath of anise and heather and add a drop or two of my blood to appease them. That chilled me. How might such powers challenge me, a woman?"

He pauses, a piece of bread halfway to his mouth. "Since then I've had reason to wonder if my offerings and prayers were sufficient, or what influence our prayers even have. Do the gods care about us? They, and Fate, drive us as they will, regardless of our sacrifices and invocations. Force and Necessity cannot be appeased. We cannot stop the Epigoni."

"You say that as a seer? Are you certain Thebes can't defend itself?"

"The Theban army, arrogant and ill prepared, will be trapped by sword and fire. When the Epigoni are near, I'll warn King Laodamas to send women and children to safety. All I can do to save the city is advise him to delegate emissaries to negotiate a peace treaty. If battle ensues, the king will not survive it."

"What about us?"

"We'll evacuate. My life will end soon after, but Cenchrias will live on and you, Manto, will carry my story far from here. Though always a priestess and seeress, you will marry a king across the seas and be renowned for your tales and your wisdom."

"You see that?"

"I do. Your path will not be easy, but you are strong."

A wife and queen? That's harder to imagine than Thebes' destruction. This prophecy seems a distraction from my true path.

Or perhaps not. As he speaks I consider how to tell his tale. So far I have a beginning. How will the Muse inspire me onward? How will his story impact my own? I sigh. For now I shall simply listen.

He finishes his bread. "Carpho recognized the ancient power of my ring. She echoed Dora, saying serpents twine through all existence: the essence of life, destiny, and death.

"She described Corinth's founding by Sisyphus, a scoundrel who made the city a center of navigation and trade who now perpetually pushes his heavy stone in Hades for attempting to trick the gods. Every hero has visited Corinth and always shall, his life changed when he departs. So too for the women blessed as priestesses of Aphrodite, and now I'd been chosen to join their rituals.

"When I asked how to proceed, Carpho described the eternal spring Peirene on the Acrocorinth that erupted where Pegasus struck his hoof. Before entering the temple, I must splash myself and drink of Peirene's sacred waters, and all would follow. Carpho's practical advice gave me confidence."

He pauses. Is that all she told him? I wouldn't consider a splash and a drink of sacred waters sufficient preparation.

His story changes direction and I don't interrupt.

"From Carpho's bluff next morning, I gazed through the shimmering heat beyond the isthmus to the expanse of water beyond, outlines of distant islands appearing and disappearing. Do you know the sea, Manto?"

"We often bathed in the waters below Eleusis."

"You were fortunate. When I saw the sea for the first time, something loosened within me. Its vastness made landlocked Thebes seem a benighted outpost cut off from infinity." He lets out a long slow breath. "How small seemed my pursuits as an upstanding man of the Cadmeia."

"Even at Eleusis one cannot grasp all the universe," I say. "That's why I left. The world held more for me to learn and experience."

"And here you are, a seeker. This is a sanctified place where pilgrims come for prophecies. In time, you will learn more about the city looming behind us, but first I'll describe Corinth and all Teira encountered there and afterwards, up to a fateful encounter with Zeus and Hera."

"Zeus and Hera?"

He laughs. "Oh yes, they play a big part in my history."

I scowl. Zeus may be Demeter's brother, but at Eleusis he and his brothers Hades, Persephone's abductor, and Poseidon Earthshaker are not held in high regard. Why would Zeus figure in Teira's life?

The sun breaks through the clouds and illuminates the ravine of Mount Cithaeron. A pair of swans plough through the air, shimmering iridescent birds of Aphrodite, and Teiresias' milky eyes follow their vanishing sound.

"I could recount the most dramatic events and have done with it, but I can't report why the gods questioned me without explaining why I answered as I did. I never experienced the kekeon enhancement of the Mysteries, but I know the godlike heights and depths revealed by visions transcending ordinary reality. So I shall proceed, with you imagining the part played by nature's hallucinatory gifts."

"Are you saying your mating serpents might have been a phantasm?"

"There's a thought," he says with a smile. "No, although the aromas of dense pine and black cedar that day did create an unearthly atmosphere. Striking apart the serpents transformed me. Visionary plants came later.

"I'll describe as succinctly as I can Aphrodite's temple and my time there. In my dreams last night I saw the faces of those I loved, in Corinth and beyond, and wept in my sleep. Yet, as you shall discover, memories, including sorrowful ones, are treasures for the old. This moment too is a treasure, with you beside me and Cenchrias looking after us."

Chapter Six: The Temple of Aphrodite

Teiresias takes a deep breath. "The temple stood on the summit above Carpho's cave, past the shrine of Ananke and Bia where I made my offering as instructed. It was as colossal and golden as if the gods laid its stones in perfect symmetry. Below stretched the wind-roughened gulf and narrow isthmus, with vineyards and orchards of the Peloponnese stretching to the south. That perfumed air would become my life breath, mingling sea, lemon blossoms, and roses sweeter than any I've known since. Those bushes"—he points over his shoulder toward a hedge of rosemary and full-blown pink and white blooms framing Cenchrias' vegetable garden—"were the closest I could find. At the gushing spring Peirene, I splashed water on my face and drank from my cupped hands.

"Inside the temple I glimpsed a statue of Aphrodite aglitter with jewels. I daren't enter, instead circling to the back courtyard where a trellised pathway led to the priestesses' dwelling house. To the trill of flute music, a line of women emerged, dressed in diaphanous gowns that caught the last rays of afternoon sun. I admired them not as Teiresias would but as my accomplished sisters and kept my distance into the temple.

"The wave design of the tile floor surrounding Aphrodite's statue evoked her rising from the sea. As the women began their dance, I recalled my dream where the goddess herself taught me the movements. I joined in, swaying to flute and drumbeat faster and faster until I lost my footing. A priestess seized my hand and held me firm as the flute slowed to a melody that rippled like splashing water.

"She, a priestess named Iole, walked me to supper. When I said a priest told me to join this sisterhood, she looked surprised.

"Only then did it occur to me that just because Mydon told me to come here didn't mean I could walk in and become a priestess of Aphrodite, even with Carpho's instruction.

"'It's Polydora you want to talk to,' Iole said. 'She doesn't call herself chief priestess, but that is how we see her. Come join us for dinner and you'll meet her.'

"At the marble threshold of the dwelling a cat glared, her tawny eyes upon me. I nodded to her, as if a sentinel cat could grant me safe entry, and stepped into a large central hall lined with tapestry-hung doorways. In the center between glimmering lamps, plates of fruit, olives, and cakes stretched down a long table with benches along the sides.

"Each priestess taking her seat at the table was stunning after a different fashion, and each intrigued me. Iole indicated the most regal among them as Polydora. I'd noticed her while dancing, with braided honey-blond hair, deep-set brown eyes lacking painted emphasis and wearing a simply decorated chiton, yet radiating a nobility that set her apart. Fear slowed my step. How dare I approach such a powerful woman?

"Iole introduced me. 'Teira hopes to join our sisterhood.'

"Polydora asked a priestess to move so we three could sit together. As she lifted her wine cup we joined her. 'To Aphrodite and Bellerophon, in celebration of his feast day.'

After we drank, the meal began with murmuring, laughter, and curious glances my way.

"'You arrived on an auspicious day, Teira,' Polydora said. 'Usually men join us in worship in the evening, but at the feast of Bellerophon they gather on their own. Only us tonight. What brought you here?'

"Of course I should have anticipated the question. After my time with Halia, Laothoë, Dora, and Carpho, I thought I was prepared. How truthful dare I be?

"I said I came from a village in Boeotia where my mother died birthing me. After my father's death, his closest friend, a revered priest, told me my destiny was as priestess of Aphrodite. When I was of age, his wagon brought me to Carpho with the message that she prepare me to climb to this temple on the Acrocorinth.'

"Polydora smiled. 'We know Carpho, a worthy teacher. What do you know of Aphrodite's rituals?'

"'Only the sacred dance.'

"'I saw Iole help you up when you danced too ardently. I'd sensed another priestess would join us, and you appear to be the one.' She looked across me to Iole. 'Teira may have the empty chamber next to Calyce's.'

"I had no appetite, but drank three goblets of a golden wine unknown in Thebes. As Iole named the priestesses around the table I was most intrigued by Calyce sitting across from us, with coppery gold curls under a bejeweled band and more adornment than the others. Suddenly, the wine and weight of perfume assaulted me. As I slipped backward, Iole caught me and helped me through one of the tapestry-draped doorways, where I collapsed on the bed.

"Lulled by women's voices, I was falling asleep when I felt warmth between my legs. I sat up in horror. In the dim light a reddish stain was spreading. Nothing to do but wad up bedclothes to absorb the blood and go to sleep. When I awoke, my first thought was I had shamed myself, and Polydora would send me away.

"Iole came in just then and laughed at the mess. 'With that much blood, it will be a short flow. Quite a welcome Aphrodite has given you!' Little did she imagine how remarkable a welcome.

"She led me to the inner courtyard lined with tables covered in creams, unguents, kohl, rouge, and decorated boxes filled with jewelry and hair ornaments. Two large chests of clothes stood against one wall. Iole told me to choose what I liked, for they were gifts to the temple. In the afternoons, priestesses arrayed themselves here to meet men who came to worship the goddess out of devotion, fear, or yearning and to experience her healing joy.

"I selected a gown of finely woven linen. Iole laid it on a bench by the central fountain and bathing tub, along with linen toweling, and left me to my bath. In the morning, priestesses wore only enough jewelry in the temple dance to please Aphrodite. In the evenings, besides dancing were the mystery rites. Iole didn't reply when I asked what preparation was required."

"Mystery rites inspired by Aphrodite?" I can't keep the shock out of my voice. They would have no resemblance to ours in Eleusis.

Teiresias ignores my outburst.

"Alone, I diverted cool water over me into the tiled tub and rubbed soap into my hair, the bubbles skimming down my body with the rinse water, their foamy traces arraying my breasts and belly. Never had I known such luxury. Would this truly be my life? It was hard to believe.

"In my chamber, sunlight angled through the window, illuminating the woven yellow and blue design on rug and cushions. The bloodied bedclothes had disappeared, and my blue serpent shawl was folded across the end of the bed. Attendants wafted in and out, young and ungainly or agèd and gracious."

"Not slaves?" I ask. We had similar attendants at Eleusis, but in most cities slaves served.

"In Corinth, our attendants were women who lived with us by choice or necessity. They ate at an adjoining table and dwelt in a comfortable house beyond.

"After the morning dance, Iole and I returned to the central hall where we breakfasted, the women's voices a melodic murmur. I sat next to Calyce, the most recently arrived before me. She praised me for knowing the dance and laughed when I told her I learned it in a dream. Nightly we would celebrate Aphrodite with dancing and sometimes in the intimacy of our chambers. When the goddess' light shone on me, I would be initiated into these rites.

"My curiosity was tinged with fear. What had Mydon sent me into?"

Chapter Seven: Sacred Dance

Cenchrias brings us chunks of watermelon, welcome in the noonday heat. He sits in a shady spot with a huge pile of melon in front of him, a look of sheer delight on his face.

Teiresias licks the last drops of juice from his lips. "I've reached a part of the story—" He looks hesitant.

"About initiation into the rites of Aphrodite. So you said."

"As I think of what words to use, I realize there are details—" He stops again.

"Details a father would not ordinarily tell his daughter?" I prompt.

"Exactly."

I laugh. "I understand you want me to create your story into a narration and convey the emotions as I will. Tell me everything, and I'll know what to say if the time comes."

At that I breathe an inward 'I hope,' then speak so he can hear. "So far your tale is etched in my imagination, but I cannot know what's significant until I hear it all. The rituals of Aphrodite must involve physical love, so I need to hear how you experienced it in Corinth."

"I'll tell it as it happened."

"It's all new to me."

"And a pleasure to recall." He takes a slow, deep breath.

"That afternoon, we relaxed into indolent conversation in the bathing courtyard, beautifying ourselves while Marpessa played her flute."

"You, a woman among the most striking women in all of Hellas. Quite a picture!"

"As I look today you can't even imagine me as an attractively agèd crone."

We both laugh. "Did being with those priestesses feel bizarre?"

"By that time, I'd embraced so much of the female that Corinth's ways were becoming mine."

"Will anyone believe this story?"

"Do you?" he counters.

"With you sitting beside me I do." I give his hand a squeeze.

"As I stood in front of a smoky mirror, Calyce combed my hair and wove in ornaments, turning my free-moving mane into a work of art, ringlets held by a woven band. I smudged kohl around my eyes. Laughing, she wiped it away and showed me how to etch the inky powder, spread a gold-tinted cream over my cheekbones, and rouge my lips. I chose a musky perfume oil which she dotted at points of warmth, even between my toes.

"She added an amethyst at my throat and bracelet on my ankle. As I examined my emerging beauty from every angle in the mirror's burnished sheen, she smiled. 'What a vain one! You must come from a village lacking mirrors. If you're so fond of mirrors, come to your chamber for a moment.'

"There Calyce took my hand and pulled me to the bed. 'Rest back on your elbows. Lift your skirt.' She aimed a hand mirror so I could see myself. 'Isn't that a beautiful petaled flower? Like an iris, pale pink shading to lavender. I'd like to see it blushing scarlet!'

"I couldn't think about what once belonged between Teiresias' muscle-knotted legs, so curious was I at this new sight, my moon flow now a mere trace. What I saw seemed a labyrinth into mystery.

""'Time to hide it away.' Calyce rearranged my skirt, 'even though I'm tempted to kiss it. When you dance, remember your beautiful hidden flower and enjoy its warmth.' She skipped away, me following, warmed through and a little shaky."

I don't interrupt the long silence that follows, with Teiresias lost in memories or musings.

He shakes himself and continues.

"As the sun fell toward the sea, attendants served dates and goblets of lemon water before the evening dance. This time we entered the temple by the wide front stairs, passing the altar attended by Polydora. Male worshipers stood beyond.

"Dancing near them, I heard the words 'beauty' and 'goddess' grace.' A man wearing the short tunic of a warrior under his bronze-threaded robe was addressing the words to me! As the music rose, I felt Aphrodite release me to him. I whirled faster and he wound me in against his chest.

"Calyce said if drawn to a man, I could bring him to my chamber. So I led this man Damysos across the courtyard, past the cat, her eyes half closed, through the carved door into the priestess dwelling, flute music muted behind us. In the empty dining hall, the table was set with wine jugs and plates of delicacies between low-burning lamps. I filled two goblets, lacing in drops of water. Drumbeats carried us to the privacy of my chamber.

"Damysos lifted his goblet to Aphrodite and to my beauty. As he spilled his libation I quavered. That night under Selene's moon, the Naiad who taught me woman's secrets seemed more spirit than human. Damysos was a flesh and blood man who could have been companion to Teiresias.

"Was it a jest of Aphrodite, that I should lose my old Teiresias self by making love with such a one? Damysos was trained in manly arts and now served King Laertes of Ithaca. But he was so unlike Teiresias as to open his dreams to Aphrodite and to me, her priestess."

For a moment I can scarcely follow what he's saying. This old man raises more questions than he answers, talking of himself as formerly Teiresias, now Teira. Here beside me, he is again Teiresias.

What happened? He relished his days as Teira and scorned the limitations of his previous male life. Yet here he is, not only male but blind, with no society but mute Cenchrias and those who come seeking his wisdom.

Unable to see my puzzled face, he clears his throat and resumes.

Chapter Eight: Rite of Aphrodite

"That night I became the goddess' true votary. The initiation that began with dancing came to fulfillment in Damysos' arms. To you, Manto, I describe encounters no woman today will experience. The temple of Aphrodite has changed irredeemably from the place Teira knew, crass in ways ours was not. In large part, I blame the so-called priestess Macaria and her love of wealth. When I arrived, Corinth's temple was a place of unsullied worship. My tale restores its innocent spirit for me and, I hope, for your eventual telling."

I touch his hand. Teiresias turns his blind face to me, transported, and speaks slowly.

"What an awe-inspiring evening Damysos and I enjoyed. He released the clasp on my girdle and sent me twirling, my skirt billowing around my bare legs and thighs. It touched me like a silken whip. As I fell laughing on the bed, the gown barely draping me, he leaned over to remove it. Aphrodite, that most abandoned goddess, gave us a voluptuous interlude beyond imagining. I resist the pain of nostalgia for joys the love goddess granted, but this memory fills my heart." He pauses, eyes closed.

"Afterwards, breathing in unison with me, Damysos murmured that he must leave at dawn on an embassy for King Laertes to the island of Cyprus. So suddenly? My heart clutched. He promised to make an offering at Aphrodite's spring outside Paphos. Scant consolation, for I would be no part of that. He told me he'd never before served the love goddess. Nor had I, but that I kept to myself. He praised her for inspiring our loving, which I echoed silently. Our love was a gift from Aphrodite.

"I enjoyed the lingering glow between us, only half listening as Damysos spoke softly. He would return to Corinth for the Isthmian Games next year—had spent so much time on embassies he never married—his brother managed their lands in Ithaca—he'd learned battlefield medicine, both practical treatments of wounds and healing rituals, from a priest of Apollo. My attention sparked when he added that an old woman tending a shrine deep in the woods who gained her knowledge from Mother Gaia was wiser than the priest.

"When I mentioned knowing such women, he nodded, unsurprised. My service too was healing, he said. I offered the comfort and inner peace a man yearns for. One who feels only an animal urge dare not approach our temple, for our rites required preparation like any sacred mystery."

I protest. "You can't be serious. You say your voluptuous interlude, as you described it with Damysos, was of the same order as Demeter's rites in Eleusis?"

"My dear Manto, don't be offended. Why do we have a pantheon if not for rites associated with many gods? Childbirth is a sacred mystery, and heroes would say the same of warfare and sailing Poseidon's seas. Much in our lives is touched with the divine."

"Until now I've known only the rites of Artemis and Demeter," I say. "Because the Eleusinian Mysteries reach essentials of life and death, they seemed the greatest. Yet I left them behind."

"Exactly. Rich in spirit as Eleusis is, you yearned for more. I asked Damysos if the temple dance had been his preparation for our ritual.

"Partially, he replied, and his dreams. Much of the pain a man seeks to heal with medicine could be vanquished through love. He stroked my back, saying I healed unaware. Men who came to me might not reveal their secret wounds, but they would be whole when they left. So it was with him. He embraced me and fell asleep, but I was too overwhelmed by sensations of mind and body.

"I heard the rustle of feet passing my doorway, bursts of laughter, music in the distance. This is my life, I thought. How remote Teiresias' boyhood games seemed, running in armor and running naked, boxing and wrestling, my pride in my ornamented sword. The combative spirit dominated Thebes since warriors sprang from Earth Herself, ready to battle to the death. In Thebes Teiresias never questioned that heritage, but in Corinth it made no sense."

"As Teira you renounced your former practices and beliefs? What about your sense of duality?"

"After I recognized Teiresias' ignorance and blinding fears, I saw how his fealty to Apollo entrapped him. That was past."

"And now?"

"Now I honor the deep wellsprings of woman's eternal power, from Gaia to Aphrodite and beyond."

"Is that how you want your story to be told?"

A long reflective pause. "As I said, it's larger than the tale of Teira. For now you must hear about my transformations. They are what I've kept to myself all these years.

"I told you I'll listen attentively."

"That's not enough. If you're committing to do this—"

I interrupt. "I haven't committed."

His blank eyes hold mine, unnerving as always. "Didn't I impress you with the urgency? My story must be told, and our time together is limited."

"I understand, but have I the skill to pass it on?"

"Have you ever listened to rhapsodes?"

"Now and then."

"What skills did they employ?"

"All stories I've heard begin by giving the listeners an idea of their argument."

"Then here's your test. Create an argument for mine. If you cannot form even a possible beginning, you need not listen to another word."

A laugh escapes me. "Oh! I have done. Here's what I came up with. *Sing of a complicated being, Muse, one who who discovered the realms of the male and the female like no mortal before or since.*" I pause. "I know more is needed."

He says nothing, and soon the next part fills my mind. "*Sing of a complicated being, Muse, one who who discovered the realms of the male and the female like no mortal before or since, gaining greater knowledge than the gods of Mount Olympus. Tell of the pain and glory of this rare lifetime and the wisdom gained.*"

"Bravo, Daughter. One more line will be needed, but I haven't reached that part of the story. You have the makings of a rhapsode." He smiles. "Don't worry about poetic expression. More important, and your second sight will be a great help, is to experience these adventures yourself. Listen with me, and you'll be able to capture the drama for your hearers. You will know how to participate in Teira's emotions."

"I was on the bed with Teira and Damysos. When you relived that night, you brought me along."

"Good start."

"You stopped with Teira lying next to sleeping Damysos."

"Yes. The sky was dark when he untangled himself from my arms. He apologized for disturbing me. I watched as he slipped on his tunic, belted it, and gathered up his robe. In spite of his warning, his departure felt abrupt.

"Damysos assured me Aphrodite would remain with him on his voyage, as would this night with me. He leaned down, brushed his lips across mine, breathed, 'I pray to return to you,' and glided out through the drapery.

"His steps faded into silence, leaving emptiness in his wake. So. Worshipers leave. Where was Aphrodite now? The dregs in my goblet smelt stale, the room hollow with abandonment. Perhaps this was Aphrodite's lesson, not what happened between Damysos and me. She doesn't wish us to despair. She merely departs, indifferent.

"I wrapped my bare body in a robe and stepped into the empty hall where oil lamps still burned and the table was littered with goblets and half full plates. In the outer courtyard I relieved myself and washed, then ate a honey cake which seemed cloying and nibbled a handful of almonds. Muffled sounds came from behind the tapestried doorways.

"Instead of taking me to my apartment, my feet moved toward the temple. Dawn was a pink glow on the horizon, the building deserted. Even here I felt Aphrodite's absence. I hurried back to my warm bed and fell asleep. And thus I was initiated into her service."

"Were you sad? I'm sad hearing this."

"After Damysos left?" Teiresias sighs. "Yes, at first. Poets sing of woman's encounters with gods, all those abductions, seductions, and rapes, but you must tell how Aphrodite preserved Teira. She—I—bore no resemblance to fated Persephone, Europa, Semele and their kin, stolen from their mortal course to be held in a passionate god's arms, then forsaken, perhaps killed. When I complained to Halia about such women's suffering, she said those tales of rapes represented Zeus taking over early shrines of woodland goddesses. Perhaps, but for myself, Teiresias' seizure by the serpents of the goddess from his male Theban life opened a miraculous new existence."

His blind eyes fill with tears. How did that existence come to an end, when its loss causes such grief?

Caught in the mood of Teira's loss of Damysos, I wonder if his memories of being a beautiful, loving woman make him regret that he's now a blind old man. Was it a punishment? True, as a warrior he would be long dead, and as an old woman? Perhaps Teira would be living in a woodland shrine or practicing the healing arts.

Instead, Teiresias is a renowned soothsayer. I take his hand, keeping questions to myself.

Cenchrias has been preparing supper, and I'm pleased when he brings us bowls of vegetable soup with the scent of dill and swirled through with goat cheese. On top floats toasted bread, a satisfying meal.

After we finish, we linger in the firelight in companionable silence. Then Cenchrias settles Teiresias for the night and I make my way to the cottage that has become mine.

Chapter Nine: *The Streets of Corinth*

Next morning a cool breeze blows. Cenchrias has left honeycomb and thickened goat's milk on our table and is at work in the garden, trusting me to take charge of his master.

We breakfast in silence. My dreams were full of dancing women and flute music. After burying the story for so long, did Teiresias dream of Damysos? I can't tell from his expression, only that he's ready to continue.

"Corinth was my new home, so I wanted to know my way around. Teiresias was the perfect man of Thebes, but I couldn't afford his blithe assumptions here. With Iole and Calyce as guides, I walked down the hill to the city proper. Under carved sun eagles, emblem of the house of King Polybus, stood the royal palace. The entrance courtyard was empty. Queen Merope would not be inviting us into her chambers as Iole hoped.

"Those names, Merope and Polybus, echo with tragic resonance these many years later, and their fateful connection to another whose name shall live forever. *Oedipus*. Have you heard of him, Manto?"

"Vague whispers. A tragic fate, I believe?"

"I shouldn't have mentioned him yet. Remember the name, but for now we'll stay with Corinth.

Cenchrias comes to move our pallets into the shade of the olive tree. Teiresias leans on me as we walk, then stretches out and lounges on one arm. I make myself comfortable with a cushion.

"I was describing Teira's walk round the city. At the stadium Calyce sprinted ahead. She'd run halfway around the track before Iole and I emerged from the entry passageway. 'Our training is all wrong,' she called as she circled back, 'dancing and making ourselves beautiful. If we practiced here every day, we could compete in the Games!'

"I'd lost the swift foot of Teiresias, but without the hindering gown, my strides would have lengthened. That hadn't mattered—except, apparently, to Calyce.

"We passed by the precinct of Aphrodite within the city walls. A narrow street opened into a bright agora surrounding a half-sized statue of the goddess decorated in intaglio and embedded gems on a low pedestal, cerise flowers arching over her.

"Iole explained that priestesses living in houses facing the square were mothers. Mothers? That was a surprise. When I asked if they were no longer priestesses, Iole named them. Two I'd seen at the temple, Rhene and Satyrea, whose motherhood surprised me the most. Satyrea with her flirtatious dark beauty? An unlikely mother, but here she lived with her little son.

"Through columns in the porticos, I glimpsed murals of flying fish, youths and maidens, bordered with vines and flowers. The lively paintings made me think of the Crete described by Dora. I wanted to talk to the women who dwelt behind these doors and meet their children, but we needed to return to the temple.

"Nightly, Aphrodite's jeweled eyes blazed down upon us as we danced. Some men who attended faithfully never accompanied a priestess to her chamber. They offered oblations to the goddess, then joined a few of us afterwards on the back steps of the temple where we talked beneath the stars.

"Zetes, son of Meteos, chief advisor to King Polybus, became my favored companion on the steps. His pensive gray eyes turned inward, as if he carried a secret wound. Sitting silent beside Zetes, I felt my separation from the festive life around us and often lay awake for hours afterward, reflecting on my womanly existence rather than simply being immersed in it."

"How do you mean?"

"The peculiarity of it all. Was Teiresias gone with so little trace? What in my mind connected to him? Nothing, in my daily life or social world nor in my spirit. Aphrodite and the moon goddesses took over from Apollo and Zeus. In body and soul I was Teira. And my mind? The duality seemingly was gone, yet my inner voice, 'me,' felt consistent. Though changed in body, I wasn't a different person. My world had simply widened, and no doubt would continue to."

In old tales, a transformed being is changed in shape only. As a cow, Io still feels a woman's pangs. Not exactly the case with Teira.

But Teiresias says no more, instead describing those gatherings on the steps.

"Priestesses spoke of their home towns. Iole came from Cythera, one of Aphrodite's islands, famed for the rare purple dye made from the mollusks that breed along its shores. Calyce was born on rocky Naxos, the island where Theseus abandoned Ariadne after she saved him from the Minotaur labyrinth. Calyce laughed that Ariadne was bored with Theseus' boasts and hid until he sailed away without her, leaving her free for Dionysus. A princess of Crete,

Ariadne preferred the long-haired god of the vine over an adventurer, however famed.

"Polydora, who joined us occasionally, came closest to being the temple leader. No male worshipers ever approached her. She expressed her devotion to Aphrodite by guiding temple events. Once she mentioned she was born in Sparta but said little else of her past.

"One twilight as a few of us gazed across the wine-dark sea, Zetes said I never spoke of my home. I replied I came from a Boetian village near Thebes and yes, I attended fetes at King Labdacus' palace and had seen Prince Laius. The finality of my tone left no more to say."

Teiresias' words make me consider my own past. I suppose men born to a famous line must fulfill their destined role, but it isn't only being an orphan that permits me to do as I wish. Most women leave home to marry, their identity shifting within the male sphere. Priestesses, however, are free. For Teira to say little about her past wouldn't likely matter. At Eleusis they knew Lydia and I had been raised in a shrine to Artemis. That she was born into a wealthy trader's family and I an orphan was insignificant.

Nor do origins matter for a soothsayer. Teiresias now sits beneath the walls of the city where he grew up, and no one knows his origins.

Chapter Ten: Spring Celebration

I shake my head to more food, and Cenchrias takes away what remains of the honeycomb.

Teiresias describes the festival of Aphrodite's renewal at the new moon before summer. As Aphrodite renewed herself in the sacred spring, her priestesses were renewed in her grace. Teira was to preside over offerings and prayers.

"The afternoon of the festival, Polydora set a woven diadem on my hair and gave me a cup of a pungent herbal drink. Walking to my place at the altar, drums pounded my head into a fever. Or was it the drink? Priestesses shimmered in the rosy light as worshipers gathered in a circle beneath the steps in the torch-lit dusk. Young girls in white carried caged doves, and priests from the temple of Helios wore azure blue and gold.

"This was my first view of Queen Merope and King Polybus, dressed in matching violet robes. Otherwise they were a study in contrasts, the bronzed face of Polybus creased with lines of perpetual good spirits lifting outward from dark brown eyes and silvery Merope, pale of skin and hair, eyes the color of her robe.

"After Merope presented a bouquet of white roses to the goddess, I offered her a kylix of water from the Peirenean spring, then to Polybus, each touching a drop of the water to their foreheads and a drop to their hearts. I knew what such a devoted couple would seek before Polybus placed his offering on the altar. A crawling baby of bronze.

"I envisioned a radiant child. 'You will have a son.' I could barely rasp out the words, my throat constricted. Only later did I recognize my burning eyes and choked breath as a warning, for this was my first vision. Still today my eyes burn when I hear the Epigoni galloping toward us."

"Your first vision came when you were a priestess of Aphrodite?"

"Yes. I didn't expect any such gift. My encounter with the serpents transformed me more than bodily—which had been dramatic enough! Uncanny forces seized me, as I experienced on my walk to Corinth between hidden shrines. Visions can sneak up on us gradually or be revelations." He pauses, looking in my direction. "How did you discover you possessed second sight, Manto?"

"At first it was simply a state of awareness. I saw beyond the surface, perceived depths I couldn't express. But visions? The first was when Demeter spoke to me from her well at Eleusis. I didn't see her, but it felt like a vision."

"You know that ominous feeling when we hear the Epigoni. So too, a flight of birds or sudden change of wind can bring an omen. Your sight will manifest in many ways and enhance your story-telling." He pauses. "Are you willing to hear more?"

"I haven't anything more important to do," I reply, my voice conveying a smile.

Teiresias describes the temple offerings, worshipers, and dancing to the music of Marpessa's flute at the celebration of Aphrodite's renewal. Three worshipers besides the royal pair would figure later in his tale: Zetes and his father Meteos, King Polybus' chief advisor, and an unnamed stocky man who held Teira with his fiery eyes.

"Singing intensified until it touched the ears of Aphrodite. A cymbal clash commanded silence for the ritual washing of the small goddess figure.

"From the altar I watched the sacred bath through the columns until the song, "*Goddess in the holy waters,*" chorused to the flutter of wings and the girls released their doves. The procession returned to the temple with Aphrodite wrapped in a damp veil.

"I longed to join the dance flowing into the courtyard but contented myself with moving where I stood. The starry stream of Python blazed across the purple sky, obscuring the outline of the new moon. Torches flashed irregularly across the courtyard with their bearers' movements. Polybus and Merope offered libations to Aphrodite and all the gods and goddesses, their voices floating toward the heavens."

His expression darkens. "Perhaps the gods, feasting on nectar and ambrosia on Mount Olympus, were deaf to our prayers."

Chapter Eleven: Masquerade

Teiresias' voice and the bees buzzing in the flowering rosemary bushes have lulled me, and I must stretch. He's content to nap, so I take a walk, examining my surroundings.

My cottage isn't the lowly cabin of my early impressions. It's sturdy, with a stout roof and stone foundation. On the far side, a stunted lemon tree is laden with fruit, as if all its resources went into producing them. Near the pathway to the privy, Cenchrias' vegetable garden is partially concealed by overgrown rosemary and roses. The yard with its olive trees and chicken coop is encircled by a hedge of bay laurel.

Yet the high wall behind belies the sense of this as a protected retreat. The road into the city is blocked by the barely visible Electran gate. Despite the illusion of peace, Thebes looms.

I return and rouse Teiresias, who looks startled, his voice groggy. Lemon water revives him, and he begins speaking.

"Summer was full upon us. Waking up dispirited one stifling day, I pictured Damysos off in Cyprus on a mission such as I might have had as Teiresias. I came late to breakfast, no one but Iole in the dining hall. I asked her what the men of Corinth did these hot nights.

"When she looked puzzled, I admitted envying them. 'Spending time on our appearance seems pointless and our dances lack energy. I wish I could break free for a while.'

"'You mean leave the temple? Go into the hills as a Maenad?'

"What I wanted was to carouse as a man for one night. I asked Iole where men drank wine and joked and lost all thought of themselves."

I laugh. "What you told me of your life on the Cadmeia as king's counselor didn't include carousing."

"No. Only royal banquets. I never wandered ordinary streets or mixed with ordinary men. In my short time in Corinth I'd seen more than I knew of Thebes."

"What about after you returned?"

"No carousing. That evening with Iole was one in a lifetime. She thought me mad for suggesting we tie our hair under men's hats, smudge our faces, and set off in dirty cloaks. But I longed to know Corinth from inside a man's clothing and convinced her this caper would delight whimsical Aphrodite. She agreed to find us the clothes.

"In her chamber after the evening dance, Iole showed me two gray cloaks as dusty as the tunics to wear beneath. I pulled the embroidered band from my forehead and stepped out of my gown. We reversed our beauty routine, wiping away kohl, removing earrings, washing off perfume, until we stood naked together. Judging by their earthy smell, these tunics belonged to farmers. Belting them loosely, we arranged the cloaks jauntily over our shoulders and added leather hats and old sandals. Looking at each other we laughed. We would pass.

"We half slid, half ran down to the city, no thought of dust.

"I spoke in a deep voice and straightened my shoulders. 'We're men now.'

"'As you say,' Iole answered in a similar tone. 'Tell me, Tereus, what's the news from Sparta?'

"'The same old thing, Iasus.'

"We headed for the port through unfamiliar streets, walking with firm steps and greeting the few men we passed. I felt at ease in my anonymity and manly stride and looked at Iasus to see if she bore a similar confidence. Her male bearing and blank face carried it off, but I caught the anxiety in her eyes.

"'I wonder who we'll meet tonight, Tereus.'

"'No one will recognize you. You aren't particularly good-looking. All you need is wine to redden your nose.'

"'You're quite the coarse fellow yourself.'

"We followed dissonant music to a wine shop, linking arms in a comradely fashion as we stepped into the noisy room. She'd thought to bring a small loop of bronze to exchange for clay goblets full of what must have been the last pressing of the wine.

"'Is this what you longed for, Tereus? Dreadful stuff!'

"'So this is men's home ground,' I said in her ear as we found a bit of wall to lean against, far from a lamp. We looked over the boisterous crowd, seeing no familiar face.

"'To Hermes, god of tricks and wiles.' Iole spilled out a libation.

"After I poured a few drops myself, I saw the man nearby watching. 'To Hermes.' The din drowned me out, but he understood, and we lifted our goblets together. In the freedom of disguise, Iole and I became part of the joviality, blending with the men around us.

"Soon patrons began spilling out of the crowded shop into the street. Goblets refilled, we were pushed into the refreshing breeze. A man took my hand. 'I see you like jewelry.' Shock pieced me. Had I forgotten a bracelet? At his next words I sighed in relief. 'May I see your ring in a better light?'

"I held up my ring finger. I told him it came from my grandmother and asked if he was a collector. Turns out I was talking to Corinth's renowned jeweler Didaeon. He said my ring was a rare treasure, surely a relic of ancient Crete from the days when the Great Goddess ruled. The gold was of the best quality and the serpent-skirt design the work of a master jeweler. His wife Leiriope, who made their designs would like to see it. He told us where to find their shop and invited us to come any time.

"I savored the sounds of rising voices, pungent air, and ribaldry of men. Iole was blustering in a winey baritone to a pair of men I recognized, Zetes' father Meteos and his friend with the fiery eyes, slapping each other on the shoulder like old friends. When I joined them, he said, 'I haven't seen you here before.' His eyes held mine. 'My name is Brovas. And yours?'

"'Tereus,' I said. 'Good to meet you.' I took Iole's empty goblet and set it on the stoop by my own. 'Time to go, Iasus.'

"'Come again, fellows.' I felt Brovas' eyes following us.

"Walking up the dark street, the noise echoing behind us was raucous enough to please Dionysus, but I was shaken by Brovas' penetrating eyes. What if he knew?

"'A fine revel,' Iole said in the voice of Iasus, 'but we'll keep it to ourselves. Those men had no idea who shared their jokes.'

"We made our way through the city and climbed to the Acrocorinth, glorying in our evening of disguise and rough wine. At the Peirenean spring we splashed our faces clean and sneaked into our building, unnoticed at that late hour.

"I awoke with a dry mouth and a headache, satisfied at having woven a loose thread from my—Teiresias'—metamorphosis. I would not again need to play the man."

I wonder to what extent he's doing so now, here beside me. He's talked about his double vision. How could it not be even more when he's again male? And how male is his body? A withered organ, I imagine. I shake myself. Manto! What a thought. But why wouldn't I be curious? Teiresias is the strangest person I've ever encountered, father or no, and I want to learn about him—and about his visions.

"One evening Zetes confided to me that a baby boy had appeared in the palace. I was puzzled. Now and then I saw Queen Merope wearing a full-flowing chiton, but didn't suspect pregnancy. Where could this baby have come from? Zetes said Merope was discreet, as she'd miscarried in the past, but soon they would celebrate an heir to the throne.

"I feared the piteous place this child held in the gods' relentless order but shrugged it off. He was their blessed son and heir."

Chapter Twelve: Swimming

As Cenchrias brings us a salad of the greens I watched him pick, Teiresias asks if I know how to swim.

"Yes, we did more than bathe in the sea below Eleusis. Swimming was one of our observances."

"I'm glad to hear it. I never learned how, so Calyce taught me. One day we walked down to the seashore, the sky sparkling and whitecaps etching the waves. I heard Aphrodite's laughter in each breaking wave. As we walked along the beach we saw a magnificent ship sailing into the harbor, a large eye painted on each side of the bow.

"'A ship of Ithaca,' remarked an old man repairing fish nets, 'loaded with treasure and news.' When we reached the dock, its sails were furled and we could hear commands to the oarsmen.

"Calyce dashed toward a cove. Around the point, I saw her folded chiton on a rock and her head surfacing from the water. Leaving my clothes beside hers, I stepped carefully into the sea. Either Calyce was an expert teacher or swimming came naturally, for soon we were frolicking like two dolphins. Waterlogged, we sat in the shade, gowns loose, hair drying in the breeze, eating almonds and peaches. I rested my head in Calyce's lap, my fingers entwined in hers against my breast. The bright air brought tantalizing provocations, and we rolled together, girlish games verging on the play of lovers, arousing and almost satisfying."

Teiresias gives me a questioning look. Perhaps he's said too much. "Go on, Father. What fun to cavort in the sunshine."

As I knew with Lydia, my swimming partner in Eleusis and dear companion after she came to live at the temple of Artemis when we were children. Our years together seem like the distant past, yet they're with me forever. Teiresias' emotional connections are more complicated and I'll never talk to him about Lydia, but she was closer to me than my sister. I smile in memory as he talks about hurrying to the temple.

"Fastening girdles over gowns dusty from our climb, we joined the evening dance as we were. The brightness of Calyce's eyes and glow of her cheeks shone more vividly than if touched by kohl and rouge. The salty tang of the sea on our skin seemed a rich perfume.

"That night the dance was gay and light, and the musicians played longer than usual. Rhene tended the altar, overseeing the largest circle of worshipers since the new moon festival. I lost myself in the joy of rhythm and movement.

"Then I sensed a familiar figure. He pulled me close as the music ended. Damysos!

"'Greetings, my sun-kissed one. I saw you in the sea today, rivaling Aphrodite as you rose from the waves.'

"I should have guessed the ship was his. As another song began, we drifted into the empty dining hall where lamps burned and baskets of late summer flowers decorated the table. Full goblets in hand, we passed through the draperies into my chamber. Flute music and incense floated in on the sea breeze.

"In Cyprus Damysos left his ship near Paphos. There, in a meadow dotted with red anemones like drops of Adonis's blood, he found Aphrodite's spring. It fed a pool under a hollow rock shaded by poplars where he could imagine the goddess bathing.

"He'd brought me a golden serpent bracelet, the treasure of a merchant from Sidon once worn by a priestess in a temple across the eastern sea. The coiled snake felt warm against my upper arm, and I recalled my dream of such a bracelet. He said it would always remind me of him. We embraced, but Damysos hesitated, reluctant to tell me he could stay only briefly.

"'Then we mustn't waste a minute!' We lay together, bodies touching. Damysos ran his fingers round the bracelet, then moved down my body. Knowing this was a farewell, every move felt piquant, a connection between equals, each other's second self.

"During his absence, I gave myself to other worshipers in the service of Aphrodite. With each I became transcendent spirit as did he, detached from our individual selves.

"Union with Damysos was different. We knew ourselves as mating serpents. I wanted him, wanted his strength and gallantry, and he wanted the goddess in me. What we had was personal, not ritual. Do you understand?"

I do, more or less, but none of this is familiar to me. I can't imagine loving a man as part of a rite. Making love with a man personally? I hadn't considered it, but such a love could be possible for me as well. Teiresias makes me understand how widely our paths may diverge from our expectations. Leaving Eleusis was only the beginning for me.

I touch his arm and he continues.

"Anticipation of loss heightened our passion. Damysos clutched my hips to him so fiercely as to imprint my flesh.

We battled like Aphrodite and Ares, unable to get enough of each other, pushing and writhing until our desire brought us to profound fulfillment." He pauses. Then, more softly: "Afterwards we held each other in perfect stillness, timeless and united.

"Too soon, he released himself from my arms. I observed every detail of his muscled body as he dressed, seemingly in slow motion, I so wanted to hold onto each remaining second. Then he leaned down to kiss me. 'Farewell to your shining grace.' I believe I heard him murmur, 'I love you.'

"I caressed his cheek. 'Farewell, beloved Damysos.'

"Despite the sadness in my heart, I was content. No need to wander in emptiness as before, the indifference of the goddess less wounding. What more could be asked from Aphrodite than this? That it might never end? No mortal receives such a boon.

"The next day, summer's end was proclaimed not by cooling sea breezes but by a thunderstorm. Damysos' ship made an early departure for Ithaca, racing the lightning that flashed across the sky and the warm rain that drenched the thirsty land and churned the sea. We priestesses remained in the temple after our morning dance to wait out the storm and admire its glory from our high vantage point, sheets of rain turning the soil dark and rich and ready for plowing."

He nods toward Cenchrias. The youth helps Teiresias to the privy and I walk around the garden, which hasn't seen rain since I arrived.

Chapter Thirteen: Demeter's Blessing

Settled on his pallet, Teiresias begins speaking.

"The Mysteries at Eleusis are the most profound worship of the cycles of Nature, but in Corinth we too held a harvest festival. Aphrodite is a goddess of fertility."

"She is?" I never considered that. So he tells me.

"We began preparing for the celebration after the rains. With cool weather ahead, we refreshed our clothing, jewelry, living quarters, and the temple itself. The day of the festival, afternoon sunshine shadowed the furrows of the thrice-plowed fields below our temple.

"Worshipers gathered in the temple courtyard, garbed as farmers in simple cloaks, many with seed-bags fastened to their waists filled with provisions for the feast. King Polybus and Queen Merope might be in the crowd, but that day everyone played rustic. Carpho, down from her windy shrine, told me I would be blessed by Demeter. I didn't pause to consider what she meant.

"As the sun set, accompanied by drums and tambourines, we danced the worshipers down the hill. When the last gold was blazing the clouds, our procession moved out the city gates and oozed toward the fields.

"Under the rising moon we formed a circle around a plowed field, our chants carrying over the furrows. Drums pounded and torches swayed as Iole moved into the field hand in hand with a priest of Poseidon. She lay in a furrow, pulled him down upon her, lifting both their robes in swift gesture. There they coupled in moon shadows as rhythmic stamping of the circle of worshipers grew louder and faster until they lay spent. When they stood, we laughed at their clothing, covered in mud like those of Demeter and her mortal lover Iasion.

"While we continued singing, maidens sprinkled seed along the furrow where Iole and the priest had lain. Wine flasks appeared from beneath cloaks and honey cakes and kisses passed through the crowd. More than a few followed the lead of Iole and the priest as the moon glimmered through clouds.

"I felt a touch on my shoulder and turned toward a man who emanated the sweet smell of soil. 'Everyone plays farmer tonight. Do I look like a man of the fields?'

"'You have the muscles and fragrance to please Demeter herself.'

"'I seek to please Demeter and Aphrodite, but especially you. A fertile moon.' He took my hand and we walked to a ploughed section with no footmarks. My body touched the earth, vibrating from drummers and dancers in distant fields. The man moved above me, the earth below, I the connection.

"There was no subtlety of caress, no lingering, provoking pleasure, only the drive of him into me and my thrusting to meet him, longer, harder, deeper, than I had known. I realized that I was sobbing; so too perhaps was he, so powerfully did we shake. I felt I could bear no more, yet opened my legs wider, cradled by the earth. The man's plunging touched my womb, and I held myself from fainting. I had to remain fully conscious when his seed filled me, though the effort was intense. I seemed to hear the goddess—'Open, open'—and I strained toward him.

"'Now!' and with a series of plunges he poured himself into me. I felt my inner walls clutching him, seeking a satisfaction I couldn't gain from his furious drive. He held himself firm, moving only with the waves from the earth, allowing me to use him as I would. I increased the momentum, and when I came, he showered my womb again with his seed.

"Sometime later I laughed. 'This is not how we serve Aphrodite in our temple!'

"'No, little Demetria. The Great Mother possessed us to her purposes.' I nestled into his arms, wishing these fields were his so we could sleep in them, for I doubted I could climb the steep path home.

"He stood, brushed himself off, and lifted me as if I weighed nothing. His embrace was comforting, and I rested my head against his chest as he carried me to a grove at the edge of the hill. Beside a stream, he made us a bed on his cloak and lay beside me, covered with my robe. I fell asleep in his protective arms.

"At dawn I felt a space beside me and opened my eyes to see my companion at the stream, naked, throwing water over himself. To capture such a picture a painter would give much, I thought, admiring his glistening back and arms, the definition of muscle and sinew highlighted in the morning's faint pink. 'A father well-chosen,' came a voice from within. When I started to rise, I felt a quaking in my womb and an ache in my thighs. He offered me a drink of water from his cupped hands. I asked him to carry me to the temple. 'With pleasure. I've carried a calf more unwieldy than you twice as far.' I was sorry to see him slip on his tunic, my eyes not sated with his beautiful form.

"After he helped me to the stream to wash my face, he smiled. 'Fresh as the dawn.' He lifted me into his arms and touched my lips with his. 'You are truly Demetria.' I rested against him as we passed through the city gates and climbed to the temple.

"Below us revelers stirred, but the way into the city was quiet and no one met us on the climb. He carried me into our silent dwelling where the long table lay bare. Shouldering the tapestry aside, he lowered me to my bed but didn't settle beside me. 'I have a long journey today and will plant at sunset. Memories of you will speed my travels. Now you must rest.'

"So he really was a farmer. I shouldn't have been surprised; there was a sense of the earth about him. With Demeter's blessing and mine, he would sow his fields with sanctified seed. He rested his head for a moment on my belly, then brushed me with gentle kisses. 'Farewell, lovely Demetria. May our union bring prosperity.'

"I felt faint and aching. The music of the morning dance sounded from a great distance as I fell asleep in the coils of Delphyne, secure and peaceful.

"You can imagine how Calyce made fun of me for sleeping the day away. That evening she gave me goat's milk and honeyed gruel, invalid's food, and helped me to the bath. My legs supported my weight, the ache in my thighs a memory."

Teiresias seems transported by his story, but I interrupt. "Did this man tell you his name?"

"What?" He shakes himself. "No, and strangely, I didn't wonder who he was. Enough that I was his Demetria."

"As Teira, you had a powerful experience with a man you didn't know, and the way you tell it, you never saw him again. Wasn't Damysos the one you wanted?"

"Yes, I valued Damysos above all other men. Ours was a unique love, but this man of the earth was vital in another way." He sighs and is still for long moments before taking a determined breath and continuing.

"The night after the festival, no worshipers came to the temple, everyone home planting their fields and pressing their grapes. An almost conspiratorial glow shone over the room of women.

"Iole winked at me. 'A good day to sleep.' She told me the proverb: she who sleeps all day after the harvest festival shall be a mother by summertime.

"Others chimed in. 'She who loves in the fields with a worshiper of Demeter gives birth to a child of the earth.' 'She who comes home from the festival begrimed with the soil of the Mother becomes a mother.' They continued in that vein until I felt their voices an assault. Iole put an arm around me, and everyone quieted.

"'What's all this?' I spluttered. 'None of you have babies!' Then I remembered the precinct of Aphrodite. If priestesses had children, of course they gave birth.

"I hadn't paid much attention to priestesses' comings and goings except for Rhene and Satyrea, who I knew lived in the precinct. The wave of nausea that caught me was a premonition: there would be more to come. I stumbled to my room, wrapped my golden girdle in a silken shawl and put it away, took off my gown, and slipped into bed.

"My dreams were alive with women and children. Children climbing on the precinct's statue of Aphrodite and playing in the spring; children clutching their mother's legs; babies crawling and crying, kicking and laughing. The serpent dance squirmed with children, the banquet table reduced to their scale. In my sleep I smiled at the joyful chaos."

Cenchrias, aware of the intensity of our conversation, quietly begins to cook what he's gathered for our evening meal.

I can't believe my ears. "You're telling me you, when Teira, were pregnant?"

"That's right."

"Where's the child? Did it survive?" My head spins, and I'm glad he's slow to reply. Do I have another sister or a brother?

"She survived. Her name is Daphne."

"You named her for a girl who would rather become a laurel tree than yield to Apollo's embrace."

"She's named for the sacred laurel. She's now a priestess."

"Where?"

"In Delphi."

I want to pursue the question, but I hear the exhaustion in his voice. "You must have felt dreadfully confused. To be a woman was extreme enough. And then you bore a child."

"My body took over, as I had learned when making love to men. My life as Teiresias was dead to me. The duality I'd felt from time to time disappeared with my pregnancy."

"So no one in Corinth truly knew you." It's not a question. How could they?

"My years as a man of Thebes were meaningless. I was a priestess of Aphrodite, not a male worshiper coming to be healed." He smiles. "Not that my old Teiresias self knew he needed healing."

Yet here he sits, male. Never could I imagine such a conversation with a man. We laugh at the absurdity.

Teiresias regains his composure. "My life changed dramatically as it does for every woman who finds herself with child. I thought I knew Corinth well, but I hadn't pursued hints of more.

"One crisp autumn day, Iole and I walked down the hill to the precinct of Aphrodite. In the center stood their goddess statue, with private courtyards branching out to individual cottages.

"Rhene greeted us at her low gate that faced a charming mural of children fishing. She wore no jewels except gold earrings with a simple linen gown, a piece of the same linen holding back her wavy black hair. She led us into a room where two children played with chunky wooden beads on the floor in front of the hearth. An older woman who seemed more friend than servant brought us a honeyed drink.

"The children, Gelon and Otrere, were indeed Rhene's, as was the house. When she became pregnant after living two years at the temple, a benefactor provided it. Votaries of Aphrodite who supported these houses weren't necessarily fathers of the children, nor did a priestess who was a mother need to live there. Polydora's two sons were being raised by her sister Ialysa.

"Would I want to live in such a place myself? I was going to have a baby! That idea was new enough, let alone what would happen after she was born. I thought of her as a girl, since all my world was female. If my baby were a boy, after a certain age he would be raised in the house of a nobleman and educated by priests.

"Rhene invited me to a banquet at her house the following evening. Banquets in Thebes admitted no women except a flute girl or hetaera. A woman as host? By Theban standards, Rhene would have been regarded as a hetaera whose beauty, conversation, and music added to men's enjoyment. But in Corinth, she was in charge. Iole wouldn't be attending the banquet, but I would have an escort.

"Winter was coming. Early morning rain made the courtyard muddy and uninviting, our inlaid chests of jewelry dull in the day's gray light. At sunset, the clouds opened, gilt-edged and beguiling, and our dance that evening was joyous. Worshipers brought offerings and drank wine around our table, a few retreating to priestesses' curtained apartments. Relishing the rain-fresh dusk, I greeted my summer's silent companion Zetes, who would escort me to the banquet."

I hope Teiresias' description of the banquet will distract me from my growling stomach with a vicarious feast.

"Iole and Calyce dressed my hair three times, each more elaborate than the last, before removing the jewels, brushing out the curls, and plaiting tiny braids under a golden diadem. The silky chiton they chose for me opened on both sides. Calyce arranged it beneath my golden girdle she'd retrieved, which still fit. Iole brought a lapis necklace from Egypt from a special jewelry chest, the golden eye of Horus set in coral and gold beads. With my eyes outlined in kohl and the snake bracelet tight on my upper arm, I could have been an Egyptian princess. They brushed black dye on my brown hair to heighten the effect."

"Brown?" I repeat. "I assumed you were blonde."

"Because my hair is white now." He laughs. "That was the only time I dyed it. Too messy. Until this—" he runs a hand through his scanty ashen mane, "I had sun-streaked brown hair that became darker as I aged.

"Calyce's idea of wishing me well for the banquet was to kiss me with a dart of her tongue. Then she rouged my lips. No more kisses. She told me to restrain my dance, like a serpent arching its body. 'Slowly, slowly, only your neck, only one shoulder, one hip at a time. None of your writhing.' I promised to try, but my free-flowing movements pleased Aphrodite and perfumed my sweat. That night in our temple dance I avoided sweating and kept my eyes on the enigmatic smile of the goddess.

"Zetes and I left for the precinct under a radiant crimson sky. Walking down the hill I asked about the other guests. He named wealthy Alcimedes and his friend Amyclas, Rhene's neighbor Satyrea, and he expected one or two others.

"Amyclas lived up to his name, the lustful one, Zetes said. A toad-faced, round-bellied fellow, he lusted after women, wine, and food. No doubt boys as well, though he never troubled Zetes himself. Alcimedes had trained as priest of Helios with King Polybus and Zetes' father Meteos.

"We entered Rhene's torchlit courtyard to the sound of lyre music and the aroma of garlic. Rhene introduced me to a distinguished man called Strophios, oiled hair and thick eyebrows above dark almond eyes. Taking my hand with a haughty half-smile, he appeared world-weary.

"Beside me Zetes tensed, no longer the amiable companion of a few moments before. He gave Strophios a curt nod. Amyclas and Alcimedes exchanged a quick startled glance before Rhene gave us each a goblet of wine. Amyclas responded with a generous smile. His twinkling green eyes and resonant voice no doubt served him well in pursuit of his lusts, despite his physique.

"Alcimedes gazed at my ring. With my diadem, ear drops, precious neckpiece, and serpent bracelet, I hadn't expected the ring to attract particular notice. He remarked that it must be old, almost from another world. Although his courtesy couldn't be faulted, Alcimedes' demeanor seemed slippery, and I wished he wouldn't touch my ring or hold my hand in his clammy one. I pulled it back more firmly than courtesy would dictate.

"Rhene introduced a young man with velvety brown eyes: Tanais, with a crown of bronze curls and a mouth fixed in a slight pout."

Tanais? The name is familiar to me, but not belonging to a pouting, beautiful youth. Could he be the same man who sometimes stopped at Eleusis?

"When I was introduced to Brovas," Teiresias continues, "I had a moment's disquiet. He gave me that sharp-eyed look and praised my necklace. He spoke softly, so I leaned closer. 'Do you know a man named Tereus?' I nodded with what must have been a guilty smile. 'I guessed that was you with your friend, out for an evening's entertainment.'

"'One silly evening,' I said. He squeezed my hand, winked, and said no more."

"Brovas didn't worry you?" I ask. When I see Teiresias' smile, I laugh. "His being in on the joke made your friendship, right?"

"Absolutely. Brovas was shorter than me and would have to be called ugly, thin black hair and beard, peering eyes under bushy brows, and a paunchy body, yet he had an odd charm. He regarded Iole's and my disguises as clever and daring."

Still smiling, Teiresias goes on to describe the evening's delights, from the lyre player, a lad with the delicacy of a girl, to the the wine and platters of food eaten in dainty morsels over the evening: spicy pastries filled with meat and parsley; sliced onions layered with cheese and herbs; honey-glazed vine birds so small they were eaten bones and all; baked fish flaked from the bones, mussels and olives. His description makes my mouth water. I'm happy to see Cenchrias assembling our meal, but the image of Amyclas crunching down a vine bird, all but its beak, kills my appetite for the moment.

"Rhene's topic for the evening was stories of women of old, divine and mortal. I'll repeat them to you, Manto, as best as I can recall. No doubt you have heard some before, but these guests gave new twists. Their versions of old myths will give you a sense of that evening and of story-telling."

That's why I'm sitting with him, after all, to hear his story and think about how to pass it on. It's been a long time since I prickled with resistance. Since I created the second part of the initial argument, I've thought differently about speaking his story. "You say guests added their own twists."

"As we do with old tales. But when you tell my story, you won't vary the significant details. That's why rhapsodes speak in verse: easier to hold in memory. Most of that night's stories weren't spoken in verse, but whether or not, I'll stick with the essence.

"When Strophios objected to the topic, Rhene said she'd had enough of sea adventures and monsters. Everyone enjoys stories about love. Strophios mumbled that love stories have their share of monsters, but if anyone else heard, they ignored him.

"Amyclas begged to begin with the story of Circe, daughter of Helios, god of the sun who blesses Corinth with his golden light. Foremost of her magic powers was transformation. Perhaps she was given the island of Aiaia because it was magical itself, but more likely to curtail her powers. She sits in the center of her circular dwelling, spinning and singing. Aiaia is full of wild beasts, but from the first day Circe walked its shores and climbed its hills, they followed her. Henceforth they fawned on her, walking on their hind legs and eating from her hand. No man can resist Circe, who seduces as she will and turns men to swine when she's done with them. He popped two vine birds into his mouth at once.

"We know that story, Amyclas," Rhene said. "What's your point?"

"The transformations wrought by love."

"Satyrea said a priestess of Aphrodite finds that ridiculous. His story has nothing to do with love, which transforms the soul. Anyway, Circe was a divinely born woman beyond mortal constraints.

"I agreed with her," Teiresias says, "but even so, Circe's transformation of her suitors made me think of my own."

"Yours was the opposite—at least into Teira," I say.

"Very true. And even this—" he gestures to his male body— "isn't porcine."

I laugh. Teiresias is not much more than skin and bones. No trace of swine in body or spirit.

"Since she found his story lacking, Amyclas urged our hostess, to speak next. Rhene said the stories about Pandora are frightening, but we shouldn't believe all we hear. Pandora's box is said to contain every ill of the world, with only the tiny gift of hope at the bottom. The way it's told, 'hope' is a paltry compensation.

"But Pandora is innocent. Disaster and suffering did not originate with woman. It's men who fail to revere the

Mother's gifts who malign her. In the original tale, Pandora's magical jar contained the lemon and the pomegranate, melon and olive, apple and grape. Having sufficient food freed mortals to grace their lives and be generous, to look beyond mere survival, to create beauty and to love, to think of the future, and yes, to hope. Pandora brought skills of molding earthen clay and firing it into pots and the gift of communal life, mortals living together in peace and plenty."

Teiresias turns to me. "Have you heard that?"

"Not connected to Pandora, no, but those are the gifts of the Great Goddess, are they not?"

"Yes, that's what moved me about Rhene's tale. In Thebes, Pandora was faulted for setting suffering loose in the world. I much preferred this version."

"Strophios asked if death was part of Pandora's bounty.

"'Death is the fate of mortals,' Rhene replied. 'The Mother creates, the Mother destroys. Pandora's gifts, woman's gifts, are for the living.'

"'I prefer Dionysus' gift of wine.' Amyclas gestured to a servant boy to refill his goblet. His face was florid, the platter of vine birds in front of him reduced to a small pile of beaks.

"Satyrea said that wine originated with love. After grapevines covered the foothills and plains, Dionysus burst into the world. His birth was a tragic love story, but that wasn't the one she would tell."

"I know how the mortal Semele asked her mysterious lover to show himself in his full glory," I say. "When he did, for he was none other than Zeus, the flames of his divine passion destroyed her."

"Satyrea didn't mention Semele. Instead, she told a less known tale about Dionysus as a god, beautiful as a woman with his long locks, yet powerful and dangerous. Did we know he invented wine out of love for Princess Ariadne of Crete? Everyone shook their heads.

"'Then I shall tell you. Alone, across the sea from her beloved family and lily-blooming island, Ariadne fell into despair unto death. Dionysus traveled to the depths of Hades to return her to the land of the living. Her tears of joy fell on the roots of vines that he used to climb down to her and on the grape leaves he wore as a crown. He took her in his arms, vines and grapes entwining them both, and from this embrace, her tears flowed deep red wine.'

"Amyclas was staring into his goblet. 'You can call your wine tears or call it blood if you like. I say Dionysus saw that the world needed intoxication, and how better for it to originate than in sorrow and love?'

"'No one who worships Dionysus can help but know his twofold nature, above and below, his pull towards love and his pull towards death,' Rhene said.

"Satyrea's style captivated as she moved so that her necklace brushed each nipple in turn while glancing at Amyclas in wide-eyed innocence. You won't employ her enticing ways, Manto, but an effective storyteller must be dramatic.

Teiresias is a canny old man, building on what started as a request that I listen with attention. In Eleusis after experiencing many Mysteries, priestesses took turns telling the story of Demeter and Persephone at festivals, then eventually as part of the initiation. I had told the simplest one myself and observed how the other women spoke. Teiresias is right: a touch of drama brings a story to life.

He interrupts my thoughts.

"Strophios said so far we'd shown how love turns man to beast or creates the miracle of wine out of suffering. Love too can lead one to the starkest depths, destroying the soul.

"Amyclas waved the wine jug in his direction. 'Is this a story or a warning, Strophios? Here, drink up.'

"Paying him no mind, Strophios said rather than an old tale, he would tell a true one that happened not so very long ago, concerning Prince Laius of Thebes. Even now, Manto, I cannot utter the name Laius without feeling a chill. But that night I was more shocked than prescient.

"Laius was the son of King Labdacus, the man I served in Thebes. Strophios described how, as a wandering youth, Lauis came to a city by the seashore where young men practiced chariot racing for the Nemean Games. None, in his opinion, was particularly skilled. Beardless Chrysippus, son of King Pelops, was watching the practice. Laius, admiring his strong arms and steady eyes, determined to make this boy the greatest charioteer of all.

"He spent long hours teaching Chrysippus skills to compensate for what he lacked in size. As spring ripened, the boy grew taller. When the time came for the Games, Laius accompanied him, and Chrysippus easily won the champion's gold tripod.

"The night after his victory, Laius followed the lead of Zeus who stole young Ganymede, though he lacked the god's eagle wings and divine immunity. He galloped with Chrysippus all night, two together on Laius' horse, until they reached Thebes. His father and all the palace slept. Laius crept to his chamber, gripping Chrysippus' hand. Before the sun lightened the sky, he had taken the boy as his lover.

"Laius continued to take his pleasures with him, but Chrysippus suffered and soon died. By his own hand, some believed, though careless horsemanship was the explanation given. Laius left the palace in secret and didn't return to Thebes until after the death of King Labdacus.

"'It was said that King Pelops cursed Thebes for Laius' abduction of his son, though to what doom no one knew. Today Laius rules the city with Queen Jocasta in seeming concord.' Strophios added that Chrysippus must have been such a rare boy that Laius could not help but love him. The intense glance he gave Zetes made me wonder what was between them. Zetes' face remained impassive but his tension was palpable.

"Amyclas accused of Strophios telling more gossip than story. After all, many a man loves a handsome youth.

"Rhene was incensed. 'He must do him no violence nor offend the gods. In this story, Laius does both. You didn't keep to our topic, Strophios. You described a tragedy of lust.'

"Strophios shrugged and said no more."

"When you lived in Thebes, did you ever see Laius?" I ask.

"Glimpses when he was a boy," Teiresias replies. "Then he went off on his travels. He was crowned after my departure."

As he takes a sip of water, the fragrance of onions cooking wafts our way.

"Brovas agreed with Rhene," he says. "In his deep voice he said we must offend no divine one. They may pursue passions and quarrels as they please, regardless of the cost to mortals.

"'Athena was outraged when Poseidon ravished her votary, the Gorgon Medusa, in the goddess' own shrine,' Brovas continued, 'but it was Medusa who suffered. Her red-gold curls turned to snakes, and her exquisite face became so terrifying that any man who looked upon it turned to stone. Mortals can suffer from the gods' wrongs, but we cannot commit the like ourselves.

"Brovas didn't see Perseus as a hero for chopping off Medusa's head. To him, she embodied all that's lovely in woman, yet the story conveys her allure as horror. He regarded her as a serpent goddess whose story was twisted over years of telling. Serpent goddess! That caught my attention.

"I was relieved Rhene didn't ask me for a tale, for I couldn't think of one that didn't reveal too much. If I thought it through, I could have taken off on Brovas' idea that ancient tales were altered through years of retelling, often discrediting female divinity and authority."

Teiresias smiles at me. "Here I am advising you to be a story-teller, Manto, but I couldn't do it myself that night. My vigilance to keep my transformation secret stifled the ability to tell any tale at all. With time I learned how, but until your arrival never told my own. Mydon has witnessed much of it. Oh yes, that old serpent priest is still alive and my oldest friend. We've had our times, Mydon and me."

He chuckles heartily, his blind eyes crinkled with jolly memories. I know better than to ask more. All in due time.

The way Teiresias describes Corinth, the temple of Aphrodite seems a place of blessèd pleasure and lightheartedness. Here outside the massive wall of Thebes, our garden is pleasant, but the atmosphere is darker. Perhaps that's to be expected in a threatened place of prophecy and omens. What lightens the mood is Cenchrias' cooking and Teiresias' affection for him. And, I suppose, his affection for me. The thought brings tears to my eyes. My abandoning father has come full circle.

"I tell you these stories because the plight of Medusa and the legacy of Pandora struck me at the time. Even though I'd met woodland priestesses and knew about the ancient Cretan sisterhood, I lacked a full understanding of how male gods, priests, and even male worshippers, are defeating the Mother's long dominion."

"You're speaking to a priestess of Demeter, Father. Her authority will last forever!"

He pats my hand. "I hope you're right, but you too fear that hierophants will take over guiding the Mysteries."

Chapter Fifteen: Motherlove

At last supper has appeared, braised roots I can't identify, served with onions, greens and a bowl of olives. Not quite Rhene's feast, but very welcome.

Taking a handful of the salty olives, Teiresias says, "Over time I heard many myths and stories at banquets, but the one that stayed with me was that tale from Strophios."

"Did Laius bring a curse on Thebes?"

"Long after you departed to Eleusis, Thebes suffered, as you will hear, but no one knew why. Do you recall the oracle from Delphi I couldn't understand?"

"Something about Hera's vengeance.

"*The Goddess seeks her own. Hera will avenge the lost youth.*"

"You said Mydon came with you to deliver it. Did he understand the meaning?"

"Perhaps, but he merely spoke it to Labdacus without interpreting. After I left, the king fell into a decline. When he was on his deathbed Laius returned and was crowned. That's all we heard in Corinth.

"The stories at Rhene's banquet showed me how completely I belonged on the side of the female. In one way and another, Pandora, Medusa, Ariadne—even Circe— spoke for me. Amyclas seemed a buffoon driven by lust; Alcimedes and Strophios were trapped in their manly shells like Teiresias in bygone days. Brovas seemed different, but I didn't know him well enough to judge. Tanais made little impression at all, more Dryad than mortal.

"Rhene called for more wine and platters of sweets. I ate a sugared date, enticing as ambrosia, and grew lightheaded. The lyre played softly and the room receded, dreamlike. With heightened consciousness I perceived a painful connection between Strophios and Zetes—a tragic, enigmatic history.

"I licked my fingers clean of the sugary powder from another date and observed each of the assembly in turn. In our long talks on the temple steps, Zetes hinted at another sorrow equal to his mother's illness, and Strophios' melancholic manner suggested a man tortured by loss.

"The fingers of the lyre player slackened; the evening was coming to an end. Strophios stood stiffly and bowed to Rhene, then to the company, barely pausing at Zetes. 'You invited me as a farewell, Rhene, and I thank you. I sail tomorrow.'

"She wished him a safe journey, echoed by the others, but he was out the door before they finished their farewells. Amyclas and Alcimedes left arm in arm, and Satyrea walked Tanais home. He hadn't uttered a word all evening.

"'Is Tanais the best or worst possible guest?' Rhene asked when no one remained but Zetes and me. 'Does beauty forgive all? He comes from an important family, but their hopes that he become a leader seem in vain. Still, he gives great pleasure to the eye.'"

"A man called Tanais stopped at Eleusis while I was there," I say. "He'd been initiated into the Mysteries some time before and was on his way home from an embassy to Athens. If he's your same Tanais, his family's hopes were fulfilled. As for the other men at your banquet, I haven't met any like them."

"Your knowledge of men is limited, with none at the shrine of Artemis and only initiates in Eleusis."

"That was the life you left me to. Of course I didn't want a lover or husband—I already told you."

"I'm not criticizing you, Manto. Take my stories as an education. Or entertainment."

"They're not the sort of education I expected. Entertainment? I suppose, but you're telling them for other reasons. I'll never be close to the likes of Damysos nor the men you describe as shelled into their manliness."

"Of all those at Rhene's banquet, only Alcimedes proved a scoundrel."

"I suppose Macaria contributed to his downfall."

"Indeed she did. Your second sight is in good working order. Let me tell you one more story before we stop for the day.

"Zetes, Rhene, and I pulled pillows close to the fire, warming our wine in its glow. His head drooped, and he fell asleep on my lap.

"Rhene asked me what I thought of her guests. 'Amyclas enjoys playing the role of satyr. The others are puzzles.'

"Rhene laughed that they had their secrets, and silent Tanais must have a private inner life. As you confirmed, Manto.

"She told me Alcimedes served as priest of Helios until he broke faith. Not enough to be banished from Corinth, but from the temple. He became obsessed with gold, which drew him to Macaria, a very different sort of votary of Aphrodite than our fellow priestesses. Rhene called them two of a kind.

"My head was spinning from wine and sugared dates. Looking down at Zetes asleep on my lap, I asked her about him and Strophios.

"Strophios had traveled to lands beyond Tyre and Phithia, and some would say he offered Zetes the world. He knew men who knew the gods. Zetes was barely full grown when he gave himself to Strophios, body, heart, and soul. But Strophios was past loving. It would have taken more than worship at our temple to heal him.

"Rhene was surprised he told us the tale of Chrysippus, a dreadful story and too close to his experience with Zetes. She hadn't expected them both to be present.

"I'd been stroking Zetes' head while Rhene talked. When he stirred, Rhene sent us off to bed.

"I nudged Zetes to his feet and led him down the shadowy corridor to a room lit by a single candle. On a chill evening, best to sleep together."

Cenchrias refills our wine cups and removes the empty dishes. Teiresias takes a few sips.

"Zetes climbed in beside me, naked and as unselfconscious as a child. We embraced, stroking each other's backs, half dozing. What followed is almost too strange for words."

I wait.

He speaks slowly. "Soon, Zetes began to nurse me like an infant. His desire created such a maternal urge that I actually produced a few drops of milk. He wasn't seeking release, but craved a healing different from any other man's I'd known. My body wanted to feed him, to give him what he so desperately needed, and in that urge was my satisfaction."

He stops. "Perhaps this is too peculiar for you to tell."

"Never have I heard the like, but I can imagine calling it motherlove." Until I said that, I imagined no such thing, and the magnitude of what he asks hits me. Everything he describes using *I*, I must change to *she* in the telling. And then at some point, *he*.

Teiresias goes on. "When I awakened, Zetes looked into my eyes. He'd dreamt that a generous mother spirit blessed him. Never again, he murmured, would he wake at dawn weeping for his mother.

"After his traumatic birth, Urania became a phantom. His father Meteos provided nurses, but she scarcely knew her child. She slept a long sleep until Zetes was half grown. His very being caused her anguish, so he rarely visited her chambers." Teiresias reaches for my hand. "You too were mother-starved, Manto. Have you forgiven me?"

"When you described Chloris' death I was horrified. Now I know that like Zetes, your heart had a void where your mother should have been. As I've said, Historis and I had an abundance of mothers at the shrine of Artemis. You say your playing mother to Zetes fulfilled you as well. Was it awkward between you afterwards?"

"No, we knew we wouldn't repeat that night, nor would our friendship suffer. Next morning we had a pleasant breakfast with Rhene. Zetes left for the palace to help his father plan the dedication ceremony for the son of King Polybus and Queen Merope. Rhene told me she'd invited Strophios at the last minute because he was about to depart for a long journey. She feared it was a mistake, but Zetes seemed well recovered."

Teiresias smiles. "I didn't whisper a word to her about what transpired between us.

"Soon, Rhene told me, a priestess living across the square would leave with her child to care for her ailing father, and her house would be mine. I would run my own domain, hosting banquets as I saw fit."

"The priestess' way to become master of revels," I say.

Teiresias laughs and beckons to Cenchrias, who's been sitting beyond us, to prepare his bed.

I make my way to the cottage, my head whirling. What a realm Teira inhabited!

Chapter Sixteen: The Radiant Child

Next morning as we enjoy our melon, Teiresias takes up his story.

"King Polybus didn't want to name the child for his father or for Queen Merope's, insisting they call him by his affectionate name, Oedipus. It means swollen-footed, though no one but me seemed to find that foreboding.

"The night before all of Corinth would celebrate their long-awaited prince, we priestesses gathered for a blessing in Merope's chambers. Our sisters from the temple and precinct were joined by Labrya, priestess of Selene, and Carpho from the shrine of Demeter. I liked Labrya, her hair tumbling in loose curls, prematurely grey, and the fabric of her bodice an iridescent silver. Fuller-figured than temple priestesses, she moved heavily to the rhythms of Mother Earth, with Carpho matching her steps. Merope danced between them, sinuous as a nymph. The rest of us danced our temple dance.

When Marpessa struck a sharp chord, Labrya presented Merope with a pale blue coverlet made on Delos. Around the hem was embroidered the serpent of the ocean stream, with a central labyrinth surrounded by the sun, moon, and stars, a protective prayer for Oedipus to live in harmony with all of Nature.

"We chanted praises of the Mother's circle of life. Was I the only one who feared for the baby? I rubbed my ring and prayed to hallowed spirits of goddesses back to the Great

One Herself. The tiny prince watched with bright eyes, entranced.

"When I saw the leggings wrapped tight around his feet and ankles, I had a fleeting vision of an infant on a windy mountain, ankles thonged together, saved from death by a shepherd. It shook me so much I had trouble focusing on the celebration."

"Another vision," I say.

He nods. "I tried to mask my fears with loving prayers for the child and to hide them even from myself from then on."

"Is that possible? To pretend we didn't see what we saw?"

"What do you think?" He gives me a sad smile. "Here in the silence, I muse on how fate coils through our lives. Prophets see fate unfolding, but we're powerless to redirect it. My time as priestess in Corinth began my entanglement with the royal house of Polybus and Merope and the fate of Oedipus.

"On the following day when the prince was officially dedicated by the priest of Apollo, the sun shone bright and crowds filled the agora. My head was throbbing and I wished I hadn't come. How could I stand through a lengthy ceremony?

"As soon as the priest began to speak, my sight became splotched with shimmering light. I couldn't breathe, I couldn't escape.

"Then I fainted dead away. Even now, I can't be certain what I dreamt and what was reported to me. I see the raven face of the priest intoning terrible words, drowned by swans' wings cutting through the air and disappearing into the mountains.

"When I opened my eyes Brovas was fanning my face as I reclined on a bench away from the crowd. He'd left the king and Meteos to look after me.

"After fresh air and a drink of cool water restored me, he walked me to my house. I stood a head taller than he, just right to lean on his shoulder as we made our uneven way to the precinct and into my bedroom, me feeling better with each step.

"Ah Brovas! He charmed me with his kindness, his irreverence and humor, his flaming eyes. That afternoon his gentle hands explored, caressed, and offered me playful satisfactions of touch and tongue. Remaining fully dressed except for his sandals, he refused any touch from me.

"He knew I was among the priestesses blessing the baby the previous evening. He said a prince cannot have too many consecrations, and those of priestesses are best of all.

"Some time later when Rhene appeared at my door, Brovas was sitting beneath the flowery mural in my central room enjoying wine and a cheese pie, quite at home. He smiled, drank a last draught of wine, and grazed a kiss on the top of my head. I watched him limp across the courtyard."

I ask him to say more about Brovas.

"He and Polybus grew up with Meteos and Alcimedes. While his friends were educated in the temple of Helios, Brovas' father took him to the East. He still traveled as far as Egypt and Byblos on King Polybus' business. Rhene had heard a whisper that as a young man he sacrificed himself to the goddess Astarte in Phoenicia.

"I should have asked her what she meant, sacrificing himself to Astarte, but only commented that he was an odd one. Rhene said that during a priestess' pregnancy, a man often made himself at home with her from time to time. Brovas would rest my heart and my baby's.

"He arrived early the next day cradling a gift. Inside the linen wrapping was a carved image of Aphrodite, the perfect size for my house. Soon I would find it difficult to climb to the temple to dance, so now I had my own statue. Placing the figure on a low table, Brovas moved the lamp so its light played over her. Then he fastened a gold chain around my neck. Hanging between my breasts I felt a cool weight: a large pearl in a golden seashell, with smaller shells worked into the chain on either side.

"He said after its being long hidden in an oyster in the foamy sea, the pearl would now be burnished by our love. He lifted my gown and kissed between my thighs. With kisses and teasing, probing fingers, he brought me to lingering satisfaction." Teiresias' laugh is throaty. "Me! Can you imagine?"

Not as he is, sitting beside me, but his words carry me to Corinth in its grandeur, visualizing Teira in her private dwelling with this curious man.

"Brovas' father granted him a very different education from his boyhood friends. Polybus became the young king of Corinth, with Meteos and Brovas as his royal counselors. As for Alcimedes, Brovas shook his head. A child of Sisyphus, Alcimedes was not to be trusted in palace or temple.

"He ran his hand down my body in farewell. When I sat up, the pearl, luminescent handiwork of the jeweler Leiriope, fell into place between my breasts.

"Wanting to meet that gifted woman, Rhene and I walked to the jewelry shop. Leiriope and Didaeon were crafting golden tripods and chains for winners in the upcoming Isthmian Games.

"After creating my necklace, she'd designed a golden goblet for Alcimedes, the renegade priest. How could he purchase such a valuable piece? Leiriope gave a wink. She had gossip to share. We followed her to the courtyard and sat under the grape arbor.

"She affirmed that Alcimedes was in league with Macaria, the ambitious woman who called herself priestess but was no more a priestess than Alcimedes was a priest. When Leiriope delivered the goblet, Alcimedes' servant pointed her toward his rooms. She found herself in the corridor outside his bedchamber with the door ajar. Macaria lay naked on the bed. She enticed him—Leiriope stopped. 'The whole scene felt sinister—almost evil. Nothing resembling love. Leaving the goblet, I fled.'

"Didaeon thought Alcimedes was simply greedy, wanting to amass gold and precious objects, but Leiriope believed he sought gold for control and dominance. As she looked closely at my ring, I winced. Didaeon saw it when I was playing the rustic Tereus. But all she said was that Alcimedes would give anything for one like it. 'Keep her safe.'

Teiresias rubs it with his opposite hand. "That didn't prove so easy. It's a miracle I still wear it.

"From Leiriope's description, I understood that Alcimedes was drawn to the Mother's dark side, a seductive, devouring viper, the force of death. His Gaia was a warped version of the Snake Mother of old. What peculiar ideas, owning and controlling! It may sound naive today, but the idea of accumulating private wealth was far from my mind, or any priestess' mind, in those days."

I see Teiresias is tempted to say more about Alcimedes and Macaria, but he speaks with finality. "Alcimedes' perverse values contributed to what happened in my own future and in our temple."

Cenchrias brings lemon water and seed cakes, and we laze, shaded from the midday heat.

Chapter Seventeen: The Games

When the sun begins its downward slant, Teiresias shakes himself awake and takes a sip of lukewarm lemon water. "Did you ever attend the Pythian Games in Delphi when you were a girl? Delphi isn't far from Thebes."

"With the priestesses of Artemis?" I laugh. "No. In Eleusis an occasional initiate had been an athlete, but they left their pasts behind. I never cared about Games or athletes, all competitive and oiled."

"You missed a fine sight, Manto. Athletes are beautiful. The day before the Isthmian Games, dignitaries and competitors began arriving from Nauplion, Mycenae, Troezen, Elis, and beyond. A striking scene, especially the Nauplion contingent in cloaks of rainbow colors, with flute-trilling musicians setting their pace. Only their racing chariots were more tasseled and beribboned than they. The Nauplions were the most flamboyant, but I was more impressed by the sober runners from Tiryns, including women, tall and sleek as the men. Naked women athletes look like goddesses. Sadly, now nakedness has become so glossed with sex and power that no woman dares compete with men in such contests, and no longer do competitors in the girls' footraces at the temple of Hera run naked."

I'm not sure what he means about sex and power except for tales like Hades' abduction of Persephone. In earthly terms?

"A Nauplion charioteer called Hiketaon caught Rhene's eye, and Calyce fancied the runner and spear-thrower Phidias from Tiryns. We didn't see Damysos and the Ithacans, but Myceneans were in full force, their disciplined uniformity more like warriors than athletes, with inlaid belts and daggers at their waists. Mycenaeans don't honor Aphrodite, dedicating themselves instead to Ares and Hera, whom they worship and fear."

"Why did you risk attending another public event? You fainted at the ceremony for Prince Oedipus."

"After the procession I intended to return home, skipping the blessing of athletes and sacrifices in the agora. Then I heard a familiar voice asking me to bless a competitor. I turned and looked into the eyes of Damysos, come to throw the discus. He addressed me with affection then stopped, noticing my swollen belly, and his smile hardened. A long painful pause. He knew what my service to Aphrodite entailed but had thought—he didn't finish his sentence. His expression made me sharply aware of the circumstances of my child's conception. All I could say was the truth. I would have chosen him as father.

"'You would have!' His laugh was harsh. 'So why didn't you?'

"I refused to say the obvious. Damysos wasn't in Corinth the night we celebrated Demeter in the freshly plowed fields. Nor would I offer an apology. I loved him, but if I was fated to carry his child, our loving would have produced one. He left me to my destiny and followed his own. 'I didn't know that in leaving you I was leaving my chance of fathering your child.'

"'Neither of us knew, Damysos.'

"His finger traced the golden serpent around my arm. 'Still you wear this.'

"'I do. You are in my heart.'"

"'In my dreams yours is the face of Aphrodite, Teira, and so it was at sacred Paphos. The goddess is with me in your image.'

"I could think of no response, the baby's kicks constricting me. Damysos held me close and kissed me so sweetly that tears came to my eyes. 'Throw me a kiss tomorrow and my discus will sail down the arena.' He walked away to join the Ithacan competitors.

"Standing alone amidst the cacophony, I felt shaken. Damysos was the mate of my heart, but life had sanctioned otherwise. He'd disappeared into the surging crowd. Would I see him again? All I knew for certain was that the dancing rhythm in my belly and the hot, dry winds were driving me home. Not for me to feast on roast flesh of sacrificed goats and lambs.

"On the day of the Games, pale morning sun shone over Rhene, Satyrea and me on our walk from the precinct to the stadium. The temple priestesses had gathered above the entry tunnel where we could see each athlete emerge, breathing deeply to summon the *theos* within.

"Among the racers in the first event was Tanais, the silent young man at Rhene's banquet. His finely trained body sprinted around the course, only the longest-legged Tyrinian woman keeping pace until the last length, where he sprinted ahead of her across the finish line. Corinthians surged forward to lift Tanais to their shoulders.

"Satyrea was the most excited during that race, wishing she were on the field herself. Yes, Satyrea, of the gossamer gowns and sultry ways, had wanted to train as a runner and race to become priestess of Hera. Her mother wouldn't permit it, saying her curls were better put to use than her legs and sent her to the temple of Aphrodite. Until that day I never guessed she had any aspiration beyond being provocative.

"Meteos, master of races, called the long-distance runners, Calyce's favorite Phidias among them as well as two Tyrinian women. Satyrea and I cheered louder for the women than Calyce did for Phidias. At the dusty finish, one of them tied him for first.

"Next, Meteos carried a round flat stone to the center of the arena. Damysos, Machaon of Pylos, and four other discus-throwers followed. Machaon stepped forward to take the first turn. He whirled as if propelled by the weight, then let the it soar down the stadium. 'A throw to beat!' The crowd cheered as a boy trotted back with the disc.

"The well-muscled thrower from Nauplion followed, his hair touching his shoulders in a multitude of tiny braids threaded with narrow ribbons. Both men and women were so enthralled watching his dancing whirl and flowing toss, arm remaining gracefully extended after the weight soared, that we barely noticed his throw fell far short of Machaon's and cheered as loudly for him.

"The throws of the next two came within inches of each other but still short of Machaon's. When Damysos accepted the disc, he smiled at me, and I threw him a kiss. Crystals in the stone caught the light as it flew down the oval, arcing as if borne on the wind. It landed two spear-lengths beyond Machaon's mark. Damysos bowed to the shouting crowd, catching my eye as he left the arena.

"At the far end of the stadium, a pigeon was being tethered to a pole. Eight archers stood in readiness. Perhaps it was the prospect of the bird's death, perhaps spending too long in the sun, but I felt unsteady. The stadium took on a reddish brilliance and I began to shake. Rhene helped me out. You're right, Manto, I should have gone home sooner, but I wanted to celebrate Damysos' victory. Instead, I came close to fainting. The chariot race came last, so if Rhene hurried, she could return in time to watch Hiketaon compete.

"A breeze blew up from the sea as she and I drank cool water in my garden. I recovered myself enough to send her back to the arena. I could hear roars for winners and cheers for those who came in last, and envisioned gleaming athletes and horses giving their all. From the open pavilion erected for the king and queen, Polydora, the priest of Poseidon, and Meteos would award gold tripods to winners, golden chains for second place, bronze vessels for third, and painted vases for fourth.

"At least I had seen Tanais and Damysos win firsts. I didn't regret skipping the rest of the Games and honors but was sorry to miss giving Damysos his victory kiss.

Chapter Eighteen: Alcimedes' Feast

"By that evening I recovered sufficiently to attend the feast at Alcimedes' house. Rhene and I were greeted by Amyclas' wine-bubbly laughter and served cups of wine as we stepped into the hall, its walls lined with embossed gold plate refracting the light of elaborate torch holders. If we in all our glamour seemed underdressed in comparison, what would those austere women from Tiryns do in such a place?

"A striking woman, imperious as an Eastern queen, stood with Alcimedes in a distant doorway. Macaria! A braided silk girdle clasped her pearlescent silk peplos, and emerald drops hung from her ears. Above her high forehead a golden wreath crowned her black hair, and her eyes shone black from their kohl outline, darker even than Satyrea's.

"Meteos stood off to the side with a frail woman, her thin, ashy hair cropped close to her head. So this was Urania. The rich robe hung loosely on her narrow frame, and she appeared wan, leaning on her husband. No one pushed against her, respecting one who spent her time abed.

"Watching Urania hobble away on Meteos' arm, I recalled my night with Zetes, the flood of motherlove welling up in response to his desperate need. I watched him greet his parents, and their brief formal exchange sorrowed me. Odd as it felt to be carrying a child, I couldn't imagine pregnancy would ruin my health as it had Urania's.

"Be careful, I cautioned myself. No woman is guaranteed safe childbirth.

"Light-headed from perfume, flute melodies, and voices darting across the dazzling room, I could have been one of Alcimedes' statues, so still was I. Guests moved hip to hip, separated, found another, flirted, withdrew. Whichever gods prevailed at the Games—Athena, Apollo, or wing-footed Hermes—this evening was Aphrodite's.

"I caught the eye of Tanais, beautiful in his white tunic. When music, drinking, and laughter resumed after Alcimedes praised the athletes, Tanais came to stand beside me. His rarely-used voice sounded strangled in his throat as he conveyed Carpho's greetings. I assumed he ran to her shrine for hill training, but he told me he often stayed on her hillside. She'd convinced him to do something. Guess, Manto."

"To go as an initiate to Eleusis."

"Exactly. Carpho said that in all of Corinth, no one would better benefit from Demeter's Mysteries. Tanais would return a new man, fit to lead. The devout silence of those nine days would teach him eloquent speech." Teiresias turns to me. "Did you ever see such a young man there?"

"I remember Tanais from his later visits to Eleusis. Priestesses serve as guides through the Mysteries, so we don't see initiates as individuals. Some we may feel closer to than others, but the experience is ours to offer, theirs to receive and make use of as they will. We didn't always know what drove pilgrims to be initiates. For Tanais, it was Carpho's advice, to his good fortune."

Teiresias nods. "At the banquet I heard that little Oedipus had already proven a prodigy. Rhene and Hiketaon, the charioteer from Nauplion, found each other, as did Calyce her Tyrinian spear-throwing runner Phidias. I could see Rhene knew Hiketaon, and Calyce appeared more enamored than usual. What either attachment might lead to who could say, but both seemed magnetic that night.

"The extravagance of Alcimedes' decor outdid the royal palace, given Queen Merope's simple tastes. Platters of garnished fowl, roast meats, rainbows of vegetables topped with flowers, aromatic sauces, olives, cheeses, and breads in every shape repelled my sensitive appetite. I would have happily skipped the meal. But Amyclas directed me to sit between Brovas and Tanais. Brovas was soon on his feet joining libations and speeches, and Tanais sat mute beside me.

"Across the table, Macaria spoke in Calyce's ear, ignoring Phidias, awed by the splendor around him. I caught her words, that we must strive for what we want, whatever it takes. That was the first I heard such a thought from a woman. *Strive for what we want?* She added that Calyce would look stunning in precious jewels, and deserved more than she could ever gain in Aphrodite's service. Calyce waved her away, but I was shocked that Macaria aspired to use our service for profit."

"Could she?" I ask. "What deity did Macaria serve? From what you say, I would guess Hermes, trickster and thief, but he's a guide of souls. Hecate?"

"No, Macaria didn't emanate her dark magic. I couldn't judge if she was missing a connection to the divine force of the cosmos or possessed something extra, a sense of her *self* as an absolute? She *wanted*, used, manipulated. I sensed in Macaria and Alcimedes a new order, a brutality of spirit and desire for personal gain. How could those living in harmony resist?

"Macaria approached Tanais, she an angler, he the iridescent swimmer in the deeps. I saw her trying to reel him in, to capture Tanais' bright beauty. He rose, arcing his body out of the water, she playing the line and drawing him closer. For a long moment he leaned toward her until, just short of drowning in her perfumed breath, he broke her taut line, pulling away abruptly. Looking angry, Macaria turned on her heel. Tanais returned to his place beside me grinning.

"That night fueled visions of the future. Macaria and Alcimedes appeared in my mind's eye as harbingers of a new age. I'd drunk the wine of prescience and thus recall images more than events, Tanais a silvery fish, Alcimedes a shrike, Macaria a vulture. Damysos, who arrived late in the festivities to bid me farewell before departing for Ithaca, a sacred bull, favored by the divine ones. He circled the table, pausing to give me a kiss on uplifted lips. He whispered loving words, and my heart followed him out the door.

"The vulture with soaring wings and an unerring sense of prey and the shrike who impales insects and lizards: Macaria and Alcimedes flew at each other warily through the evening, but for the time being, the dove of Aphrodite overpowered them.

"These guests resembled birds and beasts, but I felt like a serpent near to bursting through my skin. Yet, nearly full term, I danced, cymbals on fingers and thumb, with a prayer my daughter would be a sibyl serving the Goddess.

"Exhausted, I asked Brovas to walk me home. The waxing moon and torch at my door created a lacy bower of light in the garden. On such a lovely night, we sat outside in silent communion. I felt an indentation in my finger. At some point I must have wrenched off the ring.

"Brovas told me as a young man he gave his all in a mad sacrifice to Astarte. The greatest joy he'd known since was with me. His eyes, admiring yet clouded, startled me with the truth. I wondered at my blindness, failing to understand the nature of Brovas' sacrifice. Yet to speak of it, to alter our affectionate ways, felt impossible. I longed to say I too lost what made me man but simply embraced him. After his sojourn in Phoenicia, he found it impossible to return to Corinth. The dream cure at Epidaurus saved him, and now here he was, blessed by Aphrodite and me.

"With a smile I led him to my chamber.

"Much later, Brovas rested beside me, absently curling my hair around his finger. I lay in peace beyond thought, until he came to himself, gave me a light kiss, and departed.

"The next morning, my golden ring was still missing. I was certain I secured it in the fold in my peplos, but searched the courtyard and house with no luck. My maid Iphinoe ran to Alcimedes' house, but no one there knew anything, nor did Brovas recall when last he saw it. Rhene assured me it would turn up when I least expected."

Chapter Nineteen: Childbirth

Teiresias reaches a stopping point as Cenchrias appears with a supper of vegetables braised in olive oil.

"A welcome meal," he says, drinking deep of his wine. We dine in congenial silence, sharing Cenchrias' serene world.

Teiresias wipes his beard and continues. "I'll tell you about my late days of pregnancy, a peculiar time for one such as me." He waves his hand over his male body.

I laugh. "Hard to imagine."

"As it was for me initially, but pregnancy takes one over. I spent my days with Rhene, Satyrea, and the children of the precinct, picturing myself as a mother. The idea wasn't frightening. Just odd. The process of giving birth: that I would rather not think about. How do women do it?"

"You did," I say. "And your child survived."

"Yes. She thrived. In those days I expected to be Teira forever. In the old stories, when a mortal transforms to a new shape, he—it's usually a woman who becomes male— remains a man until death."

"Or a flower or a laurel tree," I say.

"So I assumed about my woman's body. She was me forever."

I know about childbirth only from the full-term women who came to the shrine of Artemis. Unlike Historis, fascinated by the process, I never attended a delivery.

That this old man was a mother takes my breath away. Such a drastic change from his manly self as counselor to King Labdacus and negligent father. Can I tell such a story convincingly? I'll have to carry the conviction of Teiresias himself. This is what happened.

"Carpho arrived as my labor pains began. She prayed to Eileithyia and told the nurse Anippe to fetch all that was needed to facilitate childbirth.

"The serpent of the Mother who held and comforted me through my pregnancy now seemed wrapped around my belly, tightening downward, each constriction pressing the tiny one on her voyage. A fierce contraction waved through me, and I gripped Carpho's hand. Her voice came from a great distance. 'One more push and she'll be here.'

"Not pain but a huge release opened my body, propelling the infant into the world. Carpho caught her in a linen towel. The baby's wail sounded like a laugh.

"We started laughing too, which expelled the afterbirth and contracted my womb to stop the bleeding. Weeping, laughter; pleasure, pain—who could separate them? Childbirth for a woman more than equals a warrior facing his enemy, requiring courage and bringing transcendence to another plane. Her victory, if she survives the ordeal, is the joy of an infant in her arms. In exhausted calm, I held my daughter to my chest, breasts aching to feed her.

"As soon as Carpho and Anippe tied off the cord and washed her, they helped me sit so I could nestle her into the curve of my arm for her first meal. My breast was too full for the infant to grab, but Carpho pinched it into a nipple. A squirt of thin fluid wet her cheek, and she was quick to fasten her mouth to its source. I couldn't stop smiling as I admired the perfection of her tiny mouth, traces of eyelashes, miraculous fingernails. Within seconds we both fell asleep. I sensed Carpho moving the baby and leaving me to my dreams.

"An unworldly green-black space surrounded me. There coiled the massive serpent Delphyne, shining with a soft green light. In a sibilant voice she whispered, 'Our child shall be called Daphne, after the Dryad who eluded Apollo, after the sacred laurel whose sweet smoke produces visions. From my dwelling place beneath the omphalos I bless Daphne.'

"I reached toward Delphyne, but she'd retreated into the depths, leaving me with no light, no direction, only the disorienting green and a whisper that sounded like 'Resist Apollo.'

"A blaze of radiance awakened me. I lay open-eyed in my chamber, a lamp flickering beside the basket where Daphne breathed evenly. Her name fit one destined to join the ancient sisterhood as Pythia. I welcomed the tiny mouth so real, seeking its nourishment from me." Teiresias pauses. "What do you think of this story, Manto?"

"I wonder how Daphne's birth resembles my own."

"I wish I could tell you, but I wasn't present. A priestess of Artemis attended yours and your sister's births. Our housemaid said that with you, Chloris had an easy labor. She looked happy when I arrived home to see her cradling her newborn in her arms. Chloris was a loving mother, but I don't know how she envisioned your future." He exhales a long breath. "I've described the circumstances of Historis' birth. Though she came early she was healthy, but to my shame and grief, Chloris did not survive."

Terrible as those words are, I don't add to his regrets. Much has passed since the shock of learning how my mother died.

Teiresias takes my hand and I squeeze his. I've forgiven him, as nearly as I can.

He speaks softly. "Chloris would be pleased that both her daughters became priestesses."

"Historis and I knew that was our destiny. If Daphne now presides at Delphi, all three of your daughters now serve goddesses—and you as well, in serving Aphrodite."

"The golden goddess no longer blesses me."

"You say worship in Corinth is not as you knew it."

"The sad truth. No longer do Aphrodite's priestesses possess the innocence of my day." He senses my incredulity. "Yes, innocence is the right word. Our worship was pure. Intimate and healing. It still has its sacred elements to lesser degree. Macaria and Alcimedes couldn't overpower Aphrodite, only alter her rituals and their meaning."

"Have priests taken over control of the temple in Corinth? Priests of Apollo translate the sibyl's oracles in Delphi, and one day priests will become hierophants at Eleusis. Has something like that happened in Corinth?"

"Not exactly. I'll describe the decline as I experienced it, beginning late one autumn afternoon. A cooling wind blew white across the sea after a day of stifling heat. By then, Daphne could suck a linen teat of goats' milk and honey in Anippe's arms, so I attended an evening temple dance. I was almost out the door before I remembered the girdle from Aphrodite. Fastening it around my waist made me stand straighter, again a priestess. I reached the Acrocorinth in time to dip my fingers into the sacred waters of Peirene.

"After embracing Calyce and Iole, I looked closely at the carved figures on the door to our dwelling, so familiar that when I lived there I paid them little mind. We examined the carvings in squares depicting the works of women. Weavers and potters, singers, bakers, and spinners plied their crafts, framed by the Ocean Stream.

"With one finger Calyce traced two small carved swimmers, saying she looked forward to teaching Daphne to swim. She wanted my daughter to love the water as much as we did.

"Flute music pulled us into the temple, and as the drum beat intensified, I rejoiced at returning to dance with my sister priestesses. The drum stopped abruptly. A sudden rainstorm blew past us to sheen the image of Aphrodite.

"We struggled across the courtyard against its onslaught and into our dwelling, where attendants fought to keep the fire burning through gusts of wind. Toweling, dry robes, and a big pot of soup awaited us.

"A tremor shook the building, then a second. We cried prayers for mercy to Poseidon Earthshaker. The building creaked and rocked from side to side, spilling soup down the table, and we clung to the benches in frightened silence.

"Soon after the quaking subsided, the drenched Labrya and Merope pushed through the door. They were on their way here to plan Daphne's blessing in the Queen's chambers when storm caught them, and the path rippled beneath their feet. Merope regretted leaving Oedipus below with his nurse as I regretted leaving Daphne, but now we must stay where we were, warming ourselves by the fire, drinking sweet wine, and praying. To keep up our spirits we sang old songs to the accompaniment of Labyra's lyre.

"After her last chord, fragmentary conversations began. When I touched my finger where the ring should be, I was filled with apprehension. I used to rub it while praying to the Great Goddess, and we certainly needed Her now.

"Merope sat beside me and spoke softly about her worries for Oedipus. She said I might suspect she didn't give birth to him. I squeezed her hand in affirmation. She whispered the truth. The baby had been found on a distant mountain and brought to the palace by a shepherd as heir to King Polybus. Merope welcomed the infant, believing a baby saved after being abandoned to the wolves was the Mother's blessed child."

His expression is so sorrowful I ask if Fate was unkind.

"I won't say how unkind. At that time however, Oedipus was a beloved son.

"Merope and Labrya shared a chamber that night, and we all slept two to a bed for comfort. Curled around each other, Calyce and I drifted to sleep. In the middle of the night, the sharpest quake yet shook the building. We held each other close, fearing Earth would swallow us.

"But after that jolt, all was still. Poseidon's rage had run its course. When dawn lit the sky, we stepped cautiously through the muddy courtyard to the temple. The stone steps had separated from the flooring, requiring a careful jump. Inside, a ripple cracked the floor, a giant wave across the blue-tiled ocean. I couldn't bring myself to look at Aphrodite herself.

"Only after Polydora said the statue was unharmed did I gaze at her wet face, reflecting sungold rays, her decorations in place. But the serpent on the pedestal had moved. A hairline crack angled through its coils, increasing their arc as if they might twist apart.

"In a hurry to return to Daphne, I hesitated to mention it. Avoiding fallen stones, I made my way down the hill. A figure of Hermes lay on its face in a puddle. The smiling image of Aphrodite at the center of the precinct courtyard was intact, though the flowery arc above her had shaken to the ground.

"My doorway stood firm. I opened the door and called to Anippe, my breasts heavy. I can't see your face, Manto, but I'm sure you are bemused that such a paltry figure as me was once a woman in her nurturing prime."

"So would anyone be hearing such a story."

"Yes, but you will have two advantages when you tell it to others."

"What advantages?"

"The obvious one: it's not your experience. A rhapsode plays storyteller, and everyone loves a story. You can dramatize all you like. That's what speaking before an audience requires. How much detail you include may alter each time you tell it, but add nothing of your own."

"That I can promise. I haven't the imagination of a poet. What's the other?"

"You will know the end of the story. After we hear a tale, Theseus in the labyrinth, for example, we play with our listeners' fear and ignorance to strike their emotions as we speak it. We guide their understanding until all is revealed."

"You're saying I should ignore my puzzlement as you tell it, Father, and await the next revelation."

"I may use suspense to keep you engaged."

I hope he knows I'm smiling. "I still have no idea how you ended up here, blind and male."

"Nor shall you until the time is right."

"I know, I know. Carry on."

"Anippe met me at the gate, baby in arms. She prepared our breakfast while Daphne snuggled against me, her mouth questing, gurgling in contentment when she found my nipple. What a rare feeling, to nurse an infant! Her even tugging calmed me, and my life again felt secure."

Teiresias touches his chest at the memory as if he still has breasts and who knows, perhaps remnants remain. Did he fully regain his manhood after his second transformation? Likely no old man possesses all he did when young, but perhaps Teiresias has become something of an hermaphrodite. Unseemly thoughts about a father, but who's had a father like mine? I'm relieved when he speaks.

"Within a few days, Corinth was cleared. The storm gave way to splotchy white clouds racing across the sky and a crest of whitecaps on the dark sea, the perfect day for Daphne's blessing. I wrapped her into my best cloak for our walk to the palace, joined by temple priestesses as they descended from the Acrocorinth.

"Queen Merope led us to her silvery chamber. In the adjoining room, Oedipus was being bathed by his nurse. Labrya struck a chord, and Daphne made a long oooo sound. While she sang her wordless song, we spoke prayers around the circle, wishing her moon vision and freedom, love of animals and solitude in the service of ancient goddesses." Teiresias looks at me. "Chloris must have taken you to be blessed at the shrine of Artemis. I'm ashamed I don't know."

"No doubt after Agathe brought us there, we were embraced into its fellowship with the ceremony required," I say. It makes no difference to me now. Sitting here listening to Teiresias as the Epigoni amass their forces is an interlude.

With war threatening, I can't reflect on the past or worry about my future. Might I be sibyl with Daphne in Delphi one day? A mother myself? A wandering story-teller? A worthy calling for a man, feasted and housed as he travels, but would a woman rhapsode be regarded as a beggar? In ancient times, women were the story-tellers!

Teiresias must have said more about the ritual for Daphne, but I catch only his conclusion.

"Holding Daphne in my arms at the feast after her blessing, I ate and drank little. The room was full of goddesses summoned to balance Apollo. At home that night, the god appeared to me in a dream, his presence shining, his voice reverberating. 'Daphne will bring the wisdom of light. When I speak through you, your office will be more painful.'

"How would Apollo speak through me? A mystifying, fearful thought. When Labdacus sent me, Teiresias, to Delphi, I didn't understand the oracle. I would need fuller knowledge and the god's blessing."

"You've gained renown as a soothsayer. Some god blessed you."

Why does he laugh?

Chapter Twenty: Polydora

In the cool of the evening, Teiresias continues the story.
"Losing my ring felt ominous, but the crack in the pedestal
beneath Aphrodite was a bigger crisis, precipitating major
changes. No one in Corinth knew if Poseidon's fury was
at our temple, the city, or from something beyond us. like a
quarrel with his godly brothers.

"Now and then Calyce or Iole visited me in the precinct
as I nursed fretful Daphne, grateful for their company. They
described how our temple rituals had slackened. Fewer
worshippers and no mad whirling dances, stamping feet, or
rapidly beating drums. Craftsmen from Tiryns repaired the
fissure in the tile floor, seemingly unaware they labored in
Aphrodite's domain. A priest of Apollo accompanied them,
a gaunt man called Oineus who never knew himself through
excess. We were used to Corinth's old priest of Apollo who
embraced every god and every ritual. Oineus was young,
focused, and ascetic."

I laugh along with Teiresias. Ironic for such a man to be
in the temple of Aphrodite, where healing comes through
music, dancing, and love.

"Yes, it was absurd. Oineus didn't belong there, but
Polydora couldn't force him to leave. He lodged with the
workers in the city and accompanied them daily, interfering
with Polydora's every suggestion. Finally she gave up trying,
distracted by Zetes' news that Urania died.

"Her grief puzzled me until she confided something I'd never guessed. Urania's husband Meteos was the father of her two sons. I could be of no help in combing out Polydora's tangled emotions. Her distress added to the temple's disorder. I had nightmares that Poseidon shook it to rubble on the hillside, forcing us to flee like priestesses in long ago Crete.

"At last Polydora snapped out of mourning and the rest of us our listlessness. Rhene and I returned to the temple, gathering the last of our roses as an offering. We had to jump over the gap at the top of the stone steps, but the floor was retiled, its ocean pattern more brilliant than ever.

"As Polydora arranged the flowers, already losing their petals, I looked closely at the carved serpent. The crack was still evident through its coils, but I couldn't be so consumed by melancholy as to fail to notice Aphrodite's glory, not a gemstone of her necklace missing. Our spirits rose, and the restored temple welcomed our impassioned dance. With Urania's funeral rites the following day, our exuberance celebrated our precious lives in the face of death.

"I spent the night with Calyce in the priestess dwelling. Next morning we all walked together to the burial mound outside the city walls. Mourners had clustered under a black alder tree. We scattered lavender and rosemary over Urania's gravesite and prayed for her spirit in the name of the waning moon and Hecate of the dark. The worst she would suffer in the afterlife would be darkness."

I break his long silence. "You and I both envision more than darkness beyond our earthly existence. The Mysteries offer eternal life, whatever form it takes. You must have your own consoling beliefs."

"That would be a stimulating conversation, Manto. I do. But now I want to tell you Polydora's story. Some time before she arrived in Corinth, Meteos married Urania, a beautiful wraith of a woman. Though fragile, she conceived a son and almost died birthing him. Henceforth, Urania kept to her bedchamber. The boy Zetes made do as he could, never hungry, never fully fed.

"Meteos too was starved of affection. You would think that after Urania took to her bed, he would seek solace at the temple of Aphrodite, but he focused on his responsibilities to King Polybus. He never said as much, but blamed Zetes for Urania's disabilities. He escaped from their dreary household to the palace, leaving his son in the care of servants.

"Years later, a friend brought Meteos to our temple, where he watched Polydora dance in her restrained style. Something drew them together, and Polydora invited him to her chamber. Next time Meteos visited, she was carrying his child.

"She declined his offer of a house in the precinct. Her leadership at the temple came first. Meteos carried on, neither husband, father, or lover. After Polydora sent word of Biton's birth, he visited her and and the baby and arranged for the boy to be dedicated at the temple of Helios where Meteos had been educated.

"That spring, Okyrhoe, a priestess of Paphos, brought the Cypriot festival of Adonis to Corinth, celebrating Aphrodite's annual reunion with her reborn mortal paramour Adonis. Okyrhoe led all the city to the flowery meadows for dancing, feasting, and loosening garments with a chosen lover.

"Meteos never returned home that week. He and Polydora loved to the sound of revelers' music and the lark of dawn, with others nearby and in solitude. For the first time, she was fully Aphrodite's votary. As a child, she was so early-blooming, with her golden hair and midnight blue eyes, that everyone agreed she was destined to serve Aphrodite. Yet her friend Aglaia with her ruddy skin, square hands, and stocky body was more a daughter of the love goddess than Polydora. Aglaia gloried in fabrics, makeup and scent. She peered at her eyes in the mirror to practice different expressions and crafted jewelry from pretty pebbles. Polydora would rather serve Hera. I'd sensed as much from her restraint when dancing, precise but without passion.

"Only with Meteos did she truly know Aphrodite. At the end of the week, celebrants sacrificed a boar to commemorate the beast who slew Adonis. They dined on boar's meat and the next day fasted, mourning Aphrodite's loss and Adonis' death. Polydora wept more than anyone, and afterwards she stripped her chamber of its scanty adornment. I'd always admired her striking appearance, but only then did I note that her severely banded hair, gold ear hoops and ring of small beads around her neck never varied amidst priestesses who changed hairstyles and jewelry daily.

"She wasn't surprised she conceived during that wild week. When she told Meteos, he was delighted. The night Polydora birthed their second son, Urania had a seizure, hastening her decline. That was also the night Meteos' elder son Zetes met Strophios. Polydora lamented playing even an indirect part in these tragedies. Her baby, Cleobis, was raised by Ialysa along with his brother Biton." Teiresias takes a deep breath. "I shall end here. If I continue their story I'll lose track of my own. I must return to the main thread. Or is this enough for now?"

"It's a beautiful night, Father. I'm not ready to retreat."

"You can sleep outside if you wish. Cenchrias will make ready a pallet."

"I'll ask him."

"Ah," Teiresias smiles. "You understand how to communicate."

"More or less. He pays attention to what's needed. You trained him well."

"Little training was involved. He serves me out of love and trust." Teiresias takes a sip of wine and continues.

"Summer was brief that year. Winter came early, though Poseidon shook no more. I missed Calyce but felt less inclined to climb to the temple, making my obsequies to the Aphrodite in my chamber and living quietly with Daphne, Anippe, and Iphinoe. The precinct was quiet, no guests, no banquets. Zetes hadn't visited since his mother died, and no news came from Brovas across the seas.

"He'd visited me soon after Daphne's birth, bringing her a noisy toy and a golden coin with the image of the sun. King Polybus was sending him to Egypt, a place he knew well.

"As Brovas readied for departure, I felt drawn to him as never before. Perhaps it was the aura of Egypt hanging over him, the sense that there was more to his life than could be circumscribed by Corinth. He'd sacrificed to Astarte, experienced the dream cure at Epidaurus, and revered the Great Goddess. And now this mystical, ancient place.

"As he caressed my full breasts and belly newly firm, I responded to his touch, my mind opening to the visions he brought me, Hephaestus to my Aphrodite. So had Amyclas joked: Hephaestus, the lame and adoring husband of the love goddess who could be held by no male, mortal or divine. Under the spell of Brovas' fingers in the stillness of my chamber, I saw another image of Hephaestus. His leg wasn't lame. Rather, his feet diverged, simultaneously pointing both forward and backward.

"Brovas was that sort of magician, his knowledge ranging fore and aft, above and below, sometimes impeding his movement on solid ground. But never was he awkward on my bed. I quivered at a particularly piquant touch and lost myself in the glow he aroused. As always, he denied me even a touch of his body. When release waved over me and I tried to close my legs, he renewed his taunting play until I again desired him. So passed the afternoon, Daphne's distant cries answered by Anippe.

"That was our farewell. Brovas promised to carry with him the vision of me dancing more passionately than any of Egypt would dare.

"I felt nostalgic for Zetes' company, Brovas' caresses, all our gay festivities. Perhaps Merope and Polybus spent their chilly days by the fire with Oedipus, as I did with Daphne. A storm at winter solstice blew out the torches, ending our celebration before it began.

"Sometimes I wrapped myself in my warmest cloak and walked through the city, standing long at my favorite lookout above the sea, surging wine-dark below me under gray skies briefly lit with silver. Aphrodite had flown to Ethiope to bask in sunshine, leaving us to dusky solitude. Buds stayed tightly knotted later than usual, and even red poppies, heralds of spring, were slow to burst from between the rocks.

"One afternoon Rhene and I walked up to the temple to pray for Aphrodite's return. For the first time in months, I gave attention to my appearance. I'd let my hair fall free in its own curls, but that day I plaited tiny braids, brushed a coppery glow on my pale cheeks, and fastened my golden girdle over a light blue woolen chiton, adding Brovas' pearl.

Dark clouds obscured the sun, and I wrapped my shawl from Delphi over my head and shoulders under a warm cloak.

"Torches flamed against the hazy sky. The sight of Calyce and our sisters was so welcoming that my stiff limbs relaxed. Music flowed through me, inspiring a dance of ripples and undulations. Polydora tended the altar, she too swaying with the music. The few male worshippers departed as soon as dancing ended.

"Afterward the much-missed laughter of women drifted through gossip as we dined on oranges, pomegranate seeds, and bread studded with raisins. Macaria and Alcimedes had been seen in Olympia, in Sparta, on the island of Thera. The jeweler Leiriope was expecting a baby. Oineus, priest of Apollo, remained in Corinth after the workmen returned to Tiryns, but he hadn't troubled our temple in person. We were curious what kept him here.

"That delayed spring blazes in my memory, all the world abloom. Fragile pink clusters massed on bare almond branches, and rainbows of iris, hyacinth and poppies, lilies, daisies, and asphodel covered the hillsides and drifted across the plain.

"One bright morning, Rhene, Polydora, their children and I trailed down to the aqua sea, its lacy white fringe lapping the shore. Daphne, slung against my back in the serpent shawl secured in a tight knot, chirped a song.

"No heart could remain closed indoors on such a day. When the path opened out toward the port, we passed old men and women sitting in their courtyards and younger ones outside on any pretext—to fetch water or hang clothes or repair house fronts and shop stalls. Children were everywhere, shouting, chasing, laughing. Pairs of dolphins arced through the water near bathing youths, tantalizing them, then racing away. It was all Rhene and Polydora could do to keep their children from rushing into the water to join them, leading them to calmer waters to splash in shallow waves.

"Ankle deep, I dangled Daphne's feet in the sea. She caught her breath, then made her gurgling laugh as she splashed. When others from the temple arrived, Calyce took Daphne from me, moving her across the water to imitate swimming.

"At midday, siting in the dappled shade tired and soaked through, we reveled in a day of total peace. Yet as we spread our fruit and cakes on a cloth covering the pebbly beach, a wave of dread hit me. Something ominous was coming. After Polydora spilt her libation to Aphrodite on the beach, she poured out a few more drops with a prayer to Hera, who, she said quietly, had summoned her.

"We sat stunned. Polydora would soon leave for Argos. I imagined if ever she moved from the temple dwelling, it would be into town to live with Meteos. But living in the precinct never appealed to her as much as temple life, so why would she choose to run the household of one man?

"Our faces reflected our shock and dismay. Polydora said she would be chief priestess of Hera by summer, chosen heir of the agèd one now presiding. Her words made me wonder whether I too would be called onward, and I rubbed my finger as if to summon guidance from my missing ring. The only answer was a sinking feeling in my heart. Polydora, our high priestess in all but name, shouldn't leave us. The vague future troubles I sensed would threaten our temple. We needed her.

"Reading my thoughts, she said Aphrodite would not forsake us, would bring laughter and love and its poignant pain forever. Our goddess ruled Corinth eternally.

"I wasn't consoled. Aphrodite is no fighter. Why should Hera take our strongest? I urged Polydora to stay to help defeat Macaria. When she looked surprised, I said what was obvious to me. Macaria sought to make our priestess' service a trade for gold instead of gift to the goddess. Calyce agreed. Macaria had said as much, trying to recruit her to some venture of wealth she planned, not in Corinth but somewhere more profligate.

"The temple's Aphrodite stood on a cracked pedestal, and splendid banquets in our precinct were rare. Royal guests were more likely to dine in the palace on roasted meats with women seldom present, even Queen Merope. Such times, I feared, could only help Macaria and Alcimedes corrupt worship.

"Nothing more was said. We made shady beds for the children and spent the afternoon dozing, watching clouds drift and birds fly high above, sipping wine and, for me, fighting worries about the consequences of Polydora's departure.

"A few nights later in the midst of a summer rainstorm, Meteos ventured through the showers to Polydora's chamber. As he was her first votary in the service of Aphrodite, so was he her last, arousing and exciting and exhausting as the winds. By the time he fell asleep in her arms, he understood it was farewell. During the night, Polydora's shoulder was drenched with his dreaming tears. In the morning they agreed that Meteos would raise their sons. Perhaps Zetes would join their family, all male except for a nurse and attendants.

"We made a valiant attempt to bid Polydora a loving farewell. But she was abandoning us. Did she feel no duty to our community or her sons? We hadn't imagined a priestess would leave her children behind."

"You left Historis and me, Father. Under different circumstances, I grant you." A long silence. "Don't tell me you left Daphne as well? You, her mother?"

He murmurs, "After a fashion."

I stand. "It's been a long day, and we must sleep. I hope I can, after all you told me."

"A difficult day for me as well, reliving so much. Next I must speak of the many kinds of darkness that descended on our temple. Definitely time to stop for the night."

I'm exhausted and don't wait for Cenchrias to make up a pallet for me. The cottage will suit fine.

Chapter Twenty-one: Poseidon Earthshaker

Over breakfast Teiresias tells me about the Egyptian sphinx Brovas described on his return, a colossal statue, both fierce and benign, like a guardian spirit.

"Besides bringing treasures from his voyage, he described Egypt's ornate palaces, giant pyramids built as tombs for kings and queens, wide roads, crocodiles, and the fertile floods of the Nile. He was most impressed by their hieroglyphic writing. Not only did Egyptians record shipping information as we do, but their scribes ventured into poetry."

Teiresias smiles. Perhaps I can write his story. I'm too startled to reply. One of he gifts Pharaoh gave Brovas—the best besides a jar of poppy-infused honey for his deteriorating health—was an Egyptian tablet marked with hieroglyphs.

"You don't expect me to tell your story in drawings?"

"An old man's fancy. Anyway, our language has an alphabet."

"For record keeping. Forget it, Father. Life is long. You have lived countless years yourself. But however venerable, I will not live long enough to master the art of writing. You ask me to commit your story to memory so I can speak it well. That is more than enough."

"You're right. I should be grateful you don't fall asleep while I talk. So no, I won't ask you to write, but I do wish you could. One day writing will change the world in ways

I cannot even guess. For now, my dear daughter, you need only listen."

How can I not? His story compels me beyond anything I could imagine. Besides, the teller is my own father who gave birth to a younger sister I've never met.

"You will meet Daphne one day," he says. "At this point in the story, she's learning to walk in the early mornings when there's a cool breeze. The heat troubled Brovas, so he brought the waxen tablet at dawn as I was coaxing Daphne to eat an orange slice. The hieroglyphs were beautiful but meaningless. I saw an eye, an owl, but had no idea what they signified separately or together, coming from a realm so unlike our own. Brovas dreamt that I wrote the story of Corinth. I told him such a dream means each of us writes our life, makes our mark. Besides, the alphabet Cadmus was said to have brought to Greece was nothing like what appeared on his Egyptian tablet.

"He laughed when I mentioned Cadmus, who came from Phoenicia where the chief skills were navigation and shipbuilding. Had I ever heard of a Muse dwelling in Phoenicia? I had not, nor that Cadmus' alphabet could record verses like those in these hieroglyphs.

"I can assure you there will never be writing at Eleusis," I say. "Sacred mysteries cannot be set down, even in elusive pictographs."

"No, I expect not," Teiresias says. "Brovas also brought me a neckpiece, a golden bird suspended from a golden chain, its wings studded with coral and turquoise. I felt its magic, the bird slender as a serpent. She represented me, a bird with Brovas in my chamber where he, ailing and crippled, grew wings. Perhaps this image was inspired by Egyptian magic or his jar of Egyptian honey that brings memory and forgetting. Brovas swirled his finger through the little pot and offered it to me. His finger was rough, the honey sweet and sharp. After his loving, he lay with his head beside mine, my scent lingering, his breathing soon even and deep.

"Although the honey tasted of mandragora, I felt no narcotic effect. Then, eyes wide open, I saw a vision brighter than any dream. A winged serpent hovered near the ceiling, for a moment showing the face of Damysos, then Brovas, before taking the visage of Aphrodite herself. 'Do not lose yourself in wonder,' she said. 'My worship never dies. Honor me when other gods claim you. Do not fear the gaze of the sphinx.' For one bright moment the serpent became a winged lion with a face as lovely as Aphrodite's before vanishing. She was lithe, nothing like the colossal Sphinx of Egypt, and felt ominous."

"Do you still honor Aphrodite?"

"Here?" He snorts a laugh. "Brovas' honey deluded me. Aphrodite hasn't been with me in years. I love Cenchrias like a son, but haven't known passionate love since—" He breaks off.

"Since you became a blind man."

Lips pressed together, he nods. "I could say my service to Aphrodite caused my blindness." He shakes his head. "Aphrodite's poignant joys fade."

Teiresias' words sound so final I wonder if he will stop here for the day. The sun hasn't reached its zenith, too early for food or napping.

Finally he takes a deep breath and resumes.

"Brovas made one more attempt to convince me to try my hand at writing. He brought a clay tablet with signs in an old language closer to ours, but I set it aside with barely a glance. Perhaps when I grow old, I told him, but any chance of that ended with blindness.

"He agreed the loss of my serpent ring was a dire omen. Nothing simply vanishes, so he would pursue it.

"That year rain was so delayed that seeds dried in the fields. Then a flashing storm washed away seedlings barely sprouted.

"Brovas visited the day after the storm, looking haggard. His trip to Egypt served Corinth well, for King Polybus would soon receive shipments of grain from fertile Memphis. At least Brovas had that consolation, for he doubted he himself would see the spring. As we drank wine together, he told me Leiriope had seen my ring on Macaria's finger when she came into their shop. She'd claimed it was a gift—from Egypt, of all places, though of course it came from ancient Crete.

"I did drop it at Alcimedes' banquet! Of course he would give it to Macaria. How ever would I recover it?

"Brovas came to bid me farewell and express his regrets for not being able to retrieve the ring. After dreaming of monsters, he learned to have no fear. So he advised me. The most horrifying beasts live in a realm touching our own. One can go through the veil and back again. Don't expect to encounter a being like a Gorgon or Echidne, the beautiful woman-serpent who birthed the dreadful brood including the Sphinx, until you are past suffering and can look at it unflinching.

"He said I would be his talisman when he descended to Hades where none embrace. My tears blurred the sight of his limping departure.

"Three days later Brovas was buried under a threatening sky. As he predicted, the coming winter was bitter cold. The grain of Memphis kept Corinth alive.

"One day we awakened to a pink-shot sky perfect for a celebration. Okyrhoe returned from Paphos—fortunately, as it turned out, for more than commemorating Adonis. Under shimmering clouds we danced out of the temple to the music of Marpessa's flute. Corinth and the sea below shone with an eerie light.

"On our way through the city, we gathered a procession. Meteos stood in his doorway, looking grim. Was that Zetes behind him? No one came from that house, but Queen Merope and Labrya joined us as we passed the palace. At the spring outside the city gates, we paused to drink and gather more into our number before taking a wide path to a meadow carpeted with tiny yellow and white daisies and surrounded by flowering almond trees.

"On grass soft to our bare feet we sang to Aphrodite and to Adonis, reborn each year for seven days of love and joyous freedom. I felt detached from the company and drank little wine. That double sense of Teiresias—maleness, alienation—overcame my golden life like a shell of ice around my heart. A handsome youth approached me with a branch of almond blossoms, but I waved him away. Perhaps you too sense it coming, Manto, my last season as priestess of Aphrodite. My healing power expired with Brovas, and I needed healing myself.

"I shook myself out of that bleak mood and joined the feasting and drinking as the sun fell in the west, my heart a jumble of exultation at the sheer beauty of the day and an crushing sorrow. As soon as the festivities wound down I ran to the precinct, reaching my garden before moonrise. Indoors I held Daphne against my chest and burst into tears.

"That upset Iphinoe. When I said I didn't know whether it was my loss or Adonis' that I mourned, she said I shouldn't take old tales to heart. To her, the story of Adonis was a happy one. He was beloved of the bountiful goddess, and dying young was no dreadful fate for one so chosen.

"When I lamented that Aphrodite lost him too, she laughed. He returns to her arms every spring. Her loss would have been greater had he grown old and she forever young, immortal and perfect. Aphrodite never remained with a mortal she loved."

"You called Okyrhoe's visit fortunate. You haven't named anyone who took Polydora's place. Did she?"

"Paphos couldn't spare her indefinitely, but while she was in Corinth Okyrhoe helped us open the temple, closed through the dreary winter. When we examined the jeweled statue of Aphrodite, we saw the crack through her serpent pedestal had separated. One side rose against the other, almost enough to topple her figure, but she stood firm. I prayed she would stay so."

I resist hearing of the coming misfortune. Listeners may share my tension, sensing that Teira's story is about to take a turn. How best to dramatize it? Teiresias relives it as he speaks. But me? I will need to create the drama.

Time to stretch my legs, so I head toward Cenchrias, at work in the garden. A soft breeze ruffles the leaves; no sound but crickets in the distance. Cenchrias is gathering vegetables from vines along the ground and looks up, acknowledging my presence with a shy smile. He offers me one of the vegetables. It's in the family of cucumbers, but I don't know if it's eaten raw. Perhaps not, as he puts half a dozen in the bag over his shoulder—and then he looks at me, holding it doubtfully. He takes a bite of one, and I follow suit, not certain what it's called but struck by the rosemary-tinged flavor.

He beckons me to follow him to the chicken coop on the far side of the privy. Inside he points to a nest of speckled eggs. I gather them and follow him to the table where he prepares our meals. There's nothing more for me to do, but I enjoy watching Cenchrias' deft hands at work.

When I sit back down, my pallet bumps Teiresias and his eyes pop open.

"Dreaming?" I ask.

"No, I was recalling what happened next.

"Before dawn, a deep rumble awoke me and a jolt threw me to my knees. I grabbed Daphne and ran out to where remnants of our vegetable garden straggled. The earth shook to the sound of tumbling stone. Daphne was wailing as Anippe and Iphinoe stumbled out, dragging each other clear of the house, swaying and creaking. Then a dead silence, Poseidon's fury sated for an eerie moment. We huddled together on the ground, Daphne sobbing.

"Iphinoe and I dashed inside to gather armloads of bedding. We smoothed the ground and removed rocks, as if sleeping under the stars would be a lark. I hummed to soothe Daphne, ignoring the occasional ripple beneath us. Our bed was soft and comforting, the four of us crowded together. I soon heard even breathing from each side, but I lay wakeful.

"Nearby slept Rhene and her household and beyond, Satyrea. Our houses and the others of the precinct still stood."

"So you all survived? Was this quake was more serious than before?"

"That was my worry. How had our temple fared? I watched the moon move across the blue-black sky until it faded in the faint gray of dawn, my dread at what this new day would reveal rising with the light. I shifted Daphne to Anippe's arms and peered into the house. Vases had fallen, and it would be a task to reassemble the kitchen. A red drapery was askew in my chamber and the little statue of Aphrodite had slipped to the floor, but all else looked intact.

"I washed quickly and pulled on my sturdiest chiton, gathering it carelessly under a woven girdle. I shook crumbs of our beach picnic from my serpent shawl, as tattered as I felt after that sleepless night.

"The sky glowed orange with the rising sun, the sea a pool of flame. I picked my way over rough paving and up the hill. From above the harbor, I could see a section of the city wall broken and the carved sun eagles fallen from the palace entrance. Its enclosing wall was cracked, and the wood structures behind were charred. The temple of Helios too had been shaken, two columns crumbled into its circular entry. My breath labored, I climbed over stones to the Acrocorinth.

"Iole was calling my name. She stood on the temple's wide front steps by a jagged fissure. Behind her, only wreckage. The bases and parts of columns remained, but the roof lay in pieces. Under the sheet of rosettes that had decorated the ceiling, we found our treasured Aphrodite. The snake pedestal split in half but her figure seemed whole. Then I saw it, a hairline crack around her neck, still hung with garlands, angling down to her toes where the carved gown had begun to separate.

"'If we lift her, Aphrodite will lose her head.' Iole's laughter became hysterical. I draped my shawl over the statue like a shroud and tried to calm her. She began wailing, and only then did I see the priestess' dwelling in ruins. Behind the still-standing carved door, the building was smoking rubble. Peirene's waters must have saved the door, and the courtyard bathing tub had watered the chests. Nothing else remained of the wooden structure.

"Our sisters were gathered in the grove beyond, their faces smudged, gowns torn and grimy, coughing and looking dazed. I half-carried frenzied Iole to them. Okyrhoe stepped forward, her curls ash-tarnished, her gown black and frayed. She and I settled Iole on the grass as Labrya and Queen Merope came up the hill with two basket-laden attendants.

"Okyrhoe led the women to the spring to wash while I helped Merope and Labrya spread out an embroidered cloth and set it with fruit-filled cakes and candied lemon slices, bread, cheese, figs, and sweet wine. When beauty is destroyed we need sustenance, Merope said, and directed the freshened priestesses to look toward the mountains or distant sea, their backs to the ruins.

"I reassured them that our chests of clothes, jewelry, and the temple's treasures had been spared. Somehow our worship could continue. Iole didn't seem to understand, but everyone else was relieved. They'd lost their dwelling, but Merope would house them at the palace. Anyone who wished could sail to Paphos with Okyrhoe.

"Merope looked at me with a troubled expression, and I moved apart with her. 'What a disaster! I know life beckons onward and women rarely spend a lifetime as priestesses of Aphrodite. Many ruined temples have been rebuilt more splendidly. But if you are to survive as a sisterhood without Polydora, you will need a leader. You should be the one.'

"I protested I hadn't lived at the temple since before Daphne was born and took little part in the now-shattered life on the Acrocorinth.

"Yet something sparked at her suggestion. Perhaps I could keep the sisterhood together. Teiresias' capacity as advisor and revels master for King Labdacus surfaced. Perhaps rather than my service to Aphrodite ending, it had merely changed. So fully had I rejected Teiresias' mind and soul that I barely remembered his life. The ignorant man who wandered into the deep woods a lifetime before had no part in Teira with her loving ways. But apparently his skills lingered."

Again his narration raises the question, to what extent did Teiresias and Teira share one soul? If Teira lived out her days as a woman, her male self would have disappeared. But here he sits, Teiresias without his former identities. True, he plans to warn Thebans to flee when the Epigoni are near, but has he helped the city otherwise? All I know of its recent history is war between brothers, now extended to sons and cousins. Whatever transpired between the reign of King Labdacus and the current threat to Thebes, Teiresias could not prevent.

Cenchrias is setting out the grilled vegetables and eggs he's been preparing when an ominous sound reverberates through the sanctuary.

"You hear it too," Teiresias says.

"The Epigoni?"

"Lest we forget."

"Do these omens make you feel helpless?"

"You mean because I see the workings of Fate but cannot change them? Besides seeing the future, soothsayers fully perceive the moment. And the past, of course. We know how past and present determine the future. That is one reason seekers come here: for better understanding of themselves, fuller perceptions of their earlier lives, perhaps leading them to change course. But fleeing fearful omens backfires. It's possible a seer has influence, cautioning against a war or suggesting alternatives. Other than bellicose young men, no one wants their lives disrupted by these wars of revenge and acquisition initiated by powerful men."

"You mean seers may avert a war or potential disaster?"

"It's possible. With the Epigoni, I see a way out. Negotiate. Thersander must send a peaceful delegation to Thebes. Great cities fall, but they needn't. Not by warfare."

Teiresias' milky eyes intensify his sorrowful expression. "Sins of the fathers are visited upon their sons and their sons. Seers possess more insight and self-control than do those driven by vengeance and impulse. We'll make every effort to stop the Epigoni, but I fear they will raze Thebes. The cycle of revenge and retribution leaves everyone dead."

The sound of galloping hooves fades, and we eat in silence as birds call back and forth and a breeze rustles the tree tops. Peace again reigns.

After Cenchrias removes our empty dishes, Teiresias continues.

"My duality reappeared when Merope called on me to take on responsibilities like what was required of me in Labdacus' court. As at your shrines of Artemis and Demeter, priestesses had no official hierarchy. Yet we'd looked to Polydora."

"As we looked to Chloe, our elder at Eleusis," I say, "but the priestess who leads the ritual and recites Demeter's story changes each season."

"Sacred communities aren't like kingdoms, but they do rely on talents of priestesses and priests. Merope emphasized how I was needed to guide us through this crisis, and I couldn't easily refuse. Yet how much would I be able to do? I'd soon be drawn onward. After she and Labrya and the temple priestesses left for the palace, I hurried home to Daphne.

"While I was lifting her from Anippe's arms, two youths appeared with Iole stumbling between them. They'd found her wandering in the ruins as they were moving the temple statue of Aphrodite away from the collapsed roof. All they could think was to bring her to the precinct, where they saw my light.

"You can imagine how alarmed I was. Iole's eyes were wild, her hands clutching a dried rose from the goddess' garland, and she looked on the verge of collapse. We carried her into the house and made her as comfortable as possible.

"The boys were sons of Telebus, the wealthy uncle of Rhene's friend Hiketaon. The elder brother smiled. Their father often said they could do worse than marry a priestess of Aphrodite. When I commented that marriage was a long way off, the younger one blushed.

"Did I agree that he and his brother should deliver the diadem and jewels from the statue to Telebus' house for safekeeping until a new Aphrodite could be carved or the damaged one repaired? I consented.

"We couldn't rouse Iole, so the brothers and the strongest assistants in the precinct carried her to Carpho's bluff to be looked after.

"Next day young men and women joined the servants of Corinth clearing the rubble and making the salvageable dwellings fit to live in. Aside from buildings scorched from household fires, most required less work than we feared, and workmen from Tiryns would soon arrive.

"A handful of priestesses readied themselves to sail to Paphos with Okyrhoe. On their departure day, women and children poured out of the precinct carrying flowers. As we moved through town, more joined in, singing to the goddess whose loss they'd mourned alone. The priestesses passed into to the port under a volley of flowers, but the crowd dispersed after they boarded with downcast faces.

"I climbed to my lookout over the isthmus, today crystal blue. The ship bound for Paphos, loaded with trading goods and my former companions in their flowing garments, sailed southwards. My heart weighed heavy from farewells. I expected Rhene would leave soon to join Hiketaon, and perhaps Calyce would go with Phidias. My life seemed hollow with only a handful of women to lead, relying on our hopes for rebuilding the temple and our faith in Aphrodite.

"One day I came home to find Zetes sitting in my courtyard. He greeted me with a smile and tried to jest me out of my pensive mood, something I never imagined him doing. We must laugh at ourselves, he said. Why not gamble for happiness, even if the stakes are life or death? He thanked me for reviving his long-dead heart.

"I couldn't take credit for his brightened spirits. To Zetes' surprise, Strophios returned from his sojourn with open arms. After exploring his soul he recognized how he needed him, and Zetes was willing to risk it. Grown older, he and Strophios found hope out despair. When I told Zetes I wanted him fully alive, he threw his arms around me. The chance of a loving connection with the only man he cared for would grant him a full life.

"I hadn't intended to mention my disheartened mood, but he asked why I seemed so troubled. Our temple life as we knew it hadn't ended forever. Times change, yet some forces run deep. Love redeemed him, so why wouldn't I, a priestess of Aphrodite, be saved as well?

"His words were kindly meant, so I made no effort to describe the difference between the sorts of love each of us knew."

"Much of your life as Teira stretches my imagination," I say. "When you took men to your chamber, you embodied the goddess in your healing love. Yet for you, though so intimate, that loving seemed impersonal, which I find perplexing. You loved Damysos as a woman, not a priestess. I don't desire marriage and motherhood, but I know one of the reasons women want a child is to share parenthood with their mate. You regarded Damysos as your mate, yet when you became a mother, he wasn't Daphne's father."

Teiresias nods and says nothing.

"And besides this confusion of love, you felt the old worship of Aphrodite was coming to an end, not just from the earthquake but from Macaria's polluting force. Music and dancing, love and community—so many joys you knew. But no lack of sadness and loss."

"You're right, Manto. Difficult to balance those. There are times, sitting here, when my reflections are more sad than joyful. Yet in each moment—" he smiles. "Right now, here with Cenchrias and you and my rich memories, I'm happy to have had such a life and that it continues to this precious moment.

"One afternoon Merope and I took our children to my favorite cove. Prince Oedipus ran back and forth from his mother to the seashore bringing her shells, bits of seaweed, and driftwood. Daphne stayed close by him and copied his every move, gathering pieces of shell and fishy-smelling kelp. When Oedipus dared the gentle waves, then ran back to shore, so did she.

"Merope said she was worried. The priestesses brought their fine clothes and jewels with them when they moved to the palace, but their lives had lost meaning. With no evening dance and no private chambers to retreat to with chosen worshippers, they were melancholy, especially Calyce, who I'd not seen since Okyrhoe's departure.

"We left the children to their games while we discussed possible solutions. Oedipus' shout cut across our conversation. I leapt to my feet. He was trying to drag Daphne out of the water. Merope lifted him into her arms while I seized Daphne, floating face down, barely conscious. I laid her on the beach and pressed her chest to expel the water while Oedipus wailed. After what seemed forever, Daphne began to cough and then to wail herself. Tears running down our faces, Merope and I held our children close. How fragile those tiny lives."

Teiresias turns his alert blind eyes toward me. "I tell you my story as it happened. If I describe the role I played in Oedipus' life when he grew to manhood, I'd have to skip too much of what was important. But that was a day of omens. Not about Daphne, who soon learned to swim and I knew had a blessed destiny. It was Oedipus who baffled me. He was to succeed Polybus as ruler of Corinth, but though my second sight was poorly developed in those days, I saw a break in his destiny. Turmoil and tragedy were woven into his future."

"How?"

"Think of yourself as the story teller, Manto. Wouldn't you want to keep your listeners in suspense?"

"Depending on how much time we had."

He ignores the irritation in my voice. "Yours and my time is limited in the worst way, ultimate destruction. Whatever I don't recount to you will be lost forever."

"Yet you linger on details."

"I keep pushing onward. I can't say exactly how you'll tell this, but I know you will be sought for your stories."

I'm amused. "Do you imagine me a rhapsode of such repute?"

"I do, so I must impart all that's significant.

"What a relief. Our children were safe! Merope and I put off our discussion, but not long after I found a grove perfect for chants and rituals. No pilgrims would come, no serpent dance nor private embraces, but the priestesses could keep worship alive.

"Daphne and I lived simply through the summer while workers filled Corinth. When I went to see their handiwork, they'd repaired the façade of the royal palace, so until I reached the reached the temple of Helios, all was familiar. Even there, columns stood firm. On the Acrocorinth, instead of charred wood of the priestesses' dwelling, behind the carved door the space that had been the dining hall was surrounded by pots of rose bushes to mark each priestess' chamber. In the outer court where hairstyles had been crafted and kohl carefully applied, the bathing tub was now a fountain. A small figure of Aphrodite stood in a sheltered corner with offerings of figs and flowers at her base, and I wished I thought to bring some myself.

"As I returned to the precinct, the elder son of Telebus stopped me. Our magnificent statue would soon be good as new, surely a hopeful omen. Worshippers would return to the temple.

"Among the first of these was Phidias, now King Atreus' youngest commander after leaving his simple life in Tyrins. He came seeking Calyce, for with her he would be more than a warrior. I wondered, how likely for one serving in Atreus' army? I doubted Calyce would be attracted by Mycenean wealth, outshining that of Polybus and Merope, but could Phidias charm her away from damaged Corinth?

"When Macaria and Alcimedes came to Mycenae, he'd attended the feast King Atreus hosted for them. Phidias saw that Macaria held the power in that pair. His description of the extravagance of the feast and grandeur of the palace made me see Mycenae as just the place for what Macaria called a new kind temple to Aphrodite, with a fixed set of charges and other blasphemies. I doubted any priestess from Corinth would be drawn there, but who knew how Macaria would recruit? The days of loving as a pure ritual of devotion to Aphrodite, at least beyond our temple, had passed.

"I asked Phidias if he saw Macaria's hand. He couldn't help noticing her unusual gold ring. When I said it was mine, imbued with the ancient power of the Snake Mother, he promised if he saw Macaria again, he would do his best to retrieve it."

I glance at Teiresias' ring finger. "You have it now. Another story?"

He nods, laughing. "See?" He holds up his hand. "Her serpents marked my transitions and wove through my life."

"Did they make you male again?"

"You're incorrigible, Manto. If you were telling the story, you'd silence a listener who pelted you with questions." He waves toward Cenchrias, who's already lifting the wine jug. "But a serpents' mating dance did play a part in—in this body."

I squeeze his arm with an unspoken question. A moment of silence as Cenchrias fills our cups.

"In transforming me back to male, you wonder? Yes, in a sense. Did they blind me? No."

I watch him wipe a drop of spilled wine from his beard. "You mean deities were involved in your blindness?" I take a breath. "As I must wait to hear revealed."

He smiles as he would to a child who's mastered a lesson. "I've portrayed the gentle slide of our temple: restoring what worship we could, rebuilding, carrying on. I told you about my time as priestess of Aphrodite in detail because it colored all that followed, including who I am sitting here."

"How did the temple's slide end?"

Chapter Twenty-two: Ischys

"The end wasn't dramatic. Satyrea and I maintained the rituals, prayers, and dances. Ending our intimate private worship seemed the best way to resist Macaria, nor did any of the Corinthian priestesses decamp to the grandiose temple she was building in Mycenae.

"We celebrated the midwinter festival amidst partially restored buildings, carrying green boughs and bouquets of narcissus and lilies from sheltered gardens. Townsfolk bearing baskets of food and jugs of wine gathered under stars. The temple was clean and bare, but no tiles on the floor and Aphrodite's statue still missing.

"Workmen had erected a pine pavilion in the broad yard between the temple and the partially rebuilt priestess dwelling. Torchbearers came up from the palace with King Polybus and Queen Merope, filling the space with the odor of pine sap.

"As flute and drum played, I felt myself letting go, not only of my melancholy but the boundaries of myself. Instead of a solitary earthly body gazing at distant heavens, I was part of the light and noise, fragrance and revelry.

"When I was shoved into Oineus and one of his torchbearers, I smiled as I did to every other worshiper. There was Amyclas, there Strophios with Zetes, there Telebus, his wife and the sons who safeguarded Aphrodite's jewels and girdle.

"The pine pavilion was filled with music and feasting, drinking laughing, and flirting that spilled out into the yard. A young man caressed my back as I passed near him, perhaps Zetes, but my eyes no longer focused clearly. It could as well have been Oineus.

"Remembering that sparkling night is like recalling an ancient story. A tall man reached a plump cushion just as I did. He pulled me down beside him, saying he was guided to me. His arm draped over me easily, and I warmed to him, so confident and easy in himself.

"His name was Ischys, priest at Epidaurus. He knew I was called Teira and lived in the precinct of Aphrodite with my daughter and that I'd fought melancholy since Poseidon shook down our temple. He smiled. Aphrodite can heal even her priestesses.

"I felt such trust that I walked with him into the perfumed starlight as soft voices murmured among the trees. We found a place apart where Ischys arranged a mat of pine boughs. I sat against him as I had on the cushion, my head on his shoulder, outlining the constellations above with one finger. After a long convivial silence, he told me I must bring Daphne and my healing arts to Epidaurus.

"I answered 'as the goddess wills,' but couldn't imagine how anything I practiced in Corinth would apply in Epidaurus, where Brovas experienced his dream cure.

"Ischys cradled me in his arms, sharing warmth against the growing chill, and touched his lips to mine. Perhaps because of the vast sky, the secret dark, or a longing beneath my sense of emptiness, I willingly yielded to him. Our loving on those pine boughs felt unreal, Ischys' slim body against mine, seeking, withholding, then finding all satisfactions.

"He and I sat companionably on our piney pillow, the city and bay twinkling below and stars piercing the sky above us as the moon rose from the sea. Before he walked me back to the pavilion, he repeated his invitation to Epidaurus in spring, or whenever the time felt right.

"After the festival, the measureless dark of winter came upon us. I spent most days at home with Daphne, who learned to talk early and was an avid listener to adult conversation, so silent that we forgot her presence. She plied me with questions about Apollo, asking if he was a bad god. Gods aren't good or bad, I replied, but they can do things that would be bad if we did them. She wanted to hear all about him.

"I told her Apollo likes to test himself. First the bow and arrow, until he became the farthest-shooting of any god, challenged only by his twin sister Artemis. Then music contests, where he played his tortoise-shell lyre better than anyone could play any instrument. When he heard that Pytho, a great serpent, had frightened his mother Leto, Apollo took up his bow for his biggest test yet.

"Since Daphne enjoyed Anippe's scary tales with happy endings, I described Apollo shooting the serpent Pytho full of arrows. Pytho is sacred to the Great Mother, so Apollo couldn't kill him. Wounded, he slithered into a cave under the omphalos, the navel stone. Apollo pursued him, but Pytho blazed into the sky and became a stream of stars. We can see him there still. His mate Delphyne remains deep under the omphalos, keeping secrets as she has forever, oracle of the Great Mother.

"Daphne was fascinated with oracles and the Pythia who sits in a cave above the fissure rising from the center of

Earth, source of wisdom. When she burns leaves of the laurel, visions come and she speaks them in riddling poetry.

"When Daphne asked what questions were asked of her, I kept it simple: to guide an important decision or to know the gods' will for our lives. She looked puzzled. If the Pythia's prophecies can be understood in more than one way, how does anyone knew the true meaning?"

"Your daughter was clever, even when so young," I say.

"Not my first clever daughter," Teiresias replies with a smile.

"Did you tell her seekers must trust the priests of Apollo?"

"Yes, unless they can understand Pythia's words themselves, which few do. They would have to be granted with magical hearing.

"How I wished we'd gone with Ischys to Epidaurus when first he asked. Why wait for springtime? At night I was haunted by a sense of doom hanging over the house of Polybus and over my own life. My treasured early years in Corinth couldn't be recovered, and the unknown future tormented my sleep. Carefree worship of Aphrodite belonged in the past, innocence lost and our goddess fled to sunshine lands."

"What distressing dreams," I say. "I felt no such loss when I left Eleusis. The Mysteries are ever-powerful, in Eleusis and in my soul. My only sadness came from leaving my dear friend Lydia. It was wrenching to part and I still think of her. But my time there had run its course and my path led elsewhere."

"Mine too, but I couldn't leave in the middle of winter."

"Did you believe that in Epidaurus you could forestall the calamity you feared?"

"Epidaurus offered fresh opportunities. That's as far as my thoughts carried me."

He seems fatigued, and we sit in silence while Cenchrias makes up his bed. Both of us welcome sleep.

Next day we begin early, sharing the bowl of grapes Cenchrias set out. From time to time Teiresias pops a grape between his teeth as he talks.

"Spring came at last, calling us to green hills, with poppies nodding in the breeze and the sun warm enough to bask in. Without Okyrhoe bringing her festival of Adonis, that spring promised only housecleaning and, though I kept it to myself, my departure.

"The air carried the fresh scent of growth as Calyce, Daphne, and I walked to the sapphire bay. Daphne ran into the shallow water while we stood barefoot watching her. Like me, Calyce hadn't felt herself through the winter, and with her living in Merope's wing of the palace, we rarely consoled each other in person. She was debating between sailing on the next ship to Paphos or going with Phidias. Some of our number drifted back to their villages and likely marriages. We waved them farewell with little ceremony. That day at the beach blew our troubles away on salty breezes, beckoning us to savor bright moment.

"But that night I lay sleepless, my empty ring finger aching. If you still encircled my finger, I asked, where would you lead me?

"A figure with a skirt like my Snake Goddess led me through shifting dream images. Delphyne coiled in purple iridescence in her dark cavern, which became the cave on Carpho's bluff, filled with serpents, which became an open pit with benign snakes basking in the sunshine. Around the snake pit were sun-splotched woods promising comfort. A long shadow reminded me of Ischys. It was time to go to Epidaurus.

"Daylight brought practical concerns. Easier to snuggle into warm covers, but I couldn't. The forces driving my life pushed me out of bed.

"As I moved about with an eye to what must be done before I could leave, I said nothing to my household. The house had become oppressive, a gloomy reminder of last summer and foretaste of the coming one if I remained. Every rustle of drapery or leaves sounded like Aphrodite's mocking laughter. 'No joy here for you, Teira. Follow the serpent.'

"I looked around my house with eyes of separation. Its familiar beauty, Daphne's intimacy with Anippe, Iphinoe's cooking, the delights and friendships of the precinct were coming to an end. Much as I would have liked to see Merope, Calyce, and Zetes, I couldn't bear farewells. Difficult enough to leave, without being wept out of Corinth. So I prepared in secret.

"On the departure day, I awoke before dawn, dressed, and twisted my hair under a simple band. Taking my cloak from its hook I ascended for the last time to the Acrocorinth. I was in no mood for lamentation. Recently my dreams evoked the place I first knew, making it eternal within me, as I hope I've made it live for you."

I don't tell him he's achieved that all too well, and I'm sorry he's leaving Corinth. I enjoyed being there with him.

"Hurrying through the streets I smiled at early spring flowers and appreciated the freshly painted houses, the palace with its sun eagles, and the temple of Helios gleaming in the sunrise. Climbing the hill on winged heels, I paused to catch my breath only when I reached the Peirenean spring.

Flowering rose bushes crowned the urns on each side of the carved door of the dwelling house. I picked a red rose from the bush marking the doorway to what had been my chamber. Who should I see but the sentinel cat! She rubbed on my legs, and I was glad to see her fur shone and she looked well fed. That made me hopeful for the temple, still in shadow as I entered and began to move to music playing inside my head.

"I danced on the balls of my feet, rising, arching, a serpent striving for wings. Sunlight sped my movements, and I ended twirling until I knelt at the feet of Aphrodite, face to face with her mended serpent pedestal. I sensed her saying, 'Go in strength, daughter.'

"As Demeter spoke to me when I left Eleusis."

"Yes. Visions can speak to us.

"A flock of doves fluttered from the pine-bough roof of the pavilion as I bid the temple farewell. I prayed that my golden goddess would always bless me, then dashed down the hill unobserved.

"'What makes you so happy?' Reaching my flowery dooryard, I turned toward a man's voice. Tanais! I invited him inside, past my open traveling chest. He was the first to know I was leaving.

"He said he'd always found me a mystery. When I once considered giving a banquet where everyone told secrets, he laughed, doubting I would tell my own.

"I said mine was a strange tale of abduction. He didn't press me, instead inquiring where I was bound. At 'Epidaurus,' he shrugged in puzzled acceptance.

"Early as it was, with Daphne still asleep, we drank tiny cups of sweet wine. Whether we would meet again, only the gods could say.

"'I know what Aphrodite says now.' Tanais took my hand into my private chamber. Sitting on the bed, he embraced me in love and gratitude for Aphrodite's blessings.

"'We mustn't be ceremonious or I'll weep,' I said, playing with the belt of his tunic. He loosened it, removed his clothes and mine, and nuzzled me in a tickling embrace. None but Aphrodite's lightest joys were ours. Lying contentedly in each others' arms after our gentle loving, tears came to my eyes and to his, but neither broke the silence.

"After another long embrace Tanais left my bed, wishing me safe travels on my serpent path. My farewell grace from Corinth."

Cenchrias brings us a late breakfast of bread and honey. So. Teira's only farewell to her service to Aphrodite came with Tanais.

Chapter Twenty-three: Epidaurus

Teiresias takes a deep breath. "Seeing Tanais leave, Rhene walked over to my gate where I stood watching him disappear.

"I couldn't simply abandon the precinct, so I told her my house would be empty and Anippe and Iphinoe would need employment.

"Rhene held me. 'Must you go? Will you be safe?'

"I assured her I had a destination. Epidaurus. Perhaps I would return one day."

"'I doubt it, Teira. Your time here has ended. Departure is in the air. Hiketaon invited the children and me to come to Nauplion, and I expect we will go with him soon. With our temple restored, younger women will come as priestesses. Despite changes, Aphrodite will continue to have a sacred shrine in Corinth.'

"When we were packed and ready to go, four-year old Daphne was in tears at leaving her beloved nurse. Iphinoe embraced us both.

"At the harbor, we found a ship traveling along the eastern seacoast to Epidaurus. Daphne loved the wind in her face, the dolphins off the bough, the birds who followed their bellying sails. For her, the voyage was all too short.

"Although I loved the sea, I felt less anticipation as we approached Epidaurus than I had coming to Corinth. No visions of golden splendor enticed me onward. Epidaurus would be a retreat. Was that what I wanted? Perhaps I was going there for Ischys."

"All I know about Epidaurus," I say, "is that ill people go there. It must be tranquil."

"No doubt about that!

"When we landed on the wooded shore, my doubts were eased by the dappled shade. A boy led us through pine trees and patches of rosemary. Daphne ran ahead to a bank of flowers, nearly colliding with Ischys, as appealing as I remembered him. He praised her, flowers spilling from her arms, for making herself at home. We arrived in time for the spring festival, he told us, but we shouldn't expect the pageantry of Corinth.

"This shrine was dedicated to Asclepius, healer son of Apollo. His statue stood in the central courtyard surrounded by cottages for patients and healers, each backing up to woodlands. Ischys showed Daphne and me to ours.

"I hadn't brought a nurse, since he assured me that adults looked after the children. Sometimes little ones came to Epidaurus for healing themselves, and Daphne could help cheer them.

"The serenity was welcome, but I doubted my service to Aphrodite would be of much use. Here healing might entail elixirs and assisting patients restore their limbs or their balance. Some patients slept their days away, waking to speak of their dreams, then back to sleep.

"Ischys left us at our door, the question of what he and I might be to each other unspoken.

"Celebrants dressed plainly for this festival. I wore my long saffron peplos and girdle of Aphrodite, plaiting my hair with curls around my face. Daphne was happily carefree. I could barely catch her for a moment to pull her hair back into a braid and wash her face. Perhaps I would return to a simple garment, but not for my first appearance.

"Epidaurus was indeed safe for a child. When Daphne ran off, I gave her no second thought. Caring arms abounded. The old delighted in her liveliness, and the younger felt responsible. Besides Asclepius, the Mother dwelt in the surrounding groves through the powers of his daughter Hygeia.

"Instead of a procession, the festival began with a gathering around Aesclepius' statue. A boy drummer appeared with two women who reminded me of Labrya and Merope carrying flutes. At a drumroll, everyone made room. The women played an interweaving harmony that lifted my spirit but roused no one to dance, so I stilled my lively limbs.

"Standing beside me listening to the music, Ischys gazed at Aesclepius. The statue bore some resemblance to Apollo, but with a compassionate face and draped in a humble robe.

"Ischys joined the musicians at the pine-bedecked altar and began a song of praise. Each word took on fuller meaning as the crowd sang the hymn again and again. I felt hypnotized. *Sweet mysteries, sacred healing, wise strength, eternal wisdom.* The words circled and changed, echoing, altering.

"Under the rising moon, worshippers left to fetch their gifts. Wondering what I could offer, I recalled Brovas' gift from the Pharaoh and headed purposefully to my quarters.

"After folding my contribution into my gown, I waited for the summoning drumbeat. Glancing at Aesclepius' image through eyes half-closed I saw, superimposed upon his rigid figure a more fluid deity—Aphrodite?—playing and teasing. Perhaps everyone would rather laugh than proceed so solemnly."

I chuckle. "So her golden powers followed you."

"I felt free to dance, more or less sedately. For one night, Aphrodite shed her light on Epidaurus. I took my offering from my pocket and opened the jar. Dipping a finger into precious heather honey from the bees of Acrocorinth, I moved around the circle, first touching the nose of an old man, his face reflecting the innocent rosiness of a child. Then a laden finger into Daphne's mouth. To the rest of the company I left a drop on forehead or fingertip, and on one exultant worshiper, the tip of his extended tongue.

"Ischys approached me as I glided around the circle, and I put two fingers thick with honey towards his mouth, then slid them past his chin and back in a quick gesture, giving him a moment to lick the sweetness from my fingers. I set the jar on the altar and danced my way to where he stood.

"My body continued to move in gentle circles as worshipers presented their gifts. Some I could only guess, small containers of what could be mother's milk, blood, semen, or pollen, along with sheaves of grain, flowers, herbs and seed pods; caged mice and a brilliant yellow bird who trilled above the flute melody.

"A youth and maiden began turning cartwheels and somersaults. They wore pelts of the spotted mountain lion around their waists, like votaries of Dionysus, and performed an acrobatic dance which ended up with the youth lying still upon the ground as if dead. A moment of silence before he jumped up. He and the maid made leaping arcs out of the circle."

"So Dionysus as well as Aphrodite blessed the festival," I say.

"Once we open to them, healing gods abound. Those acrobats mimed death and rebirth." He takes a long drink of water.

"That night I first glimpsed Cilissa, the girl who became Daphne's friend. She approached the altar with a snake coiled around each arm and one round her waist. As she bowed, the snakes seemed to raise their heads to Asclepius. I didn't dare move, spellbound by the arc of their bodies and their mesmerizing eyes. They were small and earth-toned rather than the copper and blue of my coupling serpents, but embodied the Mother's power.

"By now the moon was high and the torch that lit acrobats and snake-maiden guided the company out of the shrine to tables under the trees. As I watched the proceedings, overdressed and vaguely hopeful, Daphne fell asleep in the lap of an old woman.

"Ischys came to sit on the bench beside me. He echoed Tanais, that I was mysterious a mystery about me. Perhaps I would perceive it for myself there, apart from men's views. Then he said I was so luminous and giving he wanted nothing more than to love me, but Asclepius forbade it.

"I was speechless. Together we were blessed by Aphrodite, and I imagined that would continue one way or another in Epidaurus.

"I stuttered in confusion. Why had he invited me?

"He knew our temple was changing and soon I must leave Corinth. My loving heart would be helpful here, and in serving patients, I too would find healing.

"I could scarcely contain my anger at his condescending manner but worse, his rejection."

Teiresias' voice rises as he relives his distress. Never courted by a man, I've never been rejected, but I feel Teira's indignation. "Did Ischys tell you how he meant for you to help?"

"Yes, but I'd expected he wanted me there out of affection as well. Of course I could massage weak limbs and utter kindly words, but I felt deceived." Teiresias shakes his head. "Womanly pride, I suppose."

"Well deserved, for a cherished priestess of Aphrodite."

"Having dwelt in Aphrodite's grace, I suffered from her absence. I had no choice but to swallow my pride and shut my heart to Ischys, folding away my saffron peplos and girdle. I spent my days massaging and walking with patients, usually old women.

"Best of all were my solitary walks at dawn up through the trees to a jutting rock high above the cluster of dwellings. Some summery mornings I could see a sheen on the horizon to the north, perhaps the Saronic Sea, also visible from the heights of Corinth. And beyond, vanished in the distance, the city of Thebes. This lookout opened a vaster perspective than in placid Epidaurus below. I could gaze toward Crete, toward Cyprus, toward Sidon, Egypt, Mycenae, and Argos. Then I would return to our sanctuary and the patients who needed my healing touch.

At meals I sat away from Ischys and spoke to him, if at all, with formal courtesy. I never looked him in the eye so didn't know if my aloofness troubled him, but he made no warming efforts.

"Daphne spent her days with Cilissa. Her snakes were small, living in a rocky pit and requiring little care as they basked on warm rocks and caught the occasional mouse. She and Daphne laughingly wrapped them around their arms or necks. Once I watched from behind a tree, amused at the sluggish serpents' liveliness when heated by sun and the girls' touch. For most of the day, they played with stones in endless games, told stories beside the snake pit, and, when the afternoons cooled, played chase, Daphne losing in spite of the head start Cilissa allowed her. So did she thrive.

"Through the summer, everyone in Epidaurus who wasn't bedridden ate a late afternoon meal in the courtyard. Meat was roasted once or twice a week for those who needed it to regain their strength, but the rest of us ate bread, fresh-picked fruit, olives, radishes, greens from the hillsides, goats' milk and cheese. And my honey. Climbing to my vantage point one day, I found a woman who kept hives, refreshing my supply.

"None of the patients could walk up to my morning lookout, but I strolled with them around the buildings and into the trees as they leaned on my arm. Mostly we moved in silence, listening to birds, the whisper of the wind, the ripple of the slow-moving river. This simple life felt complete, except for the void where Ischys should have been. Daphne and I bathed in the river, deep enough for floating. I let my damp hair hang free in the evening under a band of fabric tied around my brow. The local cobbler supplied sturdy sandals, pressing brass studs into the straps for decoration. Soon such details mattered little, and I forgot my beauty rituals.

"During that slow, reflective summer I went into myself, sometimes sensing a deeper darkness hovering. But demands and distractions beckoned—visiting the bedside of a gray-faced woman who brightened at seeing me, or Daphne taking me to watch bees dancing in a flowery thicket or pressing a bunch of wilting daisies into my hand. As evenings turned cooler, more patients arrived, welcoming my soothing touch and joking about my favorite medicine being honey.

"Time stretched peacefully enough, thanks to my resignation about Ischys. If this was what the gods intended, so be it. One patient made a mark on me, Thoas of Argos. He recognized me as a priestess of Aphrodite and preferred my healing to the dream cure."

Noticing my sharp intake of breath, Teiresias smiles. "I don't mean Corinthian devotions. Thoas valued my sympathetic perceptions. Ischys said something similar, but he had no time for me and Thoas had nothing but time, certain that keeping company with a priestess of Aphrodite would hasten his cure.

"He knew I liked to walk. Although he couldn't climb my hill, he accompanied me elsewhere daily, sharing witty or silent company as suited the moment. Thoas resembled dear Brovas, his head coming just above my shoulder and his gait uneven. His hair too was thinning and his eyes intense. His confident dignity marked him as a royal ambassador, serving King Adrastus as Brovas served King Polybus, and as I once served King Labdacus.

"What if Teiresias of those days had come to Epidaurus? But he didn't know he needed healing. I credited Thoas for knowing he did."

"Tell me more about him."

"With me Thoas could talk and listen, another healing art. I'll pass on what of his tale was important. If I get lost in details, as I tend to," Teiresias chuckles, "stop me."

I agree, but won't interrupt if the story is good.

"On Thoas' recent embassy to Thebes, he began having such ferocious nightmares that he dared not sleep. Each time his eyelids became heavy, a beast would grab him and try to rend him. He would awaken in horror and force himself to walk for the rest of the night. Since then, his life had been such an agony that he had to come to Epidaurus. The previous evening at dinner he consumed only a pear and goats' cheese, and later, in his room under the rustling trees, fell into his first sound sleep in weeks. Yet when he woke he sensed the beast nearby.

"When I asked if he came to Epidaurus to vanquish the beast, he said he must understand her, which then would vanquish her. *Her.* She first came to him after a bountiful feast at the palace of King Laius. The story Strophios told of Laius abducting the boy Chrysippus came to mind, but Thoas gave me no time to reflect on it. He disliked Laius but didn't mention Chrysippus, faded even from gossip.

"In the talking cure, what one says brings a new awareness, which can take a moment to put in words." Teiresias pauses. "As I say that, I realize that's happening to me as I'm speaking and will to you in your time. Story has a magical effect. In the telling, we understand more than we knew. Only when describing his beast did it occur to Thoas that the house of Laius might connect to his dreams more than as simply the place where they began. I'd helped him with that insight. Seemed to me I did little, but I urged him to keep talking.

"The first time she appeared to him, her lion paws threatened to tear him apart. Then he saw above the powerful haunches and leonine body, wings and an enchanting female face. The Sphinx. He heard from toothless a old beggar woman that the she hid in a cave high on Mount Phicium, Hera's curse on Thebes biding her time.

Teiresias shakes his head. "I never encountered such a beggar there. She sounded like one of the ancient sisterhood. How else could she know about the Sphinx and Hera's curse? That was the first I'd heard of it myself.

"She didn't hint at what that curse was or the reason, and in the palace on the Cadmeia Thoas heard nothing about curses. Laius seemed edgy, which Thoas attributed to his tense reserve toward Queen Jocasta. He surrounded himself with elegant courtiers and had little to do with his wife.

"Thoas stayed in Thebes just long enough for a banquet and those nightmares. His purpose was to seal a trade agreement and convey friendship from King Adrastus, but something odd happened when he first arrived. When he told the beggar woman he came from Argos, she said one day Argos would be feared in Thebes. Thoas saw no evidence at the banquet.

"'Until you went to bed,' I replied.

"'How can we know if monsters are within ourselves?' he asked. The Sphinx was his monster, for it was his sleep she haunted. Had he committed an offense worthy punishment? He never killed anyone, not even in the name of king or honor. Nothing but the ordinary failures and unintended betrayals of a man of many years.

"Those word struck me, and I remarked on how naturally he said them. I said that in Epidaurus he could leave all that behind, but I felt uneasy.

"Thoas was tottering with fatigue, so I returned him to his cottage. Even though it was midday, I climbed to my rock. Hills rolled away from me in every direction, and I prayed to Aphrodite to show me her light. The wind caressed me into a sense of calm, but no answer emerged. I gazed over the sea until the sun began slipping downward.

"Thoas was wandering through the trees with shaky steps. The Sphinx appeared when he tried to nap. I told him when next she showed herself, he must clasp his tunic firmly around himself, stare into her eyes, and ask why she threatened him. He promised to try, and thanked me for giving him courage.

"Just then Daphne ran to me, Cilissa in hot pursuit.

""This sun-touched child is yours? You are blessed!' Thoas looked at the snake encircling Cilissa's waist. 'Are you certain this isn't venomous?'

"I extended my hand toward it and it hissed. 'Cilissa! This isn't a pet snake. It's a viper that will grow huge!'

"She protested. The snake never hissed at her. It loved her, and Daphne too.

"I didn't want to frighten the girls, and perhaps the snake was tame to their touch, but poisonous serpents don't have human feelings, not even the one winding around the statue of Asclepius who was said to grant healing. One drop of venom was among the more drastic treatments at Epidaurus.

""This snake carries great power, and you must let it go. It belongs in the woods.'

"Cilissa looked at me as if I were an ignorant adult. Her mother might be indifferent or permissive, but I couldn't allow my daughter to play with a viper. With forced equanimity, I asked Cilissa to show us her snakes.

"Every step as we walked to their pit I worried the viper would become agitated and strike. The girl was no more twelve years of age, but confident of her gift with serpents. Whether that gift could protect her from venom I doubted. I told her I enjoyed her performance with the snakes the night we arrived and asked if she knew about the snake goddess of Crete.

"Cilissa's grandmother told her snakes bonded to her because she was descended from a line of ancient serpent priestesses. I'd heard some handled venomous snakes safely, but if Cilissa were my daughter, I would ask her to keep only those without venom. At the pit, I saw that none of the rest were poisonous.

"Daphne told Cilissa she didn't like a snake who hissed at her mother, but she loved all the others. She begged her to let this one go free. Cilissa looked at her long and hard, and I saw she not only debated releasing the viper go but keeping Daphne as a friend. Finally she unwound it from her waist, walked to the edge of the clearing, and let it slip away. When she turned back, she had tears in her eyes. I embraced the girls together and thanked them for doing me such a favor.

"I bid Thoas good night, even though the meal was being laid out, and returned to our cottage, shaking and thankful that what I regarded as my serpent path had not included death of a child.

"Near my threshold I met Ischys, who commented on my special patient. He wasn't pleased that Thoas and I were engaged in some sort of talking cure. Epidaurus was famed for the dream cure. Besides, getting personally involved with a patient was discouraged. I should make more space between us.

"Then he walked away! He didn't give me a chance to reply. Ischys should have known that a priestess can't be ordered about, and certainly not by a man who brought her there under false pretenses. Needless to say, I ignored him.

"Next morning Thoas was waiting for me. His beast had appeared, stretching her her lion paw, claws extended, toward his belly. He clasped his tunic firmly and shouted 'Why?' She rested her paw on his chest so heavily he could scarcely breathe. Her breath was musky, her body sinewy. She lifted her paw, saying in a female voice that he was not her man. Only if he was skilled in riddles should he ever return to Thebes. Then she flew away, her wings beating through in the trees.

"That was the end of his beast, but Thoas was in no hurry to return to Argos. Unless he was weak within himself, such a creature wouldn't have plagued him. The peace of Epidaurus had yet to sink in, so he and I would continue our daily strolls. There must be more to this talking cure. Vanquishing the Sphinx was but the beginning.

"Thoas asked what Thebes meant to me. He visited just that once, more than enough to experience the disagreeable atmosphere in the Cadmeia and to judge Laius as arrogant and hostile. I confessed to being born there, never to return." Teiresias snorts his ironic laugh. "Short on prescience back then.

"Thoas surprised me by asking about my parentage. I didn't mention Everes or Chariclo, saying only that I considered myself daughter to the goddess, free of Thebes' bloody heritage. But I was distracted. For me too, talking brought new thoughts. Thoas' description of his Sphinx struck me with fear, which I kept to myself.

"He was curious why I came to Epidaurus, for I seemed out of my element. I showed him my empty finger. I was seeking an irreplaceable ring.

"On our next walk I told him about the spring festival at Epidaurus which he'd missed and my favorite part, the acrobats performing for Dionysus. Rather than celebrating him as the god of wine, their leaping and tumbling suggested Dionysus' joy and suffering, death and rebirth. If I remained here for the next festival, I would ask Ischys to sing the suffering of Dionysus so all might undergo his breaking apart and renewal. A healing performance would enrich Epidaurus.

"Thus did Thoas and I envision sacred tragedy long before a theatre was built there.

"On his departure day, Thoas met me on the walk to my rock. He wanted to try the climb with me, and I welcomed him. For all I cared, Ischys could see us.

"It was a day of crystalline clarity. When we reached the summit, Thoas put his arm around my waist, awestruck at the sight of all the world below, distant lands appearing as pinpoints beyond the sparkling sea. Here we felt at earth's center, with hills and sea stretching in every direction.

"He appreciated my hill cure. Silence surrounded us as the sun rose high above the trees, and the water below became a vast shining presence. Regretfully returning to the shrine below, Thoas described his last dream. The Sphinx hadn't returned, but instead a serpent. She could be one of Cilissa's pets, so gently did she move, but she seemed to be me, a guiding spirit. The snakes of Asclepius were sacred. With their shadowy powers, they could belong to the Great Mother of old, including that viper.

"He said I must trust my serpent path. If I didn't recover my ring, I would find my way without it.

"When Daphne ran up to us, Thoas presented her with a rosy stone hidden in his robe. I wished him a safe return to Argos and sound sleeps henceforth. No Sphinx, no vipers.

"He promised to remember Daphne, Cilissa and her snakes, and, especially me, kissing me and whispering a fond farewell. Ischys and the few patients who came to see him off must have noticed, but what would they expect from a priestess of Aphrodite? After all, besides the dream cure, others were tried, including tricky ones like a few crushed berries of belladonna. Toxic drops can heal, as the arrows of Asclepius both puncture and mend. What danger in affectionate listening?

"As evenings turned chill, hearty meals were served around the long table in the dining hall with roaring fires at each end of the room. The ceiling molding was decorated with carved serpents, each corner crowned with a snake head in high relief.

"One night Ischys walked me home after dinner, saying he appreciated my lightness of movement and hoped I would soon grace them with a serpent dance. I told him I'd rather watch the acrobats who inspired Thoas' and my idea for reenacting the death and rebirth of Dionysus. Ischys recoiled at the mention of Thoas, but why should he? Hadn't he noticed how marooned I felt after my only friend left?

"Ischys told me he hadn't dreamt deeply since I arrived. So, I thought with grim satisfaction, the healing priest cannot see what ails himself.

"At last Asclepius spoke to him. Sleeping in my arms would bring dreams to us both. I'd had no profound dreams either, but I wasn't there for the dream cure."

I laugh. "You were relieved Ischys finally came to his senses."

Teiresias nods with a smile. "In the adjoining room where Cilissa spent most nights, she and Daphne bade us good night. When I lit my lamp, Ischys looked surprised at the embroidered cover on my bed. Of course I kept remnants of my days in Corinth, even if my serpent armband rarely showed beneath linen garments.

"Ischys confessed he'd been unsettled by me so near and by my friendship with Thoas. Now he realized no one, divine or mortal, would care if he and I shared a bed."

"So you seduced him," I say.

"Teira did. Embracing Ischys came naturally. I could have remained in Epidaurus as his assistant and helped develop tragic dramatic performances. Sleepless after our loving, I thanked him for giving me sanctuary and a healthy place for Daphne where I could be useful, but once through the seasons was enough."

"Ischys wanted you to stay."

"Yes, but he was a less complicated person than I was. My learning there had been as steep as my daily hill climb, while his wisdom was innate."

"Yet he touched something in you."

"He took his time about it! Beside him I dreamed that the snakes along the ceiling winding up and down the columns in the dining hall began to move. Two twined up one column and faced each other. They arced their sleek heads back and together hissed, 'The goddess loves us.' 'We're sacred to Asclepius.' 'We hold eternal secrets.' They wrapped around each other and the slender column, their words echoing.

"When I woke to Ischys curled around me, I asked if he shared my dream. 'Two serpents surrounding a staff,' he said and kissed me. 'A caduceus.' We began our own serpent dance, moving together until I could barely tell which was me, which him, our sighs almost a hiss, and came together in arching union. We recognized the dream dialogue between the snakes as cryptic messages from Asclepius and the Mother.

"He suspected I wouldn't remain in Epidaurus beyond the spring festival, so we must sleep together often. And so at last we did."

"In all weathers I continued my morning climbs. Sometimes rain fell so heavily I could barely see the stepping stones. Other times in the thin clear light, distant snow caps appeared where I'd only guessed there were mountains. Ischys often visited my room, our unions snaky undulations, our sleep peaceful, our dreams variations of the first. We pleased Asclepius and Aphrodite—and ourselves.

"One night when I slept alone, I awakened from a dream of laughter. Not the familiar tones of Aphrodite or the sharper note of Asclepius, but the great blood-curdling roar of Ares. Even there we were in danger?

"As I walked up the hill next morning, I gazed at the secure community below, protected by trees and river, Asclepius and Hygeia, but my dream gave me chills. I wasn't sure it presaged war, but certainly a disruption to my life.

"That evening with Ischys I knew our nights of sleeping ardently together were numbered. From then on each moment took on a rosy aura, not only with Ischys but with Daphne and the patients who smiled when they saw me.

"A few days before the spring new moon festival, Daphne found me in the courtyard as celebrants were arriving. Behind her stood a fisherman. He said he was sent by the priestess Iole to bring me and my child to the island of Cythera. He sailed early next morning: we must be at the harbor at sunrise.

"My first feeling was relief. But Ischys had gone to gather provisions for the festival and wouldn't return for another day.

"In a daze I climbed to my rock. Only at the top did my vision clear. To the south I could almost see Cythera, island of Aphrodite. Below, a lone ship was anchored. Even as I stood there, Epidaurus, catching slashes of sunlight through the pines, was fading to memory. That night I dreamed of the caduceus as an arrow guiding me forward.

"Before dawn I packed my clothes and Daphne's, the few that still fit her. On soft dirt outside my door I scratched the image of a staff entwined with two snakes, their heads arced back, facing each other. Below I added an image of the ouroboros, serpent with its tail in its mouth.

"Daphne appeared with Cilissa, whose eyes shone with tears. Cilissa gave her one of her little snakes, and the girls petted it as it encircled Daphne's wrist. I glanced back into my empty room, my heart full of warmth and regret for leaving Ischys without a farewell.

"With a sigh I stepped into the morning."

Chapter Twenty-four: Cythera

I walk Teiresias to the privy while Cenchrias climbs the fig tree. When we return to our pallets, he brings us salad with chopped figs. We turn our faces to the cooling breeze, as if sailing ourselves.

"There's nothing like a sea voyage," Teiresias says. "We live in a land of islands. Do take any chance you're offered, Manto. In my imagination I sailed with Damysos to Cyprus and Ithaca, with Brovas to Egypt, with Tanais to Phoenicia, but all too rarely in person. I loved salty sea air in my face and the brusque camaraderie of sailors with their understanding of Poseidon, Nereus and his daughters, every whirlpool, reef, and islet, and the hazards and miracles of the depths. Daphne's and my short voyage down the coast from Epidaurus to Cythera offered only a brief taste of open waters.

"Nearing the island, I saw Iole waving, ankle deep in purplish water. All of Cythera seemed to glow lavender, unique as Epidaurus's green and Corinth's ochre. After we anchored, I waded toward her, the water swirling around us colored by mussels.

"Cythera was a blessing for Iole. She seemed younger and in robust health. Daphne stopped to pick up a spiny violet-shaded shell and, her snake encircling her wrist, and ran to catch up.

"Iole's temple of Aphrodite felt more ancient than ours at Corinth, and its statue of Aphrodite wore a helmet:

Aphrodite Urania. The building was smaller, the stones rougher, decorations simple, and no sign of earthquake damage. Priestesses were less bejeweled and their dwelling modest. No private chambers off a fine dining hall.

"Iole led us to our room, saying that after we washed in the fountain, Daphne could take a nap.

"After she fell asleep, music called the women to the temple. A girl played the flute and her brother the drums, and I moved easily with the handful of priestesses. The drum beat increased, and we danced out of the building.

"Our meal awaited under a trellis. Sipping wine and eating fruit and cakes, I felt part of an ageless sisterhood, yet detached from the women except Iole. However long I stayed in Cythera, I would be a visitor. Nothing in me wanted to become part of another community. I was on a path toward solitude."

"Like one of your woodland priestesses?" I laugh. "Or a seer outside the city walls?"

Teiresias laughs too. "That I never imagined. Cythera felt like a primordial outpost against wealth-seeking Macaria and Alcimedes. When I said something to that effect to Iole, she stopped me.

"'Haven't you heard? Alcimedes' body washed up on the shore of Ithaca, his throat cut. It was said he gambled with the wrong people for the wrong stakes, but no one knows what happened. If Macaria had anything to do with his death, she covered herself well. What a fate for a lost priest of Helios, his soul turned to a lump of gold, his heart entrusted to such a woman, and a cut throat! May he have found peace in Hades.'

"I told Iole Macaria was seen wearing my ring. Whatever she pretended, Macaria's deity was Plutus, god of wealth.

"Next morning Daphne woke me, jumping impatiently as I dressed. We made a little house for her snake, who'd crawled under her covers during the night, then walked to the beach. She scampered ahead looking for mussels. I hadn't paid much attention to the beach itself when we arrived, entranced by the lavender-tinged surf. The dark sand was ribbed with lines of rock like dragon spines, and wind-blasted bushes fringed low dunes, gray-leafed with straggly yellow flowers. The place had a defiant beauty. If not for Daphne's bouncing profile in the distance, it would appear as forbidding as the beach where Theseus abandoned Ariadne. Its barrenness spoke to my soul, my loneliness, my sense of cherished times ending, and gave me a somber strength such as Ariadne must have known on Naxos.

"An old woman appeared from behind a rocky outcropping, startling me out of my reverie. Small, with a silvery fall of hair and bright dark eyes, she reminded me of Halia, petite and motherly. Her name was Rhea, she told me with a smile. The Titan.

"I followed her through twisted bushes with their tiny buttery flowers. Some believe Aphrodite was born from the seafoam in Paphos, some say to Dione on Cythera. This was clearly the more primal place.

"Rhea and I walked toward a cluster of boulders. Hidden beneath the rocks was a spring and beyond, the entrance to a cave shrine. Inside I saw a small serpent goddess, her high breasts cupped by a tight bodice above a full skirt in the ancient style, holding a snake in each outstretched arm. The Snake Mother! I asked Rhea if she came from Crete.

"They both had, the little statue and Rhea herself. When she was young, many Cretans lived nearby. In time, they sailed home across the sea, but Rhea chose to remain behind with her prized goddess.

"While the day was bright, I must go play with my daughter. At sunset I should return alone.

"As the sun dropped toward the sea, I left Daphne with Iole and walked to Rhea's shrine, setting my basket of apples, bread, and wine at the mouth of her cave. A lamp flickered beside the figure, giving the serpents in her arms a hint of movement and her painted face an inward smile. Despite her diminutive size, this statue emanated the power of Corinth's temple Aphrodite. Rhea referred to her as Aphrodite's grandmother.

"Sitting beside me on a woven blanket spread on the sand with the food and wine, Rhea asked what I knew about Harmonia. Like all Thebans, I knew she was daughter of Aphrodite and Ares who married Cadmus after he completed his exile for slaying Ares' dragon."

Teiresias turns his milky eyes toward me. "Do you know her story?"

"Harmonia's? No. She was another part of Thebes' history ignored by priestesses of Artemis."

"Then you must hear it, Manto. Rhea described Harmonia as a blessed child, born of the union of war and love. But beauty can be a curse, divine parentage a mixed blessing, and gifts bestowed by gods ruinous. Harmonia was both blessed and cursed.

"Daughter of King Haematios and Queen Electra, she lived in Samothrace. On Cadmus' journey in search of his sister Europa, he visited their court. The royal pair listened, entranced, to the handsome young stranger, but Harmonia thought him a bore. Cadmus claimed to have slain the Typhon, a monster of many heads and mouths, who once captured Zeus and drove the gods from Olympus in fear. He was their proud rescuer.

"Harmonia, making designs of pomegranate seeds on her plate, didn't care about Zeus or this young man who bragged about saving the great god. In return, although Zeus refused to return Europa to her brother, he promised Cadmus a beautiful woman who carried the secret of cosmic harmony within her. When Cadmus saw Harmonia, he knew she was his destiny.

"The king and queen consented, Aphrodite aided his wooing, and because her divine mother warmed her heart to him, the girl agreed. Thus did Cadmus depart from Samothrace with Harmonia at his side.

"Rhea's story of their union captivated me. I expected I'd never to return to Thebes but relished her description of the magnificent city Cadmus designed, modeling the Cadmeia on the geography of the heavens and dedicating each of the seven city gates to a divinity. Veins of precious metal ran through its stones, and amethysts and garnets glittered from their surfaces.

"To me now, Thebes and the Cadmeia live in the images of Rhea's tale rather than my memories of living there. When I was a heedless young man, I ignored its sparkling walls and went about King Labdacus' business with little imagination. The Thebes I've pictured through these years of blindness has been as she described.

"There Cadmus and Harmonia celebrated their marriage. All the gods were invited to their wedding feast, the grandest gathering ever. It's risky to invite even one deity to a celebration. To dance and sing with all the divine ones, to savor roast lamb, figs, and wine while they dine on ambrosia and nectar is to court danger. Never after this feast was another such event. We mortals live—and die—to entertain the gods. They do not exist for our sakes. 'Beware divine gifts,' Rhea had said on seeing my girdle of Aphrodite.

"Hephaestus crafted the necklace that Aphrodite clasped around Harmonia's neck: two golden serpents with their joined open mouths surrounding a sapphire and bodies writhing with gems from deep underground: diamonds, chalcedony, and emeralds, never before seen by mortals. This peerless necklace safely adorned Harmonia, but every woman who wore it afterwards, beginning with her daughters, suffered its curse."

I'm puzzled. "Wasn't Harmonia meant as a gift to Cadmus? You say they knew perfect love together."

"Yes, harmony radiated from them. But even though he completed his punishment, Cadmus couldn't atone for slaying Ares' dragon. Those curses hung over their perfect marriage and their daughters, each a tragic mother in her time."

"The gods are harsh," I murmur under my breath. Teiresias may or may not have heard.

"Cadmus and Harmonia didn't die peacefully in Thebes. After the loss of all their daughters, they departed together. Some say they were transformed into a pair of blue-spotted serpents, the rarest sort, and one day they will join the blessed ones."

After a silence he says, "Rhea's goddess held an adder in each hand. They're dangerous, but no snake on Cythera was poisonous. I told her about my lost ring and how its entwined serpents had been my guide. They still are, she said. Why did I think I came there?

"My question as well. Iole didn't need me, so there must be another purpose.

"Rhea offered me a green mixture which served better than the herbs of Epidaurus for dreaming. I worked the honey-soaked concoction around my teeth. She said if I watched the sea turn silver with the moonrise, a dream would come. Then she retreated. I walked slowly along the beach, watching stars flicker more and more brightly.

"Someone touched my braceleted arm and whispered that at last he'd found me. Even in the moonlight, I shone with the grace of the goddess.

"Damysos! I couldn't speak, moving into dream. As if from a distance, I heard 'O lovely one, let me dream with you.'

"'Are you brave enough?' Can you risk vision?'

"Aphrodite once sent him to me for his reasons, and now he sought me for mine. Wherever I winged myself, he would be with me. Then he took my hand and slipped the ring onto my finger. My snake goddess!

"That shook me out of my trance, and I listened to him with keen ears.

"After Macaria and Alcimedes left Corinth with the gold they'd accumulated, they traveled from island to island, city to city, providing ingots for armies and receiving precious stones in trade, with grand entertainments, feasts, and host gifts and at each stop. When in Ithaca, they said that King Atreus agreed to build their temple, as they called it, after they returned to Mycenae after that last trading mission.

"On their travels, they met others like themselves, former priests dealing in treasure of questionable origins and ventures of questionable honor. Macaria was the only woman continually among them and considered herself their leader. Alcimedes began drinking larger and larger quantities of wine and fomenting what Macaria called his little rebellion. Damysos doubted if he was capable of taking over their venture in Mycenae.

"Macaria, dressed provocatively, paid particular attention to a young guard who reported to Damysos that she accused Alcimedes of treachery whereever they visited. Macaria feared what he would do in Ithaca. She asked the guard to keep an eye on him or even better, administer a trusty knife to his heart. The horrified guard suspected he wasn't the only one she approached.

"Damysos noticed her ring, but otherwise didn't speak to either of them or again to his guard. Then Alcimedes turned up as a corpse! Macaria's boat was already vanishing when his body was found. A messenger from the harbor brought Damysos my ring.

"Bloodshed returned my ring to me, but all else was speculation. Who committed murder? Who received the ring in payment? No one was accused, and Macaria sailed safely to Mycenae.

"I rubbed the ring, grateful and mystified, and gazed into the vast luminous skies.

"Damysos leaned over to kiss me, and we held each other, my eyes wet with tears. We made a bed of his tunic and my gown, the sand shifting into conforming hollows beneath us, the bright half-moon gleaming our skin. I was the only woman Aphrodite ever granted to him, and when I left her service, he would as well. With the familiarity of one who's long adored in person and from afar, Damysos caressed me with his entire being, tantalizing with every touch.

"He brought me to the point where the fulfillment promised, promised, holding me at its cusp. I prayed to Aphrodite to keep me there forever, my body pleasured but not satisfied, each thrust touching me deeply, until our union took us to the far realms of heaven, the depths of the sea. After measureless time, we lay side by side, washed up on shore, gasping with relief to be alive after such submersion. The sky and earth embraced us into wholeness with all of nature, from the wisp of seaweed under my hand to the tiniest star of the furthest constellation."

Teiresias pauses, lost in memory.

He takes a deep breath. "Through the night I lay in open-eyed stillness between sleep and wake, between happiness and loss, between the boundaries of myself, the gods, and the immense beyond. When dawn played across a golden sky, I felt like a tiny fragment of life yet connected to all the universe, enclosing all opposites.

"Gently extricating myself from Damysos' sleeping embrace, I kissed his forehead and walked to the spring behind the shrine. bathing in its shallow overflow pond.

"As I was drying in the early morning sunshine, Rhea appeared. I told her how, as I lay sleepless after loving the man I most cared about, my path became clear. I left Damysos dreaming on the beach, forsaking him forever. My eyes filled with tears. What compelled me?

"She took my hand. What I gained reached beyond this shrine, this island, the goddess herself. And beyond one beloved man. I must be brave, for soon I would be alone. Damysos understood. Our night together was a farewell.

"I reflected on her words, soothing my sorrow until I could dry my eyes. Soon I would be called to leave Cythera."

I shake my head. "Did you think about Daphne at all? All this about 'my path' and 'I must be brave' and 'I would omitted your daughter."

"Calyce didn't teach Daphne to swim in the bay of Corinth," he says—which seems no answer at all—"but Iole did that day in Cythera's shallow waters. Daphne crowed with delight when she managed to paddle herself after Iole loosened her supporting hands. The moment was eternal, the image of woman and happy child, lavender sea and sunbright air, the sea lapping and hearts carefree."

He sighs and turns to me. "My pending departure would flavor the day's joys, as pending loss intensified my pleasure in Damysos' arms. I didn't leave Daphne behind. She would accompany me on my next step, wherever it led.

Chapter Twenty-five: Alecto

"Iole knew meeting Rhea would shake me. She couldn't imagine what would follow, but understood she and I must part.

"We danced in her ancient temple one last time and poured grateful libations to Aphrodite for all we had shared. Before bed we kissed goodbye.

"Next morning Daphne and I boarded a waiting boat. She showed me a bag of stones from Rhea, who called them magical. Daphne added the rosy one from Thoas, the funny man in Epidaurus.

"Rhea told her she could predict the future by bouncing them in water and watching their pattern form. The boatman gave Daphne his drinking bowl and poured in a little water. Daphne set it on a rowing bench, dropped her handful of stones into it and watched.

"The brightest agate, a glittering brown, was her guide and a green-streaked black pebble an obstacle to overcome. Others would help her—the blue-gray, the yellow, and the rose from Thoas. She wanted to know more, so I studied them closely. With trepidation, I told her what I saw. Even if I had to leave her one day, Daphne would always be blessed by priestesses. Whatever her trials, she would be loved, so she mustn't be afraid.

"When I said she could learn to read the stones by studying their patterns and listening to the voice within her she nodded. As Pythia she would foretell the destinies of others, and Rhea gave her these to practice.

"The captain saw how we used the pebbles and offered to show us another way to predict the future. He poured knucklebones from a small leather pouch. I closed my hand over them. Not for a child. Men played them for stakes of gold. But these were different, he said. They came from a bull sacrificed to the gods and had the power to reveal divine will. He told Daphne to open her hand. She should feel the surfaces, the ridges and hollows, then ask a question and throw them onto a cloth, where the answer would appear.

"He spread a cloth on the bench asked me for a question. Rolling them in my hand I looked toward Cythera, becoming smaller and smaller behind us. Where will this ship take me? I heard the young sailor mumble that was a question for the captain, not knuckle bones, but he didn't interrupt.

"I threw the bones onto red square of cloth where they fell into a circular pattern. Daphne saw it immediately. A labyrinth. She traced the circle with her finger.

"'We follow circular routes into the inner realms: the way of the serpent,' I said. A lurch of the boat rolled the bones toward me, scrambling them.

"Daphne said Cilissa drew labyrinths in the dirt in Epidaurus. On her grandmother's island was a stone labyrinth, and they existed many other places in honor of the Mother. The pit where her snakes lived had been one.

"As we neared an unfamiliar shore, she happily accepted the pouch of knuckle bones from the captain, who said she'd learn more as she played with them. With magic pebbles and knuckle bones and the covered basket with her snake, Daphne was well-gifted.

"Men and mules waited on the shore to carry goods to the city beyond. One trader, charmed by Daphne's appreciation of the pretty white mule in his small herd, presented it to her, the perfect mount for a small girl. He lifted her onto its back and strapped on our travel bag.

"I thanked that sunburnt man who served Hermes and gave him a conch shell from the beach at Cythera and a kiss on the cheek from Aphrodite. Daphne waved from her commanding seat on muleback as we left the harbor, turning onto a smaller path to the north, away from the city road.

"Looking for a place to spend the night, we took a trail into the woods. No hidden shrines appeared, only darkness falling between trees around a small clearing. I assured her we were safe in this grove. I lifted her down and led the mule to the stream. Tethering her in the grass, I spread my cloak nearby and set out our figs, cheese, and bread like a fine feast.

"Next morning as she fed her mule handfuls of grass, Daphne said her name must be Poppy. The red poppy was Cilissa's favorite flower, and that way she would travel with us. Daphne took her place on Poppy's back, her snake basket on her lap and the path wide enough through the pines for me to walk beside her.

"Although the Mother guarded us the previous night, we needed to find a sanctuary. At the end of a long day of walking, I spotted a narrow path along the edge of a running brook. I led Poppy with exhausted Daphne rocking on her back to the headwaters. Daphne glanced around, alert. Was this a secret shrine? Was there a priestess?

"A bony dark-browed woman with flowing white hair appeared from the shadows. Were we looking for her?

Though startled, I said yes, and she welcomed us in a rusty voice. Never before had a mother and daughter visited. When I asked why there was no sacred image, her face screwed into a smile. Few cared to contemplate them, but her shrine honored the Erinyes. She was Alecto, named for one of them.

"The Erinyes! I wondered at our landing in such a place. Alecto explained to Daphne they were the Furies, protectors of family bonds who exacted fierce punishments on any who violate the laws of the Great Mother.

"I held Daphne's hand reassuringly but she showed no fear of this forbidding woman. A family of bats lived above the shrine, and owls, Alecto said. In reply, a haunting call echoed through the moonless dark.

"In truth, no place could have been safer. Alecto fed us barley soup as we sat by a her fire. Daphne didn't take her eyes off her. 'Never seen anyone like me, eh? What did your mother tell you?'

"Daphne said she knew all about priestesses in secret shrines, and she had something special in her basket. 'My very own Snake Mother.'

"Alecto smiled. Rare to hear mention of the Snake Mother, and never from a child. But Daphne was an unusual girl with a priestess mother who took her traveling.

"'And I'm not afraid of you.'

"'Not afraid!' Alecto cackled. 'Why should you be afraid?'

"'You're dressed all in black and your eyes look orange as the fire.'

"'Some children would be afraid, but you know better. The Erinyes are frightening only to those who violate their law. To those who revere them, they are kind.'

"Saying 'I like you' Daphne took Alecto's hand. 'Why didn't the Erinyes punish Apollo for killing the Python?'

"'Apollo was a god himself, so he built a temple and stayed free. Now the Pythia speaks the Mother's wisdom from Delphyne underground. The Erinyes enforce Her laws.'

"Daphne wanted to stay up to listen to the owls, but I said she could hear them from her woodland bed and tucked a cover around her.

"In the long shadows of the early morning sun, I opened my eyes to Daphne sitting beside me caressing her snake into movement. A quick splash on my face and drink from the spring seemed too little refreshment when I looked at my dusty gown and feet, but she was already bounding toward the wooden shelter where we found Alecto.

"Daphne held her snake out toward a giant tree stump decorated with offerings of dry flowers and shoots of green leaves sprouting from its base. 'I'll give her to the Erinyes,' she said to Alecto. 'She can live in the hollow under the roots. That's what my dream told me.'

"'May your offering be blessed and may you live in the grace of the Mother,' Alecto intoned. For a moment as she stood, arm extended holding the snake, Daphne resembled the goddess figure in Rhea's rock cave. Then she let it go and it slithered into its new home."

Teiresias turns to me. "Remember Alecto's shrine of the Furies outside Colonus. Oedipus came there long after."

"Why Oedipus?" I don't finish my thought. Why should I care?

"I'm describing my transformations, Manto. Only Mydon knows about them, and he's no story-teller. The house of Oedipus weaves into the story of Teira and Teiresias, eventually leading to the Epigoni. Mine is a tale of the gods' involvement in human affairs."

"Go ahead. I'll see what I can make of it all."

"Still dusty, we left Alecto and headed the direction she pointed, avoiding the town of Colonus. Clutching her basket, now holding only Rhea's stones and the knuckle bones, Daphne was rocked to drowsiness on Poppy's back. I maintained a rapid pace until we came to a sacred laurel grove."

Chapter twenty-six: Maia

"Maia, priestess with a gentler demeanor than Alecto, invited Daphne to jump off her mule and come into the shade. Maia told the girl she loved her name. They would become great friends in days to come in this grove sacred to Dryads.

"She showed us a spring hidden in the rocks. After Maia said perhaps a Naiad lived there, Daphne leaned closer. 'I think I see her shadow.'

"Maia walked us to a woodsy cottage surrounded by flowering rosemary, our home for as long as we liked. I'd never lingered in a woodland shrine but agreed without a thought.

"Daphne sang, 'We'll stay here, we'll stay here!' while I found a place for Poppy to graze. By evening, the grove was home.

"After Daphne fell asleep, Maia told me to trust my serpent guide, for this was but a stop on my journey. To better understand, I must pick a laurel leaf and chew it.

"A distant nightingale sounded in the treetops as I chewed my leaf, releasing a flow of bitter juice. Daphne breathed evenly in sleep as I lay beside her, my breaths matching hers, until dream possessed me.

"Wind blew through the grove, but instead of harmonious swaying, each branch moved by itself. Surely they weren't human, yet they gave the impression of nymphs trapped within. A river rose around me, swirling over my bare feet in the sandy bed.

"Downstream I glimpsed an otherworldly golden man, coldly beautiful and terrifying. I splashed away from him, tripping on rocks and hollows, catching myself and splashing on. His strides were long, easily outpacing my frantic efforts. Floundering on slippery stones I shrieked, 'No, Apollo! Mother Gaia save me!' Then all went dark.

"I came to with the words ringing in my ears. Moonlight shone through the open door of the cottage as Daphne slept. I went out to sit on the doorsill. Did I chew your laurel to know your plight? I asked the laurel by the door. The moon passed beyond view as I reflected on the meaning of such a dream. How would I be pursued by Apollo? Would the Mother save me?

"The taste of laurel lingered and my head felt light. I knew Apollo was as a force to be reckoned with, but otherwise was mystified. What do you make of that dream, Manto?"

"I haven't the advantage of chewing a laurel leaf." After a moment I say, "You left Apollo behind when, as Teira, you fled Thebes. Apollo's priest Oineus felt like a threat to your temple in Corinth, but in this dream Apollo was as dangerous to your very being as he was to Daphne in the old tale. I suspect he represented another kind of threat."

"Well said, Daughter. At the time, the dream felt like empathy for mythic Daphne and a warning about my vulnerability to the forces of Apollo, however they might appear. I kept vigil till dawn, then slept until the sun was high.

"Watching Daphne sing to us now who inched along the grass, Maia told me she loved her. We could stay here as long as we wished. I understood her to mean whether or not I remained."

"Were you thinking about leaving Daphne?"

"I began to sense I would need to. I had no plan but fear made me value my time with her more than ever.

"On the spring equinox, day of perfect balance, Maia led me to tree-shaded steps not far from the spring. They led to a network of rocky outcroppings and hidden caves I'd never noticed. When I said I was glad Daphne hadn't found them, Maia assured me no one could who wasn't meant to. It would be easy for me to make my way back, so she left me to explore.

"I climbed to a sunny rock by the largest cave, the sound of dripping water echoing up from its depths. 'Not yet time, not time,' it seemed to say. I felt the sun on my back, my face in shadow. The sunshine world was mine to savor, but one day I would descend. It was as if the cave was beckoning me.

"When I returned to Maia's grove I thought more about savoring my time with Daphne than puzzling over that call onward."

"Sunshine moments rather than darkness," I say.

Teiresias smiles. "That's why you're the one to tell my story, Manto. You have the words.

"As days grew longer, Daphne lost interest in her pebbles and knuckle bones and trailed me. One morning she climbed onto my lap, big as she was, and asked if I'd take her with me.

"I could only say how much I loved her. We must trust our guides, and hers was Delphyne beneath the navel stone. She kissed my cheek and skipped off, but I felt chilled. Even my daughter sensed a coming change.

"Midsummer eve was also new moon, when the great sky serpent was its most intense. I lay sleepless with burning eyes and at dawn walked to the overflow pool of Maia's spring. A line of gold on the horizon sheened my skin as I bathed. When I looked at my reflection, I felt the blend of awe and alienation of my first viewing my female body.

"The shimmering water showed me as dancer, lover, celebrant. In the trick of a wave, I looked old and wrinkled. The image disappeared instantly, as if woman's old age would never be mine. I left my damp hair free, but fastened the girdle of Aphrodite around my sturdy chiton.

"Late that afternoon, Maia lit laurel leaves in a hollow stone, telling Daphne that their aroma would become familiar, but for now she must sit upwind to avoid inhaling the fumes. I, however, should breathe deeply of the smoke. I inhaled, imagining the cave at the center of the earth until I felt myself there. The fire cooled to ash, Maia and Daphne sitting together, the girl's drowsy head on Maia's lap.

"I stood, and Maia waved me on my way.

"Walking to the hillside I felt weightless. Never had it been so easy to climb through overgrown brush and rocks. In the soft soil near the mouth of the cave grew a cluster of amanita. The mushroom caps in a ray of orange sunshine looked enticing. I picked two, chewing them slowly. Their rich sharpness made my saliva flow and filled my throat with a thick, earthen sensation. I tucked more into my pocket fold.

"As the sound of Maia's distant flute song wafted through the trees, the veins in the boulder beside me came alive with crawling ants. A swarm of bees buzzed, and birds twittered a chorus.

"I gazed at the setting sun. My eyes held its fire until a cloud eclipsed it, leaving black disks impressed everywhere I looked. Instead of the blackness I expected, the cave was streaked with reddish light, much like the sky moments before. I moved over its uneven floor into glimmering darkness.

"When my eyes adjusted, I eased my way forward. The floor became smoother, leading to a bank of stairs. On the way down I touched a wall where cool water trickled. A gust of dank air pierced the earthy warmth as the narrow passageway opened into a cavern. An indentation in the wall invited me to sit. My aimless fingers touched the amanita in my gown and I put one in my mouth, chewing and swallowing slowly.

"I can't what followed into words—I think you've known something similar in your Mysteries."

"An altered sense of yourself?"

"Yes. A song reverberated through me, through the cave."

"Do you remember it?"

He begins to chant, almost too low and soft for me to hear.

Shall you die—
Shed this life's skin
To be born anew?

Shall you become body—
Part of the Mother
In her dark womb?

Shall your dances
Freeze forever,
Your woman's life gone?

Shall your vision,
Sunlight and moonlight,
Turn to blind darkness?

Shall your full heart
Forgo all loving,
And cede its passion?

A long silence. I look at Teiresias, entranced as he sat on his pallet. I hope I won't disturb him by speaking, dangerous for a soul hanging between realms. I whisper his name. When he turns his head, I ask if answers came.

"If I focused on my death I wouldn't die, so I pictured the Snake Mother with her vipers and the toxic drops of venom that heal. With the words echoing in my head, I imagined losing life and breath, movement and sight, love and my very body. When I felt still and cold as a corpse, the words began repeating. My breaths were shallow, my limbs still and heavy, my eyes blank, and my heart empty.

"Then light surrounded me, and I felt the serpent of destiny. I must follow it into the woods, leaving Daphne and all I knew.

"Would I be able to climb out of the cave?

"Near my perch I found a staff with coiling marks up its length. With its help, I made my slow way upward.

"The pale light of early morning greeted me. I dipped my hands into the spring, the water clear and gleaming, and drank. Then I grasped the staff and began walking on my solitary path."

He exhales a long sigh.

"That's all for tonight."

Chapter Twenty-seven: Coupling Serpents

As dawn breaks, I see Cenchrias walking Teiresias to the well and helping him bathe. He wears a linen undergarment that appears to hold skin and bones together. Perhaps the Epigoni will not cause his end. He could waste away before my eyes.

But he won't, not with a story to finish.

"I feel rested," Teiresias says as he sits down to our barley gruel. "I walked into dense alder and pine woods, no sign of human tread. Why did such an untouched place seem familiar? Half blind in the primeval shadows, I followed the tapping of my staff.

"One step and I was upon them, two coppery-blue snakes knotted together in a love dance amidst gnarled tree roots. With all my womanly strength, I struck my staff between them and held it firm. They arced up each side of the staff, two suspended coils of muscle, heads facing each other like Ischys' caduceus, then down to earth again. From the spot where I struck burst a multitude of tiny snakes, flashing off in every direction.

"In the hollow silence I stumbled forward and fell, Earth reverberating as I hit the ground. My last conscious awareness was being swallowed into the abrading leaves.

"I awoke to the sound of a male voice weeping—coming from my own throat. The nest of leaves and pebbles where I fell rubbed me free of all I'd been. I ran my hands down my body and touched my manly part, alien yet decidedly mine.

"The wind in the woods laughed my name. 'Teiresias!' I couldn't join the laughter.

My breath catches. For this to happen to Teiresias twice defies understanding. I whisper "Why?"

"What remained of my chiton was streaked with dirt," he continues, "and my golden girdle lay tarnished. I left it on the ground and shook out the chiton, hanging from my shoulders like a man's tunic. Folded into its pocket I found a flecked amanita. I dropped it as if it were hot.

"Now you know, Manto. Teira didn't die in the cave flooded with mushroom memories but in the deep woods.

"My skin felt loose and leathery, my limbs bony. Teira was gone forever. Did any of her beauty and joy remain? My arm was no longer encircled by the bracelet from Damysos, scoured off in the rough undergrowth. Never again would I know such a man as he, never hold another beloved in loving embrace.

"I was a man with coarsened clothing, no girdle, no bracelet, and no wish to examine my visage. At least the serpent ring remained on my toughened hand. I sighed in relief for that much but could make no other sound, even a prayer.

"Studying my staff, I saw the carved intervals marked Teira's life: her monthly flows, her loves, her pregnancy, the birth and growth of Daphne. Daphne! She too was lost to me. I wept.

"When I found words, I prayed my Daphne to thrive in Maia's care. I'd been much closer to her than to you, Manto, but even so, Fate took her from me."

Was it Fate I wonder? I feel sad for him, never a chance to do right by Historis and me and then to lose Daphne, fulfillment of Teira's motherhood.

"Could you explain this to yourself?" I ask.

"Why it happened?" His snort of a laugh. "Old stories are full of transformations, but none like mine. The easy answer would be my serpent path played a trick on me. Serpents can't be trusted."

"But you don't believe that."

"No. At times I thought Aphrodite granted me so much she got bored. Or, as we said during cold winters in Corinth, she flew off on her swan chariot to the warm lands of Ethiope uncaring. As things turned out, Fate opened another path for me"

"You became a blind seer."

He nods. "My urge was to cast off the staff after it became a weapon, but I couldn't fall in that trackless place. The wind whispered 'Thebes, Thebes.' Not an encouraging prospect, yet that was where my feet were carrying me.

"In the woodland dusk, opposites combined as in the dripping cave above Maia's spring. Neither night nor day, sun nor moon, male nor female, alone nor in company, sighted nor blind, but both, all.

"This thought rose in a crescendo, hammering in my ears. *Both! All!*

"Darkness fell. Through the foliage I saw a crescent moon and, with the help of the staff, stumbled to a clearing. The silvery moon illuminated a path between silent trees. I followed it along a gently moving stream like a sleepwalker.

"Where it widened into a deep pool, a perfect female form emerged from the water, her back to me. She stepped onto the bank and turned, her eyes shining fire in the pale night, radiating immortality in the chaste nakedness of divinity.

"She faced me full on, and for a terrifying moment I saw her glory—and then fell forward, blinded.

"A slant of warmth awakened me on the cold ground. Dare I open my eyes? I pulled my cloak over my head until I found the courage to sit up, eyes open. Alders and pines surrounded the empty pool. I could see!

"I credit my mother, the nymph Chariclo, for saving me. No mortal encounters the naked goddess and survives. For one glimpse of Artemis, Actaeon was turned into a stag and torn limb from limb by his own hunting dogs.

"Chariclo left me long before, yet at that moment she was my guardian. I fell to my knees to thank her for preserving my sight after I witnessed the forbidden. Then, a ragged man, I strode toward Thebes."

"What a story," I say. "No woman could live so fully in seven years. The end of Teira—" I can't finish. I mourn her loss, so how much more must he?

"I'll never understand," he says. "Somehow I was compelled to strike the serpents, unthinking. Teira in full possession of herself couldn't have done it." He shakes his head. "You'll find a way to tell this, Manto. You wouldn't describe your Eleusinian Mysteries. Perhaps regard this the same."

It isn't at all the same, I think, but certainly a mystery in itself. The inexplicable role of Fate.

"Telling you about this transformation distracted us from all else," Teiresias says. "We can't forget the Epigoni."

"Why will they attack Thebes? You said you'd explain— and tell me how you were blinded."

"Those come next."

Our midday refreshment is slices of watermelon. With the last bite, he begins speaking.

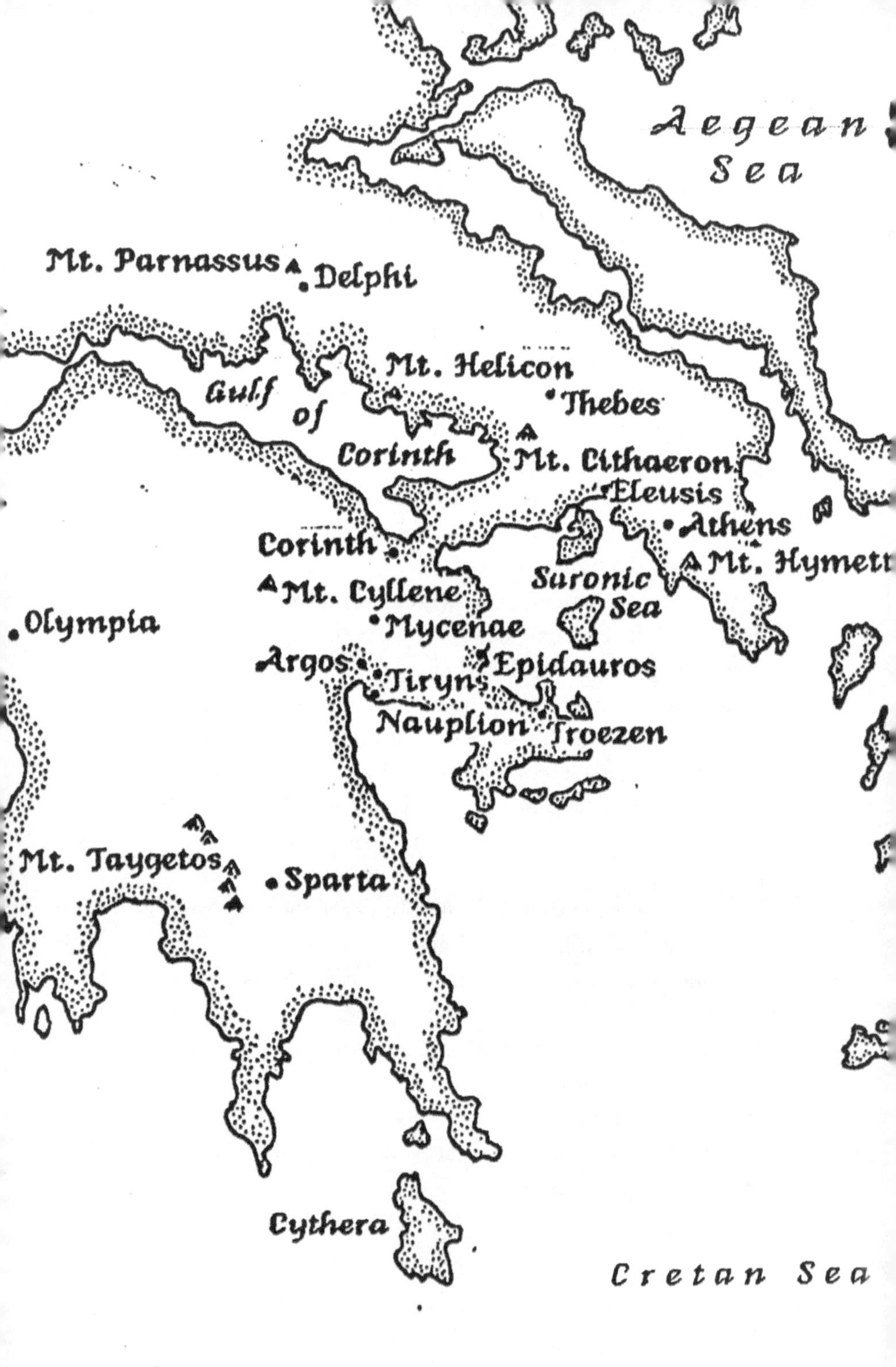

Aegean Sea
Mt. Parnassus
Delphi
Gulf of Corinth
Mt. Helicon
Thebes
Mt. Cithaeron
Eleusis
Athens
Mt. Hymett
Corinth
Mt. Cyllene
Suronic Sea
Olympia
Mycenae
Argos
Tiryns
Epidauros
Nauplion
Troezen
Mt. Taygetos
Sparta
Cythera
Cretan Sea

Part II: Riddling the Sphinx

O Teiresias,
master of all the mysteries of our life,
all you teach and all you dare not tell,
signs in the heavens, signs that walk the earth!
Blind as you are, you can feel all the more . . .
   Oedipus in Sophocles' *Oedipus Rex*
     translated by Robert Fagles

(And I Teiresias have foresuffered all . . . ;
I who have sat by Thebes below the wall
And walked among the lowest of the dead.)
   T.S. Eliot, *The Wasteland*

Chapter Twenty-eight: The Debate

I ask Teiresias if he could have gone any place other than Thebes.

"I never imagined returning there, but that's where Fate led me. For reasons I didn't understand, I was needed in Thebes. But as a man, I didn't feel the ease of Teira walking through woods where priestesses of the ancient sisterhood offered shelter. Would any do so for me now?"

I laugh. "You had the opposite worry when you left for Corinth, a woman traveling alone."

He smiles. "I suppose that's another duality. Like Teira, I prayed to Earth's powers to show me the serpent way. Walking on with as much confidence as I could summon, I came upon a trail running along a stream and followed it until I encountered a woman in a robe as green as the mossy tree trunks.

"Macris greeted me as Pilgrim in a voice cracked from disuse and offered me food and rest in her shrine of Hera, daughter of the Great Mother.

"At her invitation I cooled my hands in the stream and splashed water on my face, surprised at my short hair. The late afternoon light didn't allow for a clear reflection in the water's surface. Just as well, I thought, looking at the stringy muscles of my legs. In her transformation, Teira gained the freshness of a young woman. My male face must be aged beyond my years.

"Macris offered me a bowl of peaches, grain, and milk, filling the bowl twice over when she saw I was half-starved. Few travelers came this way, only a rare worshiper and the boy from the village who brought her goat's milk and fruit. My destination must be distant for me to have found such a remote place.

"When I told her I was bound for seven-gated Thebes, she said she hoped I was wise, for that city desperately needed wisdom.

"'I know what I know,' I replied in a husky male voice. An old man who seemed to have skipped decades of living, what wisdom did I possess?

"As dusk fell, I made my bed near Macris' shrine. The features of the roughly carved Hera within were blurred in the dim remains of the day but her figure emanated authority. She seemed not simply daughter of the Great Mother but the Mother herself. Yet despite being one of the goddesses of childbirth, fierce Hera punished women Zeus impregnated.

"Limbs aching, I spread my cloak over myself. Through the darkness, I heard the mocking laughter that haunted me after I first struck the serpents. Now it said, 'No more joy of love. No more. No more.'

"Why would Aphrodite taunt me? The years I spent as a woman felt like my true life, and I was all too aware it was over. Such is Fate, I reminded myself, and it wasn't done with me."

"How much of your female sensibility remained?"

"My memories as Teira were vivid so yes, I can say that existence remained. But as you would imagine, I was agitated. My hand fell into my folded pocket and found the last amanita. I popped it into my mouth, its earthen taste bringing back the sensations from the cave and the shock of that sudden metamorphosis.

"Dancing images of Teira's life played through my mind until sleep came.

"Hera loomed over me, not the crude goddess in Macris' shrine but the ox-eyed queen of Mount Olympus. She spoke to me in her divine voice. 'I drank too much nectar, Teiresias, and got into the worst quarrel with his cloudy majesty, Zeus of the thunderbolt. We cannot find Hermes, so I am in the humiliating position of serving as messenger. Only you can answer our question.'

"She vanished into a cloud leaving an echo of 'only you.'

"From the cloud came a thundering male voice. 'You provoked this quarrel, my queen, and Teiresias will settle it. None of your tricks.'

"Dream this must surely be. Lying still, I overheard two voices arguing. Could they really be Zeus and Hera? He roared, 'Ruthless Hera, you're jealous as a housewife. I shall defeat you once and for all.'

"She countered, 'When the Great Goddess ruled, there was no winning, neither of female or male.'

"'Times have changed since goddesses were were all-powerful.'

"'You marshalled your thunder clouds against us, your indomitable male authority displacing our deep connection to all. Vile usurper!'

"'Calm yourself, Hera. Are you not goddess of the golden throne?'

"'A smaller throne than yours, Zeus, and my power is lesser. You rule.'

"'But you must agree, in the embrace of sex, woman enjoys the most pleasure.' His voice was goading. 'You should have heard Leda—'

"'Enough! Women fake it to make you stop, you fool. You came to Leda as a swan! If you weren't taking pleasure from abducting mortal women, why do you persist in doing so?'

"'After we resolve this question, my formidable queen, you shall hold your peace.'

"'Resolve it if you can, I shall not hold my peace!'

"'No more wrangling. You agreed to heed the answer of the person who has known both ways.'"

"'I consented under protest.'"

"I heard my name on the wind in long extended syllables. 'Tei-reee-see-as!'

"Quivering, I said nothing. Again Zeus called my name. I hoped against hope this was an amanita nightmare. Were the gods playing with me because I was newly male, or did this scene come from my troubled soul? For me to speak with the rulers of high Olympus would resemble the wedding feast of Cadmus and Harmonia. If deities and mortals mingle, those who lack immortality are in danger. Macris was no part of this dream, if dream it was. I was alone in the most perilous place a mortal could be, the divine clouds of Mount Olympus. I couldn't see the divine pair but their voices were eerily powerful.

"Zeus spoke. 'Tell us, Teiresias. Who gains more delight in the embrace of love, man or woman?'

"Without hesitating, I replied 'Woman.'

"Manly laughter thundered through the skies. 'Woman's pleasure is greater, greater, greater!'

"Hera's voice: 'Dare he say so? For this impertinence, Teiresias shall never look upon woman nor man again. The queen has spoken.'

"Zeus' voice rumbled, penetrating my world now darker than the midnight sky. 'I cannot change your curse, wife, but I can grant him the most profound second sight of any living person. You, Teiresias, who have experienced the ways of both man and woman: your blindness shall be of the outer eye merely. Henceforth your sight shall be greater than that of mortals caught in the glittering charm of the moment. Yours is the knowledge of past, present, and future. You shall speak in the voice of a prophet.'

"I sat up from my bed in Macris' shrine, facing the rising sun that pressed on my eyes but revealed nothing. Rubbing the ring, I prayed. Was this to be my serpent path, with none but birdsong to guide me? I groped for my staff."

"So that wasn't merely a dream. Here you sit blind, with the seer's vision." I shake my head in confusion. "Why did you answer so?"

"Zeus asked me to speak from my experience of living as both male and female. As a young man, I never worshipped Aphrodite, and to my shame knew nothing of the nuances of loving beyond my own satisfaction. Teira's loves were fuller, deeper, more complete than anything I knew or could have imagined as Teiresias."

"As priestess of Aphrodite you healed men through the embrace of love."

"We priestesses healed wounded men wise enough to recognize their insufficiency, as do initiates to Eleusinian mysteries. My mistake in that celestial debate was failing to employ the diplomacy I mastered as a royal counselor. Zeus may have begun the argument as drunken jest, but Hera took it seriously. She's a goddess and I a paltry mortal. I should have conciliated her."

"Could you? You had to speak the truth as you knew it."

"Yes, I spoke true. But when priestess of Aphrodite, I was as limited as I was when a young male votary of Apollo. Teira experienced the best faces of love. Never raped, never subordinated to a man. Mortal rapists seek something other than pleasure. In his endless pursuit of Titans and mortal women, Zeus acted from lust and godly power. Men who follow his example are driven by cruel impulse, and their victims feel violated. Neither side has engaged in anything Aphrodite would recognize as a loving embrace." He smiles. "I couldn't have said that to Zeus and Hera, could I? Anyway, that was long ago, and I'm not one for regrets."

He exhales a long breath. "Zeus and Hera's debate began as godly banter. Another proof of how we suffer from the gods' jests and whims."

"Which you forgot."

"I did, for an ominous moment."

I take his hand. "Was that the worst day of your life?"

"Let's say one of the most extraordinary days." He pauses. "There was something more that I didn't understand. Hera told me that when the Sphinx riddled Thebes, I wouldn't know the answer."

Chapter twenty-nine: *The Sphinx*

"Next morning when Macris greeted me," Teiresias continues, "she said she'd felt Hera's presence in the night and knew my blindness was her doing. My ears and inner eye would become stronger without sight, she said, and she would enlist Phrastos from nearby Glisas, a lad with a quick wit and sure foot, to lead me onward.

"When he arrived with the morning's milk, Phrastos agreed. After he bid his mother farewell, he would return at midday, and so he did. He let me feel his face and get a sense of him, smiling and wiry.

"With my staff and Phrastos' strong arm, I made my way to Thebes, trusting my feet on the earthen path, understanding the subtle messages of shadows and air currents, and fighting my misgivings. Phrastos kept up steady chatter. His mother told him to behave himself and stay as long as he needed to. He couldn't say how long that would be because Macris asked him to remain with me after we reached Thebes.

"He laughed when I asked if he knew much about snakes. Anyone with open eyes did. Snakes were his friends, and poisonous ones slithered away from him.

"Just eleven years old, Phrastos knew the Goddess herself loved serpents. He once caught a pretty little one he let go in Macris' shrine. It curled around the figure of Hera, then slipped away, quick as anything.

"We talked about finding a place to live outside Thebes' walls, for a city is no place for a blind man and a child.

"Phrastos told me not to worry about my blindness. He was happy to see the city for both of us. Thebes must be like Glisas, but bigger and more beautiful. He was sure he could find his way around, get us food—oh yes, he knew how to cook—and watch and listen. Living with me outside the walls, he would report the news from within.

"I followed him onto a path so narrow I had to put a hand on his shoulder. It led to a shine tended by a priestess called Ida, devoted to Aphrodite. Aphrodite? In the woods?

"Ida laughed. Why not? Thebes had no temple to Aphrodite, their mistake. Few pilgrims came here, but the love goddess smiled at those who did. She guided my hands over her waist-high Aphrodite statue, not a jewel decorating her simply carved wooden figure.

"'Your vision is inward, Teiresias,' Ida said when I held out my ring finger. She repeated that Thebes needed wisdom, but she couldn't explain why, for she know little of what went on inside the walls.

"That night we slept in her pilgrim's shelter. I would have happily remained, listening to the stream cutting between fragrant banks of dill and mint. Calmed by the sound of Phrastos' even breathing and the moving water, I welcomed sleep and didn't stir until birdsong heralded daybreak.

"Phrastos left us, promising to bring back something tasty. By the time he returned with all the fruit and bread he could carry, I'd memorized our little territory. The farmer who gave him our food said it was for his old master. Perhaps he was the wise man they hoped for.

"After I became accustomed to lacking eyesight, I moved with Phrastos to this sanctuary. I became reconciled to my body's losing its fluidity and warm female center. All I had was this little serpent," he touches his penis through his tunic, "impotent witness." If blind eyes can twinkle, his do.

"I wondered if the Goddess intended this fate. Without my staff and Phrastos, I couldn't go anyplace. My inner path would have to guide me, a blind visionary. I prayed to be delivered from self-pity, to regard my new life as a blessing. Only a fool blames the gods."

Teiresias sets down his empty cup. "One day the sky darkened and an uncanny whirring cut through the air, skimming around Thebe's walls three times. In the vacant silence that followed, I shivered. I looked toward the orange light of the sinking sun, picturing a beast more fearful than any that appeared to my sighted eyes. Surely that apparition had been the iridescent-winged Sphinx.

"Yet so far as I knew, King Laius never questioned why such a being circled above his city. He above all others should have."

Chapter thirty: King Laius

"You won't be surprised to hear that Phrastos quickly learned his way around Cadmeia. An old guard let him pass, and he was small enough to escape anyone else's notice.

"He'd never seen so much splendor, but found it odd that Queen Jocasta barely spoke to her husband. Laius seemed a strange sort of king, braiding his black beard into points and seeming to care only for pleasure. His noble attendants fascinated Phrastos, jewels in their ears and woven into their girdles over fine linen tunics that smelled of sandalwood. They wore diadems of golden leaves and flowers, plaited their hair with ribbons, and lined their eyes with kohl. They were more beautiful than any woman Phrastos had seen."

Teiresias turns to me. "Do you recall Strophios' story at Rhene's banquet? Hearing Phrastos describe Laius and his courtiers reminded me of it."

"How could I forget his rape of Chrysippus?."

"Strophios told us the boy's father King Pelops cursed Laius and his descendants. But Laius was married to Jocasta, daughter of the former king Menoeceus, with no apparent dire consequences."

"Do you think Jocasta heard about the curse?"

"Much she didn't know about the charmer she married.

"So far from court life, I sat for long hours outside my cottage, sometimes twisting my ring round and round my finger. Phrastos' Thebes little resembled the one where I grew to manhood. I wondered about you and your sister. Were you living inside the walls? I didn't ask him."

"Do you know if Historis still lives here? You said you'd tell me her story."

"She does not. Hers will be our last story of the evening, one that happened long ago. Historis never mothered a child of her own, but she gained renown for safe deliveries and preserving mothers' lives. If a baby were born in the palace, she would have been summoned, but Laius and Jocasta were childless. Historis immersed herself in her worship, caring for little but midwifery.

"You wouldn't expect her arm to bear a shield, but she used one to catch a newborn: Heracles. Have you heard of him?"

"A man of amazing strength, he was fathered by Zeus and born of a mortal queen."

"Yes. Zeus came to Alcmene in the guise of her husband King Amphytrion. Long after, I heard about Historis' role in Heracles' birth. Hera had enlisted the goddess Eileithyia to prevent it. Historis had to outsmart a goddess—and she did."

"With a shield ready to catch the baby?"

Teiresias laughs. "So it seems.

"Afterwards, Historis remained in Amphytrion's household. Heracles' name makes him sound like the darling of Hera but that's far from the truth."

My sister made a notable life for herself, but I'm sorry she lives so far away. "Then I won't see her."

"No Manto, nor shall I. Wouldn't we love to hear the story from her lips! But it happened in another lifetime. I've told you all I know, and now we must retire."

Cenchrias comes to help him, and I make my way to my familiar cottage.

After breakfast next morning, I ask when pilgrims began coming here.

"Phrastos spoke of his master, how he fathomed the future from the sounds of birds and, though blind, read signs and portents. I doubt he bragged, but folk crave to know what lies ahead.

"The curious and needy began to appear at my cottage. No one wants the full truth about the workings of Fate. If one asked my advice on a decision or wanted a personal prediction, I replied easily, hoping for no more unsettling questions.

"The first were easy to answer. "Shall I have a baby this year?" *The seed fertilized with love shall thrive and come forth at the dark of the moon.* "Will my grapes flourish?" *Shade and drought bless the vine.* "Must my husband forgive his brother?" *Animosity plunges us into the abyss unless harmony creates a bridge.*

"This question put a dread image in my mind, unconnected to the woman who asked it. I envisioned brother threatening brother at Thebes' walls while the city quaked."

In the silence following his words we hear distant galloping. This is what battling brothers have brought about.

"One day a seeker asked, what is the meaning of the whir of wings above the city? I told her to return the following day.

"That night I stilled my mind to prepare for a dream. It came as a chant:

We live in Sphinx shadow
Beneath high Mount Phicium,

She who roars on the wind
Sweeps past our gates
Soon shall remain.
We live in Sphinx shadow
Goddess of death
Claiming our sons
Till the destined one comes
To hurl her to ruin
From her sheer heights.

'Can I do nothing?' my heart cried.

"The voice of Hera spoke. 'You, Teiresias, defied me when Zeus questioned you. Thebes earned my curse, and you will not know the Sphinx' riddle.' A terrible droning sound assaulted my ears, followed by an even louder silence.

"When I told the seeker she heard the wings of the Sphinx, she fled in terror. Strangely, no one else asked, and pilgrims continued. After I replied about love and parenting, planting and property, they left satisfied. I should have been relieved, but fear took root deep within.

"One day a mother walked from distant hills with her small son strapped to her back. Her precious babe, Narcissus, possessed such uncanny beauty she wondered if he would thrive.

"He will, I replied, if he never knows himself. She must harbor my prophecy and raise the boy with cautious love.

"'And so I shall, and so I shall.' As she walked away with her child, a wave of dread passed through me for the boy and for his mother's lack of understanding. I said a prayer for him.

"Suppliants began describing terrifying dreams, fears for child or husband, and anxiety about the ill wind blowing on Thebes as if from high Olympus. It blasted the fields, burning crops and killing newborn lambs. To those sufferers I could offer few words of comfort, only that we lived in a shadow.

"One morning Phrastos came running from an errand inside the walls. 'Master, Master. While Belus was walking near the topmost gate of the city, a giant winged creature swooped down, grasped him in her claws, and threw him over the cliff.'

"My heart seized. The Sphinx had arrived.

"After he caught his breath, Phrastos told me no one agreed what she looked like, though some said she had a pretty woman's face. Others believed she was a cat-monster, Hecate, or a spirit from Hades. Her wings were broad and purply, streaked with the golden rose of sunrise, and she was like a giant winged lion, much larger than an eagle.

"Everyone who saw her spoke of their fright, the chill wind stirred by her wings, and her odor of blood and decay. One witness saw the monster speak to Belus before she thrust her claws into him.

"Phrastos was afraid. Belus wasn't much larger than he was. But he refused to stay home. How I would know the news? I could only advise him to be careful and use his best judgment.

"The Sphinx was relentless. After she hurled Belus from the high gate, other youths followed. Not every day, so for brief interludes folk would believe the gods heeded their prayers. But the harvest was scanty, the herds dying, and even on the brightest day, the shadow of two broad wings hovered over Thebes.

"When this onslaught began, the mothers and fathers of Thebes came to ask how to protect their sons. Not their daughters. The Sphinx never posed her riddle to a girl. They were safe but powerless, as was I."

"Couldn't you save those youths?"

"Hera put a weight on my tongue. My mind remained lucid, but if the Sphinx came into my thoughts, my vision clouded over. All I could say, she would not be destroyed until someone answered her riddle correctly.

"Soon no more suppliants came, not even maidens in love, though this threat would make queries about their lovers more poignant. Nor did mothers ask the fortunes of their unborn babies, for no babies were conceived under Sphinx' shadow.

"Phrastos reported that the men of King Laius' court, once gorgeously arrayed, now wore plain tunics edged in black. Their rings and pendants bore protective signs, even the sign of the Sphinx to appease her. Nothing helped.

"One day I had a welcome surprise. A familiar voice broke into my melancholy musings. None other than Mydon the serpent priest! He'd heard of a blind seer outside the city walls, but not my name until that day.

"Much of the time he served Dionysus, whose ecstasies and slippery nature called to him. Dionysus couldn't be held to one mode, reason or common sense, male or female. From time to time Dionysus called Mydon into the woods and, he confessed, maddened him.

"He regretted I couldn't see him and how he'd changed since the old days. But what happened to lissome Teira, who walked off to Corinth on her serpent path wearing a girdle from Aphrodite? I held up my ring finger. His gift still led me.

"Beyond that I couldn't reply. Mydon said my face still had eerie moments of beauty, even if those who didn't look closely saw only an old man. To him I didn't seem old, though my hair was now the color of sand and lime dust. I wondered about his eyesight. Of course I looked old, with eyes dulled in blindness.

"Mydon asked me to feel his face. His beard was thick, and leaves and acorns stuck in his hair. When I pulled out a sprig, he laughed. These days he lived in the forest more than town and resembled an old satyr.

I asked if he was quite sane.

"'Absolutely not,' he replied. Often he lived in Dionysus' ecstasy, but he could speak sensibly enough when he wished. I didn't know how seriously to take him. Mydon was unnerving, but he was the only Theban who knew about my former life as Teiresias and had seen me as Teira.

"He said his clothes were more tattered than mine, and he walked about with a thyrsus like my staff but more magical. To be as I was, I must have descended into a darkness near death. So had he, feeling rent like a sacrificed animal, like the god himself. Through Dionysus he learned what lay beyond death."

I don't interrupt, but I know what the Mysteries tell us lies beyond death and doubt Mydon shares those perceptions. But who am I to say? Dionysus himself is a mystery, spiritually torn and reborn.

"Mydon was an easy visitor," Teiresias says, "both of us possessing vision, useless as it was at the time.

"Death hung over Thebes on the wings of the Sphinx, and the city sank in grief. Old Menoeceus, father of Queen Jocasta, hoping to appease her with blood of Cadmus' royal line, threw himself from Thebes' high wall. The Sphinx responded by seizing another youth that very day, posing her riddle and flinging him to his death. Prayers and supplications offered no comfort, and priests could say only that the city suffered from a curse.

Mydon and I agreed that Laius must go to Delphi for an oracle. When Queen Jocasta sent a priestess to me as suppliant, I told her Laius must approach the Pythia with a humble heart and ask what we can do to save our city."

Chapter thirty-one: Hecate's Cauldron

I'm caught up in the story, but it's distressing and we need a break. I wave to Cenchrias, who appears with wine and a bowl of cheese and grapes.

"So you were nothing a helpless bystander with no influence?"

"Influence?" Teiresias gives me a sideways glance. "I was the one who advised Laius to go to Delphi." He's shivering, and gulps his wine.

"Are you all right?"

"I can't ignore the truth. Fate used me. I know. I've described the bane of the soothsayer's gift, sensing what Fate holds yet powerless. In this case, at best, my advice changed the course of Thebes' suffering. Listen to the rest of the story before drawing conclusions."

I wait while he takes a piece of cheese and washes it down with wine.

"Hiding in the throne room, Phrastos watched Laius rage when Jocasta told him he must go Delphi. There he would learn the gods' will. She added a taunt Phrastos didn't understand about a boy stolen and a baby exposed. Fire flashed from her eyes as she said she could never forgive him. Laius had no choice but to consult the sibyl. Though puzzled, Phrastos did his best to report their words accurately.

"Preparations began immediately for Laius' departure. He would take a small company in a single chariot. In his absence, Jocasta and her brother Creon would rule.

"The day Laius rode out, thunder cracked across the high mountains. Phrastos was jumpy, describing the sky as an odd kind of silver. My blind eyes pictured two regal birds flying toward each other. All the vast sky was theirs, yet they soared on a collision course. Wings clashed, deadly beaks contended.

"Phrastos saw nothing but a blur and then a fierce clamor above the trees. My sharp ears detected the soft thud of a feathered body hitting the ground."

"One of the royal eagles," I murmur.

"So it seemed.

"All was still at the palace, Creon in his quarters and Jocasta living quietly with the priestesses of Selene. One of them succeeded Halia at the first sanctuary I—Teira— discovered outside the city. Also named Halia, she moved her shrine to a glen at the foot of the Cadmeia for Jocasta and her ladies.

"One day Mydon brought Halia to my cottage, and she became a valued friend."

"Did she know you visited her woodland shrine as Teira?"

He laughs. "Too long before, and no priestess knew of my past. Now that Halia and her priestesses spent the nights with the queen, she hoped their rituals would bring the goddess' healing powers to Thebes.

"With Laius gone, Jocasta felt a weight lift. His court had honored no goddess nor woman, not even her, though Jocasta's blood was as noble his.

"Hot blasts seared the long airless days. I sat here, still as the world around me. No birdsong, no cries of goats on the hillside, no market sounds floating over the city walls nor playing children's' voices. Only the occasional rumble of thunder.

"As Laius' absence extended, Thebans began to wonder if he'd met with an accident. I knew no more than anyone else and Mydon was no wiser. We still feared the Sphinx, but after Laius' departure she bided her time.

"It wasn't that monster who haunted my dreams but an old woman stirring her cauldron in the dark of the moon at a crossroads. Her visage was more frightening than Alecto's at the sanctuary of the Furies. Daphne said Alecto's eyes shone orange, as did this dream woman's. Perhaps she served Hecate or perhaps she *was* Hecate, her appearance that alarming. Stirring her cauldron where three roads met, she spun the future into being.

"One night as I fell asleep, a ghostly song pierced the still night air. My dream found me standing behind a branchless tree trunk at the edge of a dirt circle edged in stunted trees. In the center the woman stirred her cauldron over glowing coals, singing verses I couldn't understand. A young man, disheveled and frantic, approached. When she addressed him as son, he said he dared not be a son.

"'You are my son. All young men who seek truth in darkness are my sons. You are the Divine Child.' Her eyes shone out of her shadowy face with tan unholy light.

"'Speak no such nonsense to me, reverend one,' he said. 'I come from Delphi where I heard more truth than I can bear. When I asked about my parentage, the Pythia said I would kill my father and bed my mother. The rumor that I was not my father's son drove me to seek the sibyl's wisdom, but now I cannot return to the parents I love."

"The crone lifted her stirring stick, the broth in the blackened pot still swirling. She told him to look into the bubbling cauldron and find clarity. He stepped into the light of the fire and glanced into the great pot, then jumped back. 'I've seen enough. It looks like blood, the blood that even now stains my hands. On my return from the heights of Delphi, a man tried to run me down. He'll never do such a thing again! What is this vile mixture?'

"'Blood and more, stirred and transformed, stirred and transformed.' She resumed stirring and chanting, but I heard the young man's words over hers.

"'O Polybus, Merope, forgive me for leaving you, for leaving golden Corinth I was meant to rule. I cannot return, not at such cost.'

"'What blood did you shed, Child?'

"'A stranger's. But surely Apollo guides me, for I am Prince Oedipus.'

"She stirred on, muttering, 'Forget answers. Ask the right question.' The word 'question' echoing in the still night air, the young man slipped into the shadows.

"'Stay!' my dreaming mind called to him. 'Stay and look!' I awakened, a soft robe thrown over me and the sky impenetrable. Was that truly Oedipus, the baby we blessed, the boy who played at the seashore with Daphne?

"I pillowed my head on my folded arm, sensing someone had stumbled into my yard and fallen asleep. Or perhaps what sounded like human breathing came from the night itself.

"During that restless night I had a ghastly dream of a chariot tumbling down a hill leaving bloody bodies behind, the horses galloping into the hills. A young man stood breathless, staring at his blood red hands.

"Then I saw the Sphinx sitting at the top of the wheel of Fate. Her face became that of Queen Merope, then the Pythia, then Jocasta above the fatal wheel. I lay sleepless until birds heralded dawn.

"The sleeper in my courtyard roused himself and slipped away."

Chapter thirty-two: The King is Dead; Long Live the King

"What a dream!"

"Unforgettable—as were its reverberations. Not long after, a song rang out through the streets:

Sing woe, the king is dead.
Rejoice, the Sphinx has gone.
Glory the youth who saved us.
Glory the gods who saved us.

"I sent Phrastos to the Cadmeia. Were we truly saved?

"Past midday he returned. A noble young man was brought with honor to Jocasta and Creon. He'd solved the riddle and sent the Sphinx screaming to her death. Phrastos' voice rose in excitement. Creon had decreed that the man who vanquished the Sphinx would marry Jocasta and be crowned king of Thebes, and here he was. The queen seemed pleased, and Creon planned to retreat into shadows. The new king was named Oedipus.

"Oedipus! Stunned into silence, I felt the airless grief so long oppressing Thebes settle within me. I fought the heaviness in my chest, straining for breath, afraid I'd faint. Images swirled, then all was dark.

"When I emerged from my trance, Ida was ministering to me. I'd been so frozen with terror that Phrastos feared for my life. He fetched her here, where I lay unmoving through the stifling heat as day turned to night three times over.

"I heard skylarks singing, felt a soft breeze. My health had been restored.

"Mydon came to tell me the riddle. 'What walks on four legs at dawn, two at midday, three at sunset, and speaks with a single voice?' The Sphinx leapt to her death when Oedipus replied Man.

"All rejoiced that the Sphinx was gone. Thebes was bright, from the lowest dooryard to the great hall, and the city smelled wholesome, like a temple faintly incensed. Oedipus adored Jocasta. He looked to her in every decision, ruling together in harmony.

"To me all was not flowers and sunshine, but I held my tongue. Soon Phrastos told me that Jocasta was pregnant. She had been a woman of grief, but no longer. Is that what they're saying I asked? She was childless because Laius turned her from his bed? A gossipy palace maid whispered that Laius feared to father a child on her because of a frightening oracle. The girl knew no more, only that some said he was not inclined toward women."

Teiresias catches the savory scent of our afternoon meal before I do, relieved to take a break. Cenchrias had roasted a small fowl, fragrant with sage. He cuts it apart, laying the pieces on a pile of greens in our bowls, with chunks of bread to wipe our fingers. The chicken's flavorful oil seeps into the greens, and I savor every bite.

After Cenchrias removes our empty bowls, Teiresias says, "One day a man called Glaucus came to here, saying he'd asked Queen Jocasta to send him to the furthest pastures. He was on his way, never to return. When a boy, he was a shepherd with a flute. Later he served in King Laius' court, but now he wanted nothing more than to return to the hills.

"Why leave, when Thebes is jubilant, I asked him. He'd made a mistake to return after witnessing something so frightening that he barely escaped with his life. When Glaucus tried to describe that shocking deed, he broke off with a sob. After he recovered, he swore that henceforth he would speak only to his sheep and goats.

"I insisted he tell me and be done. That was his reason for coming here. Reluctantly, Glaucus agreed to pass his burden to me.

"Riding as herald on Laius' royal chariot on their return from Delphi, they encountered a young man on foot at the place where three roads meet. Laius refused to give way, striking him with his whip. The stranger pulled Laius from the chariot, killing him along with the driver who tried to protect him.

"Glaucus rolled into the ditch before the crazed horses broke their traces. From his hiding place he watched the young man shed his madness. He looked so dazed it was clear he'd never before killed.

"After he walked away on unsteady feet, Glaucus buried the bodies. He stayed some weeks at an abandoned shepherds' shelter among the trees, fearing to bring such evil tidings to Sphinx-ridden Thebes. Better to spend the summer living on wild apples and stolen goats' milk.

"When he finally made his way back to the Cadmeia, Glaucus was shaken to see that very young man, more dignified but definitely the murderer, sitting upon the throne beside Queen Jocasta, smiling and full-bellied on his arm. No doubt Oedipus was the better king, and all Thebes celebrated him. But Glaucus could not remain.

"I sat paralyzed. Busy filling Glaucus' bags with provisions, Phrastos overheard little of what he told me.

In his youth, Glaucus watched sheep and goats on high mountains. Except for one strange occurrence, he knew no adventures. He would now return to that quiet life."

I don't know how to respond. Oedipus wouldn't have become king by solving the riddle if Laius had lived. He saved the city but killed the king unknowing. I wondered what Glaucus meant about the one strange occurrence as a shepherd. Teiresias didn't pursue it, so it must not have been significant.

He senses my disquiet. "After Glaucus left, I had an ill feeling. He knew more than he said. My visions had become hazy, and I feared I'd lost my gift. But as Glaucus described Laius' murder, I saw more clearly.

"I don't know how I will tell you the next part of the story, Manto, and my role was small. Often I was a witness, choosing silence or forced into it. I felt cut off from the Great Mother. Jocasta and Halia served as priestesses of Selene and Ida of Aphrodite, all closer to the goddess than I was."

"How much could you be involved, sitting here with Phrastos as newsgatherer and visits from the occasional pilgrim?"

"Oh, I was involved, indeed I was! Oedipus and Jocasta raised four children, sons Polyneices and Eteocles, daughters Ismene and Antigone. For years they lived blissfully in the Cadmeia and Thebes thrived. That could have been that, no Epigoni."

"But they threaten us now, Father. You said they're sons of the seven against Thebes. Did the trouble start with Oedipus' sons? Which one inherited the throne?"

"You jump ahead to Oedipus' death."

"If he and Jocasta lived so happily, what more to say?"

"Oedipus did not have an easy old age. How likely is that for a murderer? Nor was his killing of Laius simply an outburst of anger that left two men dead, as Glaucus reported."

"Was Oedipus a man of rage?"

"No one in Thebes would have said so. He was built like a god, courageous and intelligent, and solved Sphinx' riddle. He ruled judiciously, but—" Teiresias breaks off.

"There was something he didn't know," I say.

"Remember my story of the lovely child Narcissus? He did come to know himself. When he saw his reflection in a clear pond, Narcissus fell in love with the image, embraced it, and drowned. Oedipus didn't know himself either, not the identity of his parents nor who he killed at the crossroads nor who Jocasta was. The force of destiny brought him face to face with the Sphinx."

"Destiny and Fate are as ruthless as the gods."

Teiresias nods. "Oedipus was more virtuous than Laius, abducting Chrysippus against all moral codes and exposing his son because he feared the prophecy that the boy would kill him. Later he lashed out at that son at the crossroads. Much blame to be laid at Laius' feet. But when provoked, Oedipus proved capable of murderous rage. Another sin of the father.

"No one but me heard Glaucus' story, and Oedipus and Jocasta continued to rule in peace and plenty. Thebans saw their king as flawless, and as the royal children grew, Laius' death faded into history.

"Phrastos joined Oedipus' court and brought me his cousin Cenchrias, who's been with me ever since, my helper and friend. When I was summoned to the Cadmeia, Cenchrias guided me."

"You went into the city? Why?"

"My advice was demanded. Royalty do not come to the soothsayer."

Chapter thirty-three: All is Revealed

"Apollo began to plague us with his arrows. First animals started dying, then babies and elders. The blight on the land aroused fears of another curse.

"The old song kept running through my head, 'Sing woe, woe, but may the good prevail.' We must discover the reason for our suffering. I sent word that Oedipus should send Creon to Delphi. Let the Pythia reveal the truth.

"The oracle said Thebes was polluted because the murder of King Laius was never solved. Murder? Oedipus demanded why no effort was made to discover what happened. The answer was simple. After he solved her riddle, the old king was forgotten and his widow Jocasta happy to marry the city's savior.

"The glare of Apollo dazzled my blind eyes. I trembled, feeling as the Pythia must when shaken with divine truth. Now I was summoned to speak what I knew.

"Cenchrias brushed my clothes and led me to the spring to wash. As he walked me to the Cadmeia, a cold wind blew. From their moans I could picture the citizens outside the palace dressed in rags, sick babes in their arms, illness and grief etched on their faces.

"Cenchrias halted when King Oedipus appeared in the palace doorway. The wails and prayers of the crowd silenced at the sound of his voice.

"'Oh my suffering people. You call upon the gods, as so we must. But I shall save you. I, Oedipus who vanquished the Sphinx, shall again be your salvation. We must discover who killed King Laius. Only after that villain is punished will great Apollo lift this plague. I, Oedipus, curse that lawless man and resolve to search him out. Perhaps he is concealed here in Thebes, waiting to strike again, or perhaps he fled to distant mountains. Anyone who offers a clue to the murderer's identity will be richly rewarded and the culprit banished forever from the sight of man. So is my royal decree.'

"Hearing his pronouncement, I stepped back, wishing to disappear. My movement caught the king's eye. 'You there, on the arm of the mute. You are the one I have been waiting for. Come closer.'

"I didn't move, and Cenchrias was deaf to Oedipus' command.

"'You, Teiresias, must help us solve the mystery of the murder of Laius. Tell me what you know.'

"'You do not want to hear.'

"'Don't be insolent. Speak!'

"'All will happen as fated, whether or not I foretell it.'

"When Oedipus repeated his command, I begged him to allow me to return to my cottage. He took my words as defiance and accused me of concealing my knowledge and conspiring against him. We faced each other in the crackling silence, me gripping Cenchrias' arm. This angry man was the tiny prince playing at the seashore with Daphne the day she nearly drowned. His young image superimposed itself upon this livid king. Oh my dear Merope, that your precious son has come to this.

"The more I protested that he didn't want the hear, the more he demanded. What could I tell him? I've spoken of the cloud that sometimes obscures my inner vision. Much worse when it does not. I dared not say what I knew. A cruel ruler applies torture in such a case."

"Did he threaten you?"

"Enough so that I was forced to tell him, first obliquely but then, after he mocked and derided my skills, directly."

Teiresias stops, pain pinching his face. His voice breaks as he repeats what he told Oedipus.

"You are the murderer you seek."

"Father! How could you—" I break off. Glaucus said as much.

"Oedipus called me a detestable traitor for keeping silent and then speaking riddling words. He demanded I return to my hovel out of the sight of man, collecting no reward from Creon or whoever put me up to this. Why was I called wise? I was nothing but a blind old fool.

"After I told him he would wish he suffered my blindness, Oedipus accused me of taunting him. His guards shoved Cenchrias and me out while he shouted 'Be gone forever, you despicable liar.'

"I retorted that his vaunted answer to the Sphinx had saved neither Thebes nor himself, then seized Cenchrias' arm and propelled us out of the palace.

"Near the city gates, Mydon met us and reached for my arm. He must have looked more like a madman than usual, because Cenchrias didn't want to let me go. I assured him it was safe to leave me. When I touched Mydon's hair a shower of leaves fell, but he was the one I wanted to guide me home. Cenchrias had been through enough.

"Somehow Mydon knew what happened at the palace. He settled me and returned to the Cadmeia.

"Through the eternal afternoon, I sat alone waiting, wrapping my cloak tight around me in the unseasonably chill wind, too distraught to drink the warm broth Cenchrias brought me. At last I heard Mydon's returning footsteps and knew. Oedipus solved the mystery.

"Determined to lose no moment in searching, he summoned the shepherd who accompanied Laius the day the king was killed."

"Glaucus," I say.

"Yes, Glaucus. He'd lived as a shepherd since Jocasta sent him out to the mountains. Now in his relentless search for clues, Oedipus summoned him to the palace.

"The question troubling Oedipus was whether one or several men killed Laius, for it was said a band of thieves murdered him. Oedipus became uneasy when he heard Laius was killed at the place where three roads meet. If a band of thieves set upon the royal party, he could forget his fears. Glaucus told him—"

"There was but one," I finish.

"Oedipus forced him to tell the story.

"Through Glaucus' recital, Jocasta held Oedipus' hand. She recalled sending Glaucus out as shepherd in their early days on the throne. Mydon saw she never gave Laius a thought after his death. Her eyes were all for Oedipus, pleading with him to stop his questioning.

"Creon reminded her that the plague would end only after Laius' murder was solved and the killer punished. Even when Glaucus' story proved that Oedipus was the man, Jocasta showed nothing but love for him. Laius had been a poor husband and committed a terrible crime against her motherhood.

"Jocasta protested every step of the investigation, claiming the priest at Delphi misunderstood the words of the Pythia. The prophecies of the Great Mother were the only ones to heed. She seemed almost grateful that Oedipus killed Laius. He was meant to be king of Thebes. His destiny could be fulfilled only if Laius died, as in the old saying, 'The king must die. Long live the king.'

"What Jocasta said next brought a gasp from the court. An oracle warned Laius against fathering children. Once in drunken confusion he bedded her and, fearing the prophecy, exposed the issue of their union to die on barren Cithaeron. Exposing their infant, and here she choked back tears, meant Laius would have no son and heir. The one who solved the Sphinx' riddle was fated to rule Thebes, an exceptional man who would father her children. She leaned over to kiss Oedipus. He must not bring down the curse he unknowingly proclaimed upon his own head. His repentance would save himself as well as Thebes.

"Worse was to come, as I knew all too well. A messenger from Corinth arrived at the palace to tell Oedipus that his father King Polybus was dead. The citizens of Corinth wanted Oedipus to return and rule their city. The messenger added that Polybus would have died peacefully, but he grieved the absence of his son at his bedside.

"Distraught, Oedipus muttered that he stayed away from Corinth for love of his parents. A drunken fool said he was a foundling, not related to Polybus and Merope. When he went to Delphi seeking the truth of his parentage, the Pythia replied only that he would kill his father and couple with his mother. Now, even though Polybus died safe from his hand, Oedipus feared his mother Merope.

"The messenger laughed. He needn't fear. Oedipus possessed no more blood of Polybus and Merope than he did. In his youth, the Corinthian explained, he served as a shepherd wandering with his flocks far from the city. Sometimes he shared distant shelters with shepherds from other kingdoms.

"One day a shepherd of Thebes brought an infant to a shelter, its ankles cruelly pinned together. Glaucus, given the child to expose on Mount Cithaeron, couldn't bring himself to abandon an innocent babe. He asked the Corinthian to take the him to his city where the infant would live safely. So it happened, and the childless king and queen welcomed him as their own."

Teiresias turns to me, his milky eyes glistening.

"Was Oedipus returning from hearing that oracle when he—" I stop, overwhelmed by the horror of fate.

"Yes. When he met Laius at the crossroads."

Neither of us speaks for long minutes.

"Have you guessed what came next?" Teiresias asks quietly.

"I think so, but you must say it."

"When the old Corinthian looked closely at Glaucus, he asked whether he wasn't the very shepherd who gave him the infant. Glaucus protested it was so long ago he couldn't remember, but the Corinthian was certain and reminded him. At that, Glaucus shouted he should never again mention it and tried to leave the room.

"Oedipus signaled his guards to seize him, demanding he tell what he knew. Glaucus kept repeating, 'No matter, no matter,' but Oedipus wouldn't let him be. 'Where did you get that baby?'

"Finally Glaucus whispered, 'From the hands of King Laius.'

"Jocasta cried, 'Oh save us from bright Apollo!' and ran from the room.

"Oedipus grasped the truth. Prince Oedipus of Corinth who struck down King Laius at the crossroads was Laius' son, Prince Oedipus of Thebes. The riddle-solver who married Jocasta was her firstborn, seized from her. His shattering prophecy had come to pass.

"Oedipus cried, 'O Mother, Mother,' and dashed after Jocasta. He found her in their chamber, hanging from the neck by her own veils. He cut her down, grabbed the golden brooches that clasped her gown, and drove them into his eyes.

"Oedipus returned to the throne room, eyes streaming blood. 'When sighted I couldn't see. Blind I see the truth.'

"Creon tried to send him away to be looked after, but he demanded his children be brought to him. Eteocles and Polyneices stood manly and pale as Antigone and Ismene clung to their father weeping. Mydon hoped he would never witness a more grievous moment."

"Was the story over?" I choke out the words.

"Oedipus wanted to suffer the banishment he pronounced on Laius' killer, but Creon ordered him to stay in the palace until the gods' will be known. Oedipus begged to leave, saying he'd been spared for a wondrous fate. Nothing could have sounded more pitiful from the lips of that shamed, blind man.

"Henceforth Oedipus would see as I see, by every means but eyesight. He would live as I live, in the realm of the moon. At that thought I pulled myself to my feet. Jocasta! Mydon said Oedipus cut her down from where she hung. I felt certain she lived. He must discover what happened to her.

"When I said so, Mydon shook his head. How could he pass the guards again on such a dreadful day? I insisted a priest of Dionysus could go anywhere. I lent him my serpent-skirted ring. If Dionysus didn't serve as his guide and protector, the Great Mother would.

"Through the night I prayed. 'So much you teach, O Goddess. You lighten my pain of blindness and grant me wisdom and courage. I beg you to save Jocasta and assuage Oedipus' suffering, O Goddess!' I kept repeating my prayer for the queen and the sufferer who in a single day became the three-legged man of the Sphinx' riddle: the crawling baby with painful ankles in Polybus' court who became the young man of action and power, now the blind one tapping his staff before uncertain steps.

"The only notice I took of time passing that endless night was the progress of moonlight across the sky until Mydon's footsteps sounded. He discovered that a healing woman revived Jocasta, and Halia hid her in a secret refuge.

"Chaos reigned in the palace. Oedipus raged at himself, at the curse on his family and his life, and begged to be cast out or imprisoned. In spite of the people's urging, Creon was reluctant to assume the throne. Polyneices claimed he was old enough to rule, which Eteocles disputed. Oedipus cursed them both for overreaching ambition.

"Jocasta lived, thanks to the goddess' grace," I say. "What about Oedipus and Thebes?"

He sighs. "I can say no more tonight. I must sleep, though my rest, I fear, will be haunted."

My curiosity will not easily be lulled by sleep. How did this drama play out in Thebes subsequent tragic history?

When I say the story is chilling, Teiresias replies, "Then Cenchrias will give you a blanket." We laugh to the point of tears.

Chapter thirty-four: Seven Against Thebes

Next morning we linger over breakfast. The food must sustain us through a difficult day with the sound of galloping getting louder and louder.

After Teiresias tosses away the last peach pit and wipes juice from his beard, he says, "News trickled in. Creon would rule as regent for Eteocles and Polyneices, raising them and their sisters with his children by Eurydice.

"All seemed placid for a while, but the Furies invaded my dreams. Quarrels between the brothers intensified as they grew older. When they came of age, who would be king?

"Creon summoned me to his reception hall. Eteocles demanded sole rule. The best solution, he thought, was for Eteocles and Polyneices to alternate sovereignty year by year, beginning with Eteocles. He called Polyneices a hothead, so for his brother to reign tranquilly, he must leave Thebes immediately."

"That sounds like a terrible idea," I say. "Creon should have summoned you before making that decision. What did you suggest?"

"The most precious possession of the house of Cadmus was Harmonia's necklace. He should give it to Polyneices with sufficient gold to marry and prosper elsewhere."

"Didn't the necklace carry a curse?"

"Yes, but only Harmonia's daughters suffered from it. Polyneices accepted, leaving with a band of warrior companions, the necklace, and a treasure chest.

"Phrastos left with Polyneices' band. I didn't understand why he banished himself, but he was a young man with an adventurous soul and no fondness for Eteocles or Creon. He kissed my cheek and promised to be my eyes in the world.

"I feared for his safe return but kept ill omens to myself. Time passed as I sat with my thoughts.

"One day I heard the steps of a man rapping his cane and the soft voice of a girl, the pair I'd dreamt of. Blind Oedipus and his daughter Antigone.

"When the maiden told him they'd reached the sanctuary of Teiresias, Oedipus cried, 'Teiresias, sage who pronounced my doom!' When last we met, he mocked my blindness. Now he walked on three legs himself, with the aid of a girl.

"Creon had cast him out of the city, cruel timing. Long before Oedipus asked to be allowed to leave, but in his old age he wanted to live out his days in the Cadmeia.

"Before he left Thebes, Jocasta sent him a message begging him to retract his curse on Eteocles and Polyneices. He refused, but at least he knew she was alive.

"With Antigone beside him, Oedipus couldn't dwell on his pain. She said she feared war between her brothers was inevitable and Thebes risked destruction.

"I couldn't assure her otherwise, only that her father's death would be extraordinary and his burial place confer blessing. Oedipus knew that his life would end miraculously. That sounded strange from such a ragged man, but I knew somehow it would come to pass.

"He called Antigone his crown and then paused, sniffing the air. Although he couldn't see my sanctuary, he pictured it in moonlight. Had he been here before?"

I know before Teiresias tells me. "Oedipus was the person who took refuge here in his flight."

"The night he ran from Hecate after he killed Laius at the crossroads, he slept a few hours in this very place. He bathed in our fountain and hastened on to brave the Sphinx. His destiny changed that day, as did mine in the deep woods."

"Twice," I say.

"Even more for Oedipus. From a privileged child to a youth fleeing murders committed in wrath to solving the deadly riddle and winning crown and queen, he now stumbled on foot, a blind old man whose death would bring transcendence. I advised Antigone to trust the serpent way to guide them to the place of blessing.

"As Cenchrias packed food and drink for their journey, I described woodland shrines where they could rest. I bid them farewell with mixed emotions. Oedipus' banishment was pitiful, after all he won and lost, but his daughter loved him dearly and would see him through to his end."

"So you could neither mourn or rejoice. Nor can I. I'm puzzled how to tell this story."

"Yes, it's moved far beyond Teira."

"A story-teller recites their tales and poems," I say, "and lets the audience draw their own conclusions. I only need to remember the stories."

"Like me, Manto, you will puzzle about fate and the ways of the gods. Finding the best words is enough."

He inhales the spicy air. "Ah. One of Cenchrias' tasty soups."

"It can wait," I say. "Do you know what happened to Oedipus and Antigone after they left you?"

"Nearing Athens, Ismene joined them. She and Antigone stopped here on their return to Thebes and described their father's last days.

"Creon and Polyneices knew about the prophecy that the place where Oedipus died would bring victory. Separately they sought him out in the grove of the Furies near Colonus."

"Alecto's sanctuary."

"The very place. First Polyneices came to ask his father's blessing in the coming war. He left with curses ringing in his ears. Antigone felt sorry for him, for all her family was precious to her.

"But when Creon brought armed guards, she was furious. He intended to return Oedipus to Thebes, but not inside the city. If Oedipus died in the battlefield outside the walls, Thebes would defeat her enemies, so there he must breathe his last. Creon went so far as to seize Ismene and Antigone and lay hands on Oedipus himself.

"To their surprise, King Theseus of Athens arrived as Creon was accusing Oedipus of bloodshed and incest. Antigone said her father's response was his shining hour.

"Creon blamed his mother Jocasta as well, but Oedipus said both she and Oedipus were innocent. Their crimes were unintentional. The oracle predicting Laius' death at the hands of his son was uttered before Oedipus was born. Taken from his mother at birth, he found himself in a world of pain that blinded him to the meaning of his involuntary acts. Their crimes were not willful.

"In contrast, Creon's slander was willful blasphemy and seizing the three a violation of the Furies' laws.

"Oedipus was absolutely right. Our fates lie in the hands of the gods. But besides Fate, we have the power of choice.

Oedipus and Jocasta did not knowingly do wrong, whereas Creon chose to berate Oedipus."

"Did Oedipus chose to blind himself? Can we always tell the difference between choice and fate?"

"Now there's a question for a soothsayer," Teiresias replies. "What has Fate in store for us? Can we alter it? The bleakest answer would be we cannot. Not every action is determined by fate, but those that are—" He shrugs and takes a long drink of water before continuing.

"No wonder seers carry a touch of doom. Laius and his descendants thought they could avoid fated consequences. Could they have acted differently? Oedipus would say no. In reply to Creon, he defended himself for killing an aggressive man without investigating who he was, and marrying the queen of Thebes without knowing who she was.

"Our second sight can break our hearts, Manto, but not in the case of Oedipus' end. His death was miraculous as foretold.

"Antigone described the thunder and lightning that signaled death was imminent. Oedipus walked away from her and Ismene with firm steps, saying he was being led by Hermes, escort of the dead, and Persephone, queen of the dead. They wept as he bid them a loving farewell.

"Theseus followed behind. In the silence she heard an otherworldly voice. 'Oedipus, what are we waiting for? We must move on, move on.' The two men disappeared.

"All Antigone could see was the silhouette of Theseus shielding his eyes from a blinding marvel. The Mother in deep Earth took Oedipus unto Herself in a blaze of glory.

"Theseus vowed to Oedipus never to show anyone the place where he died, so he refused his daughters' most fervent wish. But he agreed to send Antigone and Ismene home to Thebes to dissuade their brothers from battling one another, and here they were. Bidding me farewell, they and turned toward the city gates."

We sit in silence until Cenchrias brings bowls of soup and a loaf of bread. He sits beside Teiresias, who sops up his soup with the bread. Caught up in the tale I hadn't noticed my hunger, but the meal is welcome.

When we're pleasantly satisfied, the sun is setting.

"Sometime later," Teiresias says, "I heard Polyneices' troops arrive. A familiar voice called 'Master' in the darkness. Phrastos!

"He was camping nearby with the Argives. Because he served me for years, Phrastos was sent by Polyneices for a prophecy. I embraced him, touching his face with its warrior's beard and asking him about his adventures.

"Leaving Thebes, he accompanied Polyneices' band to Hera's city of Argos. On the steps of King Adrastus' palace, Polyneices was challenged to fight by a strong young man called Tydeus. Because he dreamed of two such outstanding warriors, the king stopped their battle and married each to one of his daughters. There they stayed, two captains of Adrastus' army assembling their troops to attack Thebes.

"Phrastos described their strategy for this attack. Each of seven captains would lead a force against one of the seven gates of Thebes. One Argive captain objected: the warrior seer Amphiaraus. Assigned to lead the attack at the Homoloian Gate, he despaired of an Argive victory. Amphiaraus knew the gods opposed the war and only King Adrastus of the seven commanders would survive.

"Like me, Amphiaraus was granted the gift of prophecy by Zeus. His wife, sister of King Adrastus, tricked him into joining the army, so all he could do was fight with valor, knowing the inevitable outcome.

"I agreed that no good could come it and told Phrastos they still had a chance to avert war. Tydeus should enter Thebes with a small unarmed company to negotiate peace with Eteocles, accompanied by a small unarmed band. Mydon told me Jocasta left her sanctuary to try to make peace. Perhaps such an embassy, in addition to her pleas, would convince Eteocles.

"Phrastos was surprised to hear Jocasta lived. Eteocles had been startled when she appeared like an apparition. She said she'd stayed alive to save him and Polyneices. Eteocles shouted that she must never again mention that hated name. When Jocasta took him in her arms, he held himself rigid, then pushed her away, no longer her son.

"Phrastos agreed to carry my message. Polyneices must send Tydeus into the city to negotiate peace."

"What a sorry situation," I say. "Power felt sweeter than family to those brothers, so they dragged their followers to their deaths as well. But why did Phrastos join Polyneices?"

"For a time, their enterprise seemed an adventure. Before Polyneices sought Adrastus' help, they stopped in Mycenae. How else would Phrastos ever see that famed city? There, King Atreus offered no assistance, suspecting they came from his banished brother Thyestes."

Teiresias shakes his head at the name. "Atreus and Thyestes, another fraternal rivalry with deadly consequences. Others will tell the stories of Mycenae's rulers, Atreus and his son Agamemnon, whose time will extend long beyond ours."

We sip our wine, me reflecting on men and their power struggles. "Let's return to Oedipus."

"I didn't stop the story from forgetfulness or fatigue. I have a vivid memory of Phrastos' account of coming to the Furies' grove outside Colonus and an even more vivid picture in my inner eye. Oedipus' curses followed Polyneices and his army like an icy wind.

"They found a sheltered place to camp not far from the Furies' sanctuary. Phrastos guarded the camp that night, nostalgic for those early days after Oedipus saved Thebes from the Sphinx, when Jocasta was content and the city thrived under their rule.

"Standing sentry, he saw a shaft of silver light break through the dark above the grove. It cracked to the ground, penetrating deep into Earth. The winds stilled, and the air was fragrant with a musky dampness. Phrastos held his breath. Surely a divinity or the Great One Herself was present. He didn't know what happened in that brilliant instant, but it must have been momentous.

"When the relief guard came to take over, Phrastos couldn't speak of what he'd seem, nor did he tell Polyneices, who lay ill from his father's curses."

Teiresias sighs, as if what's coming exhausts him in advance.

"When Tydeus and his unarmed men came to Thebes to sue for peace, Eteocles refused to speak with them. After being ambushed by Thebans outside the city gates, they retrieved their hidden weapons and fought so fiercely that only one of the fifty Theban warriors survived to tell the tale. Eteocles, too stubborn to see this defeat as a warning, proceeded with war preparations.

"Argives, all but Amphiaraus, expected victory. Phrastos told me to listen for the voice of Capaneus attacking the Electran Gate. He would be the loudest, defying not only

Eteocles and his troops but raging at the gods themselves. If Capaneus could breach the gates, bloodthirsty Ares would glut himself on Thebes' blood.

"Phrastos planned to stand by Polyneices in the battle but would not strike a Theban. I couldn't dissuade him. He'd come that far and would see it through. I gave him a farewell kiss and said a prayer for him as he rushed to his fate."

"A war between brothers grants no honor from gods or men," I say.

"So did Jocasta cry, begging them to make peace for her sake. As Oedipus told Polyneices at Colonus before pouring curses on him, Eteocles ought to have summoned his father back to Thebes, canceled the battle, and welcomed Polyneices into the city. Instead, he made his brother a mortal enemy and Oedipus an outcast forever.

"Jocasta valued familial love above all, but when she said so to Eteocles, he spit on the ground and turned his back on her. When Antigone and Ismene returned to Thebes and repeated Jocasta's pleas for peace, they too failed. Eteocles continued assembling his army."

"Thanks to the blessed goddess for daughters," I say—hearing how odd that sounds from the daughter of this man.

"Sadly, daughters and mothers cannot always save the day," Teiresias replies. "Jocasta, Antigone, and Ismene did their best, but they were helpless against fraternal wrath. Polyneices suspected he would die in the effort, for when he saw Antigone at Colonus, he asked her to see to his burial. But he couldn't give up the fight, nor could Eteocles. The outcome was inescapable."

"You tried."

"Yes, that much a seer can do. It was in their nature to refuse to negotiate. Often our fates spring from our characters."

"But the gods involve themselves," I protest.

"That can come from our characters as well. We offend the gods, knowingly or not.

"A spy reported the Argive strategy to Eteocles, so with ceremony he chose the leader to defend each of Thebes' seven gates. The spy described the prowess of the attacking Argive captains, and Eteocles chose a comparable captain to lead each defense. As King Adrastus was the most noble of the adversaries and Creon's son Megareus was Thebes' most royal save Eteocles himself, Megareus would face Adrastus. So were all the rest of the defenders named, inevitably matching Eteocles with Polyneices.

"During the preparations, Mydon gave Cenchrias and me refuge in the woods away from our sanctuary which, so near the Electran Gate, would likely become a battle field.

"From the woodland refuge we heard the wheels of Argive chariots charging toward Thebes. As each captain assaulted his gate, driven back by the Theban defender, I envisioned the battle as if the contenders were athletes competing in deadly Games, falling at each others' hands.

"Above clash of swords and groans of the dying we heard Capaneus taunting Zeus, Ares, and all the gods. The sky echoed with thunder as Zeus struck Capaneus. On the field below, Tydeus lay mortally wounded by Melanippus, who he killed at the same moment.

"A lightening bolt opened the earth for the seer Amphiaraus, sparing him death on the battlefield. Still fighting raged. The brave runner Atalanta would mourn her son Parthenopaeus bleeding his life away, and Hippomedon too lay slain. Of the seven captains of the Argive host, only Adrastus and Polyneices still breathed. Adrastus killed their eldest son, a blow for Creon and Eurydice.

"No more battle cries. Eteocles and Polyneices remained in the field, locked in a duel to death. What Jocasta tried so desperately to prevent came to pass. Brother slew brother, no mercy.

"Jocasta descended to the field, followed by Antigone, imploring her to return to the palace. Tear-blinded, Jocasta embraced her dying sons. 'Most doomed mother am I.' Eteocles looked at her with grieving eyes. With his last breath, Polyneices told her how much he loved her and Thebes and begged to be buried in its soil.

"In despair, Jocasta cried 'Oedipus, 'Oedipus,' as she ran through the field of corpses before Antigone could stop her. From the Sphinx' precipice, she threw herself into the ravine.

"Time stopped, the sun swallowed into blackness. Jocasta's daughters in their earth-stained gowns couldn't cease weeping. The cherished princesses Antigone and Ismene were orphans All could have turned out differently, as Amphiaraus and I tried to tell those bellicose brothers, and as Jocasta cried from her mother's heart."

He exhales a long breath. "I waste my breath talking about what might have happened. Seers must look unflinching at what is."

"I'm not sure I can do that, Father, so opposed to the hopes of the Eleusinian Mysteries. The only mystery about Thebes is why the city couldn't transcend her cursed past. Eleusis has purification rituals."

"Suffering purified Oedipus."

"With Hermes and Persephone escorting him into death, he was purified indeed," I say. "I've never heard of death as a divine transfiguration."

"Nothing was divine about that war nor its aftermath. Nearly a generation later we await the full consequences. The Epigoni are sons of those defeated captains, and this peaceful sanctuary will again be a battlefield."

Chapter thirty-five: Antigone

I inhale the fresh morning air as Cenchrias serves breakfast.

"After the war, we couldn't catch a pure breath," Teiresias says. "Argive bodies lay rotting where they fell, so Cenchrias and I stayed at Mydon's forest retreat. Creon decreed no enemy could be buried. He singled out Polyneices who, Theban born, was a traitor to the city. Eteocles would be given funeral honors and a hero's burial while Polyneices was left to putrefy. Anyone who tried to bury him would die a traitor's death.

"Mydon and I tried to burn offerings to the gods, but the flame wouldn't take. Carrion polluted holy altars. He was on his way to the Cadmeia to warn Creon about this desecration when he heard that Antigone was arrested for scattering dust over Polyneices' body and conducting funeral rites.

"Mydon arrived at the palace in time to hear that, young as she was and Creon's ward since her parents' deaths—and soon to wed his son Haemon—Creon sentenced Antigone to death. He was especially infuriated that a girl dared to break the laws of the state, His laws, His state, in attempting to bury her brother.

"When Mydon protested her sentence, Creon said gods do not condone rebellion. Antigone retorted that death knows no rebels, which further outraged Creon. Not only was she determined to oppose him in everything, but she'd persuaded Haemon to join her.

"Haemon objected. Creon was father and king, but he must listen to voices besides his own before making such an ungodly pronouncement. All Thebes, if they dared, would bless Antigone.

"Creon cut him off. 'Death to the lot of them, Antigone and Ismene and Hae—'

"'No! Do not commit the crime of condemning your son,' Halia cried. 'And spare Antigone and Ismene.'

"Creon barked to the guards, 'Free Ismene and lay no hand on Haemon. But take Antigone to the rocky cavern above the gates, leave food and water sufficient for one night, and seal the opening. Since she so loves the dead, Antigone may join them. Go!'

"Mydon and Halia wailed as the soldiers marched out, half-dragging the girl.

"When he finished telling this grievous story, I dried my eyes, pulled myself to my feet and stamped my staff. Taking Cenchrias' arm, I set off for the palace. No one was about, the entire city behind doors.

"In the palace I didn't mince words. Thebes' high altars were defiled by carrion. The gods of Olympus and the Underworld were repulsed. Antigone was innocent of treachery and Polyneices must be properly buried and all the Argive warriors. If he didn't revoke these impious acts, Creon would bring Oedipus' curse upon himself and his family. Pride was a crime and stubbornness showed stupidity.

"When I charged him with lacking judgement, Creon accused me of taking bribes. Me, bribed? I let the arrows fly. He'd left bodies unburied and unhallowed and was thrusting a living girl into a grave, causing hatred to rise against him on earth and in the heavens. The Furies lay in wait to smite him with the pains he inflicted. Denounced forever, Creon would lose all that was dear to him.

"I walked away from the palace, leaning lightly on Cenchrias as anger pushed us through a city reeking of death.

"That evening Halia brought bitter news. After we left, even the most timid of Creon's advisors joined her chanting, 'Heed wise Teiresias.'

"Creon silenced them. 'I cannot bear to give way, but you force me to. We shall do as the prophet says, bury Polyneices and the Argives and free headstrong Antigone.' He moaned, 'How painful for a king to yield!'

"Thebans dashed into the putrid field to bury Polyneices in a shared tomb with his brother. Argive suppliants built a great pyre for their fallen warriors. Great was the sound of mourning, but there was also a kind of joy for doing right by the dead.

"Creon strode ahead to the living tomb of Antigone. When others caught up, they saw the great rock at the mouth of the cave rolled away and Creon standing in the opening. From within they heard Haemon's cries and were confronted by an abysmal sight.

"Haemon held Antigone's lifeless body in his arms, hanged by a noose she'd made from her veil.

"Crying 'My bride, my bride,' he laid her gently on a rocky ledge. 'Here I wed you.' His dagger was drawn and aimed at his own heart, but when he saw Creon, he charged at him. 'This is the wedding you gave me!' Then, horrified at threatening his father, Haemon fell upon his dagger.

"Creon knelt, trying to staunch the flow of his lifeblood. He lifted Haemon's face to his own, his kiss the final touch Haemon knew. Creon walked from the cave carrying his body. Halia and another priestess carried Antigone, her young face covered, and the crowd followed them into the city.

"Their songs of lamentation reached the palace before they did. The priestess who'd hurried to console Eurydice arrived too late. She had seen the procession, her beloved son in Creon's arms and Antigone behind. Rushing to her chamber, she seized a dagger and plunged it into her heart, cursing Creon with her final breath.

"They laid Eurydice's body on the palace steps beside Haemon and Antigone. No one uttered a sound. Creon fell down before them with his face on the stones."

Teiresias touches my hand. "I'm sorry to tell you such a tragic story, Manto, and to relive it in memory."

"All this began with the oracle to Laius that a son he fathered would kill him."

"Laius' actions, not a random destiny, began that stream of tragic events."

"His abduction of Chrysippus?"

Teiresias gives me a look that from a sighted person would be condescending. "Of course. Deities work in mysterious ways, but they can punish. Hera punished me with blindness."

I'd wondered why his answer to the gods' debate so outraged her, so at last, a chance to ask him.

"Because I sided with Zeus and challenged her. How could the women he abducted have enjoyed his embrace? Hera herself didn't. As I said, I could have been more diplomatic, but even with the gift of second sight, I couldn't see inside Hera's mind and spoke the truth I'd experienced."

Teiresias' eyes glisten with tears. "Antigone entered the realm of the dead with no god showing her a sign that she fulfilled their law. I pray that the Death Mother conducted her to the Elysian Fields with other blessed mortals. The only earthly monument to her sacrifice is the bleeding pomegranate springing from the shared tomb of Eteocles and Polyneices and hers beside them."

I anticipate what he will say when he recovers himself. The cycle of death and destruction hasn't ended.

Chapter thirty-six: The Coming of War

Teiresias doesn't expect an attack today, but I'm not comforted. We can practically hear the army's horses snorting. Cenchrias moves stiffly. He too has had a bad night. We eat breakfast in silence.

A voice calls from the road. "Any food left?"

Cenchrias runs to the man, sunburnt and grizzled but clearly a warrior. As they embrace, Teiresias calls out 'Phrastos! Come, sit with us. Meet my daughter Manto.'"

So this is Phrastos, Teiresias' long-ago guide who left Thebes with Polyneices before the war of the seven captains. At 'daughter' he gives me a curious look. I nod a greeting.

"I can't believe you're here," Teiresias says. "I thought your body was consumed in the burial fire after Polyneices' defeat."

Phrastos tells how he survived and stumbled to a village where a healing woman looked after his wounds.

Teiresias asks why he's returned.

"I came to die. I kept my word and lifted no hand against a Theban. But with Creon's decrees about rebels, I dared not return until I was old."

"Old?" Teiresias laughs. "Look at me!"

"You are ageless, Master."

Teiresias smiles, shaking his head "Tell us how you spent your exile."

"All I could think was to return to the court of Argos, where Adrastus' son Aegialeus was the boy prince and

Polyneices' son Thersander grew. It was a sorry time with, I regret, a sorrier outcome. You know who those boys have become: captains of the Epigoni. They trained with the Mycenaean army, longing to avenge their fathers. The most reckless warrior to join them is Tydeus' son Diomedes."

"We expect them here soon."

"It breaks my heart that Thersander and his cousin Laodamas doomed themselves to their heritage," Phrastos says. "They're all doomed to die. Or almost all. An oracle said if Alkmeon, son of the warrior seer Amphiaraus leads the Argive troops, they'll destroy Thebes. If not?" He shrugs. "I can't join another attack on our city, so here I shall breathe my last."

"That's premature, Phrastos."

"Not if I die defending you."

"Don't. Return to Glisas."

"My mother is dead. My home is here."

"I'm well looked after with Cenchrias and Manto."

"Your eyes are opaque, Master, but you have a radiance about you still. You have been touched by the gods."

"So speaks a loving heart."

"Do suppliants still seek your wisdom?"

"Rarely. Since the death of Antigone, every thinking person can see the truth for themselves. When Creon married her to Death and gentle Haemon with her, prophecies became unnecessary."

"And now?"

"Can you imagine Laodamas summoning me?"

"So you must go to him. It's never too late to try. Don't you agree, Manto?"

I'm surprised Phrastos addresses me. "From what I hear, Laodamas is a rash young man, but perhaps he will welcome the chance to avoid war."

"He will if he assesses the risks," Teiresias says.

"As long as we're alive, isn't there a chance to change outcomes?" Phrastos asks.

"So we hope."

"You must go to the Cadmeia, Master. Tell Laodamas it isn't too late to negotiate peace."

"Tydeus tried that with Eteocles before the last war. I doubt negotiations with Laodamas will be more successful."

"Just try."

"I never expected to enter the gates of Thebes again."

I don't say so, but neither had I. It won't be the city I knew as a girl nor any of its incarnations in Teiresias' story.

"I'll wait here," Phrastos says. "Tell me if you think a returning exile will be safe. Does Thebes have a strong army?"

"Laodamas is raising one. Thersander can rely on the sons of the captains killed in the battle of their fathers to rally. Sons of the Thebans have also grown to manhood, but victors aren't fueled by revenge."

"And Creon will be no help. I hear he's faded into the shadows."

Teiresias nods. "He gave Laodamas no guidance in ruling. Creon's hair turned white after the deaths of Eurydice, Haemon, and Antigone, and his vitality perished with it. Laodamas was an infant when Eteocles died. His mother, too young to be a widow, went her own way. He is proud, ambitious, and aggressive."

This is my first visit to the Cadmeia, looming and irrelevant when I was a girl. Today, no odor of unburied bodies, but still the city emits an unpleasant aroma, like a rich wine gone sour in its golden chalice.

We're promptly received into the central hall. An attendant presents Teiresias to the king, ignoring Cenchrias and me.

Laodamas addresses him without ceremony. "I thought you were a legend, old man."

"I breathe Thebes's air from outside her gates."

"Even there you can savor its freshness, now that I rule."

Teiresias doesn't respond.

Laodamas raises his voice. "I am sole ruler, you old fool! I assemble our troops. We shall easily drive back the Epigone. The brave men of Thebes will defend our city."

"You wish for glory and triumph," Teiresias says. "Can't you enjoy your palace life? Can't you live in the splendor of the fragile poppy that blooms for a day, the smile of your beloved wife? What more dominion do you require than this, warmth and contentment under the bright sun and silvery moon? Though sightless, I thank the Great Mother daily for blessings of love and compassion.

"Make peace with Thersander. Send an embassy to negotiate. Otherwise, the full measure of Fate falls upon you and your city, Laodamas. You can change that if you will, oh mighty king."

Teiresias speaks strong words, but I hear a tremor of hopelessness.

Laodamas sneers. "You live in a myth with your Great Mother. Who is She compared to Ares? An ancient goddess no longer worshiped. Our god is Ares. You rave about poppies, Teiresias. Go back to your poppy fields and sleep your drugged sleep in your Mother's arms. I hear the ringing call to war!"

"I must appeal to your care of your people, King. When the Argives are near, send the women, children, and elders away to safety. An old friend has returned to help with the evacuation. He once served your grandfather Oedipus and is still strong and able. Phrastos and I will arrange transport out of Thebes when necessary."

"Yes, yes, go ahead. Send off all who would interfere with the defenders."

"Please make the proclamation."

"Tell the herald yourself, old man. I have an army to command."

"I see the herald," I whisper in Teiresias' ear.

Laodamas has turned to speak with an armed man, so, without farewells, we tell the herald his order. "Everyone not fighting must prepare to evacuate."

Outside the palace, Teiresias says, "Describe the temples and houses of Thebes on our walk home, Manto. They'll not be here long."

My description feels like a eulogy to the painted columns lining the palace corridor and the wide marble steps that once held the bodies of Antigone, Eurydice, and Haemon. As we descend from the Cadmeia, we pass stone shrines and adorned altars, twining rose vines on the low walls, and courtyards with fragrant herb gardens and woven blankets airing in the sunshine, blankets to soon be packed.

The sentries doze at the Electran Gate, oblivious to our passing.

Teiresias describes our visit to Phrastos, sitting in the pale sunshine.

"I'd rather not go into Laodamas' Thebes," he says. "It's a young man's town, a warrior town."

"You were young at a rare time, when Thebes was filled with lovelight.

"That proved empty."

"No, Phrastos. Our hearts retain our love eternally, like a serpent arcing through our essence."

"You and your snakes, Master. Sometimes you look like one yourself, silvery and supple. Perhaps it's a serpent light I see shining in you."

Teiresias laughs. "Perhaps so, but soon it will consume me. I can hear the warriors' horses champing at the bit. Both sides are prepared. And you have a duty."

"To spy? I know of a hiding place."

"First you must help us to move all to safety."

Phrastos is keen to watch the battle, but we need him, so he consents.

"Cenchrias will pack our food and supplies. Tell Thebans to bring essentials they can carry. All with donkeys and carts should have them ready to go."

Cenchrias looks alert: he's understood.

Mydon joins Phrastos and me to warn Thebans to be ready on the morrow, and word travels fast. On the following day or soon after, the Epigoni will assault the walls with pitch torches. Buildings will blaze, pillars fall, altars be consumed.

Moving through the city we discover that townsfolk have ignored Laodamas' confidence in victory and are prepared to escape. Mothers of boys have made sure of their safety by securing them girls' clothes. I can't imagine the people's final nights in homes they've known and loved for generations. For now, they're focusing on their final preparations, exhilarated. Whatever their thoughts, these hardy folk will eat and sleep as well as they can to ready themselves for an unknown future.

I look around our sanctuary, the comfortable home I'll be leaving. Teiresias' face is serene—because he's finished telling me his story, because he's doing right by Thebes, because he faces death unafraid? Perhaps all.

Chapter Thirty-seven: The Battle

Our dinner is communal, with Mydon, Ida, Halia, and two priestesses of Selene joining us for the huge pot of soup Cenchrias cooked with the remaining garden vegetables, seasoned with bunches of herbs. We sit in a circle, a silent embrace enveloping us.

After the meal, Ida sings a hymn to Aphrodite, linking her to Demeter, Persephone, and Artemis: a chant to the Great Mother and her divine daughters. Phrastos, the priestesses, and Mydon arrange their sleeping mats under the trees.

The ominous clamor of galloping toward us is silenced by the troops proximity. I imagine I hear the warriors' cries to Ares and the wild dancing that will last all night.

Unable to sleep, I go to the fire. Teiresias is sitting upright on his pallet, blind eyes open. He pats the pillow beside him as he has so many times before, and I sit.

"I was imagining Antigone with a crown of stars standing on a silver curve of moon," he says. "Thank you for keeping watch with me. Better to riddle out our lives together than toss sleepless. This war is a foolish waste, revenge enacted by heedless young brutes. Alkmeon, Thersander, Diomedes and the Argives believe they're driven by honor and righteous vengeance, but their attack is no more than a bitter fulfillment of their fathers' and grandfathers' sins."

"Every episode in the fall of the house of Cadmus has been dramatic, Father. I know the history by heart."

"So much tragedy."

"I thought of an addition to my argument. Remember my idea for the beginning?"

"I know it started 'Sing of a complicated being, Muse, one who discovered the realms of the male and the female like no mortal before or since.'"

"Here's the rest. *Sing of a complicated being, Muse, one who who discovered the realms of the male and the female like no mortal before or since, gaining greater knowledge than the gods of Mount Olympus. Tell of the suffering and glory of this rare lifetime and the wisdom gained. Sing of Thebes' doomed house of Cadmus, its triumphs and its anguish.*"

"Yes, you must include Thebes' tragedies."

"I need to ask you, Father. What do your prescient eyes see in my future?"

"You will be blessed."

"As your story-teller?"

"More than a story-teller, Manto. You came here because you sought a fuller path than you found at sacred Eleusis. I gratefully engaged you as listener and recorder of my story, for your second sight enabled you to see into what I described, to feel it yourself.

"I grant you a gift in return. You will save my story from being lost forever, but my gift of prophecy shall be lost unless I pass it to you. You possess more vision than you've employed until now, partly out of respect for me. Now you must assume your full prophetic strength. Look into this fire and silence your mind. Breathe quietly and deeply. Then tell me what you see."

Gazing into the fire isn't calming. Breathing slowly and looking inward, I see warriors rushing toward me, not the walls of Thebes.

"This is frightening!"

"Wait. See what more appears."

The battle rages, and then images become disjointed.

"Calm your heart, Manto. From strife comes a rich destiny."

Is that all he can say? I see a cavern and prophetic rock, such as I imagine at Delphi, and inhale sacred fumes. Out of the smoke a man with loving eyes appears. His regal bearing suggests he's king of a distant land, descended from Crete of our foremothers. I see myself wearing the antique garb of Rhea's little statue, tight bodice and full skirt, tending a shrine near the sea where I'm priestess and story-teller. The image shifts, and I'm wearing a crown in a splendid palace.

When the images fade I ask, "Did you share my vision? Do you know the meaning?"

"Those images portend your future. I understand them better than you do, but will say no more. Your life will unfold as Fate determines. Day to day you will thrive in the joys and sorrows of the moment."

Too vague, but in truth I wouldn't want to know all in advance. I have just one question. "Will I become a mother?"

Teiresias smiles. "You will birth a son, a worthy prince blessed with second sight himself."

I take Teiresias' hand in mine. "You can rest content, knowing your story and your gifts endure beyond your death."

At 'death,' I sit up sharply. "Oh Father. What if I can't be with you in your final moments?"

"That is possible."

"I cannot leave you!"

"We won't waste what time remains to us lamenting. I've more to say."

I wait, still holding his hand.

"Thebes' destruction presages future bloody battles on the plains of Troy before the gods' inciting eyes. Further into the future, I foresee enlightened days of Hellas and a luminous definition of humanity—of thinking *man,* which misses the mark, omitting woman, omitting wholeness. And further yet, to new faiths, a new logic of sacrifice and mercy. The serpent wheel ever turns, human suffering and learning, failures and success, divine powers within and without."

"We two know our lives consist of the shedding of skins," I say. "Serpents run through all: old skins rubbed off and the eternal cycles of the ouroborous."

He pulls his ring from his finger. "This is for you, may it protect and guide you on your own serpent path. I hope to watch you from Hades."

"Your blind eyes see what sighted ones cannot. If anyone can observe us from Hades, it will be you."

We embrace and I stumble to my bed where I reflect on all we spoke of. I want to hold Teiresias until his life departs. Yet my heart fears this is his final blessing.

Early next morning the wagons pulled by donkeys freshly brushed rumble out the gate. Mydon, who left us before dawn, rides beside the driver of the first cart in the procession. We have two wagons between us, one driven by Ida, with Teiresias beside her and Cenchrias and me behind. I expected Phrastos to drive the other carrying Halia and the priestesses of Selene, but he departed in the night to his vantage point. The stronger priestess takes the reins. Behind us stretches an orderly line, moving rapidly.

Only when we are well past Thebes do we stop to breakfast by a spring under trees swaying in the breeze. I recognize the place as one where Historis and I played as girls.

Voices are muted, and we eat lightly while our donkeys graze. How can we feel such equanimity when war drove us from home? Credit goes to Teiresias, who advised Theban refugees to found a new city with no tragic history. We move steadily, stopping now and then for water. No one laments what they left behind. Their silent worry is for the fate of Thebes.

We sleep in a grove and move on next morning. On we go, sleeping in another grove, and by the end of the second day are nearing the spring of Tilphussa.

Phrastos finds us there, and we gather around the fire to hear his account. Faces in the firelight look rapt as he begins speaking. Seeing how they love a story teller encourages me on my own path.

"I hid in a tangle of brush on a high hill as horses thundered from both sides. From Argos rode Thersander and the Epigoni led by Alkmaeon. Confronting them came an advance Theban troop, hoping to head them off outside the gates. They faced each other, both armies confident their invincibility, until they came face to face. Beneath their helmets I sensed their shock. Battle was real; pain and blood and death threatened.

"Shrieking their battle cries, the armies charged. I couldn't blink, watching the Epigoni gallop into the Thebans, scattering them, bringing them down. I kept an eye on Aigialeos, the son of Adrastus, who I'd trained since he was a child wielding a stick spear. King Laodamas swooped in on him, knocking him from his horse, dragging him, spearing him. Aigialeos' blood trailed across the field until the harness broke and his dusty body came to rest. I wept for my sweet Aigialeos.

"Then Alkmeon rushed Laodamas and cut him down with his sword. When the Thebans saw their leader dead, they fled in disarray. The Epigoni built a pyre and burned the dead, their own and Thebans alike, honoring the slain."

At a moan from the listeners, for surely some of their men were among those slain, Phrastos says, "I came to be with you instead of watching to the end, for I know the outcome."

"What do you mean, you know the outcome?" an old woman asks.

"Your city remains safe so long as any of the seven captains who besieged her in the old days still lives. King Adrastus was the sole survivor of that war. When he hears about his son Aigialeos' fate, he will die of grief and Thebes will fall. News of Aigialeos' death will reach Adrastus by dawn."

Chapter Thirty Eight: Seized

Next day we move slowly, our thoughts on the walls of Thebes. I report to Teiresias what I see.

Two eagles fly at each other and strike midair. The imperial Theban eagle fights beak and claw, but the golden Argive eagle deals the killing blow. Its victim falls from the sky, trailing gleaming feathers. "Thebes is burning," I say to Teiresias, and we cover our heads in mourning.

Phrastos drives our wagon. He knows the outcome, and perhaps the donkeys as well, for they plod. Nothing will induce them to move faster. Our procession slows and slows until the sky clouds over and we stop by a running stream to camp and make supper.

Teiresias instructed the refugees to build their city at an auspicious place beyond the spring of Tilphussa, which they will recognize when they see it. Phrastos confers with him apart from the group, making plans. They don't include me and no one needs my help, so I walk along the stream feeling aimless. Perhaps Teiresias will die in my arms at Tilphussa after all.

At supper I dip a piece of bread into the big pot of soup, not bothering to fetch my bowl. My feet twitch restlessly.

"Are you all right?" Phrastos asks.

"Not really."

"Why don't you and Cenchrias go brush the donkeys?"

Cenchrias and I break off pieces of a scruffy bush to use for brushes and set to work, a soothing task for beast and for us.

A cloud of dust rises in the distance, and I hear a sound eerily like the surreal galloping we heard so often in our sanctuary. But these are earthly horses who race toward us, with warriors upon their backs. Cenchrias jumps behind the bush. It's too low to conceal us both, so I remain where I am, the donkeys shying away.

Although they wear no helmets, these horsemen are warriors through and through. Their leader has thick black hair, black eyes, and a fierce expression. His voice as he reins in is loud, but his words are gentle. "Are you the priestess Manto?"

I nod. "Who are you?"

"Sthenelus, son of Capaneus. I've come for you."

Capaneus! I remember that name, the captain attacking Thebes in the earlier war struck down by Zeus for blaspheming the gods.

Their horses are sweaty, and, along with his fellows, Sthenelus dismounts. They take their horses to the stream, leaving him facing me.

"You must go with us."

I stand firmly, arms folded across my chest.

"We mean you no harm, Manto, but you have no choice."

"You seem too civilized to seize me by force." My words are foolish I know. Sthenelus is a victorious Epigoni who left Thebes in ruins and can do exactly as he wishes with me.

"I'll seize you if I must. We are taking you to Delphi as an offering to Apollo. You are to serve as priestess and sybil."

I keep my face immobile though my heart is pounding. "Why?"

"You are my captive. I don't have to tell you anything," he bellows. Then, more softly. "I owe you to the gods to atone for my father's blasphemy."

I start laughing. Cenchrias can't hear me, but he sees my growing hysteria and takes my arm, looking worried. I reassure him, wishing I could explain. The joke is Fate's.

"Stop that right now," Sthenelus commands. "We return the way we came, and you'll soon have a wagon to ride in. For now, you ride behind me."

"Now?"

"Now, woman."

The warriors return from watering their horses. Sthenelus jumps onto his and a companion boosts me up. I turn to Cenchrias in dismay and see the youth's eyes filling with tears.

Teiresias and Phrastos are nowhere in sight, and clutching Sthenelus I cannot cry. The protective skin I developed living in Teiresias' sanctuary is blasted off in the harsh wind. I grip Sthenelus, empty of all but hope.

Epilogue: Manto

I look into the eyes of my son Mopsus, now taller than I.
Since a small child, he exhibited the prescient gifts predicted
by his grandfather Teiresias. Each summer he accompanies
me to our shrine to the Great Mother in Claros overlooking
the Aegean. Born a prince, heir to King Rhacius, Mopsus
prefers our time by the seaside to the rest of the year at our
palace in Halicarnassus. He tells me his visions and listens
with silent attention while I prophesy to pilgrims.

Nothing he's said before matches the vision he just
described.

"Please say it again, Mopsus, slowly and clearly. How
did you know you were envisioning Hades? How did you
recognize the shade who spoke to you as your grandfather?"

"You said Hades is a twilight place where spirits wander,
recalling their lives and curious about their loved ones as
they drift in solitude."

"Yes, so it is for most souls. When Queen Persephone
descends a silvery light shines, opening a richer afterlife for
some."

"This Hades was dusky. No silvery light or Elysian fields.
I recognized the shade as Teiresias because only he, in the
throng of wandering spirits, had bright eyes. He told me that
from that dim place he can behold us in our sunlit world.

"When a mortal named Odysseus came seeking his
advice, he tasted blood order to speak to one from the world
of the living. Ever since Odysseus left Hades, Teiresias'

vision of our realm has been fading. He expects it will soon be gone."

"Who was Odysseus and how dared he visit the Underworld?"

"A warrior in some battle yet to come. Circe told Odysseus to descend to Hades seek Teiresias' advice. For years Odysseus tried to return home after his victorious war over a city called Troy, but his ships were struck again and again by forces of nature and the gods. When he descended to Hades, Grandfather told him how to reach his home safely."

"What a peculiar vision, Mopsus. So far in the future! I must contemplate it. Teiresias said his advice would be sought in Hades, but once he tasted the blood and spoke to a living person, his ability to observe us would weaken."

"Perhaps that explains his sadness when he told me about Odysseus."

I retreat to my private pavilion on the edge of the cliff as I always do for a few days at the end of our time at Claros, deepening my bond to the Great Mother and my inner understandings, so that when I return to the palace, royal duties won't overwhelm my spirit. After a summer of seeing suppliants and daily bathing in the sea, I look forward to this precious time alone. Mopsus' story sends my thoughts in unexpected directions.

Although I developed my second sight in Teiresias' sanctuary, rarely in Claros do I reflect on that time. In Halicarnassus I relive his story as I recite it, episode by episode. Perhaps Teiresias came into Mopsus' dream rather than mine because he's so far from my mind here.

On my second solitary day, I understand how to connect to my father. This time, I shall begin telling the story of

Teiresias' life at the end: how we fled Thebes to escape the battle that left the city in ruins and Teiresias' death at the spring of Tilphussa.

Only one difficulty. I was seized by Sthenelus and the Argives before he and the Theban refugees reached Tilphussa. Alone in this pavilion, I must let the vision of his final day fill me.

Let me experience your death, Teiresias. Grant me the daughter's right of seeing you into the Underworld.

Manto's Tale, as She Recites it in the Royal Palace of Halicarnassus

At the spring of Tilphussa, Cenchrias guided Teiresias to the water and scooped up a cupful for him. A blue and copper-spangled snake dropped from a cypress tree above the spring and landed with a gentle thud beside them. Sensing it, Teiresias held out his arm, and it coiled around his waist like the girdle of Aphrodite that once enmeshed Teira.

There by the willows and rising water, Teiresias danced slowly to the Death Mother, his staff no longer needed. His blind eyes were brilliant as he sang and swayed.

Burning, burning,
we blaze from ashes,
serpent into phoenix.

Turning, turning
 on the bitter wheel

Turning, turning,
man woman
inner outer
all nothing.

I am the serpents mating,
I am man and woman,
mind made holy
in Zeus and Apollo,
body holy
in Aphrodite's service,
daughter of the Serpent Goddess.

I, Teiresias, knew both sides:

I, Teira, knew the love,
the spirit animating all,
god and mortal,
gold and ivory,
musk and roses,
cloud and gushing spring:
the Great Mother,
Essence of soul and spirit,
love and wholeness:
She, our dwelling place
in all generations.

I AM
all
I AM
nothing.
I AM
has no meaning
in the tender air
which breathes me to my last.

Her serpent holds me
Steals my breath.
  Tight
     Tight
        Tight

Release.

In my soul I move with him in his dance, tears flowing. Teiresias' words, his divine possession burns into my heart. I hold his breathless body, the moon rising, its fullness reflected in the pool, shadowing the image, woman holding in her arms a child, a bag of bones, an empty snakeskin, crying farewell, dear Teira, dear Teiresias, as his soul emblazons Hades, an echo through the trees.

Author's Note

The earliest recorded sources for Greek myths are Homer's *Iliad* and *Odyssey,* approximately 8th century BC, and the Homeric hymns and works of Hesiod, slightly later; fifth-century Greek tragedians Aeschylus, Sophocles, and Euripides, and early Roman writers including Ovid, Apollodorus, and Plutarch. Some bring an androcentric or misogynist perspective to the stories.

Myths spring from long oral traditions, so not only are there several versions of many, but hints in archaeology and within the stories themselves suggest earlier Mediterranean antecedents before the pantheon we see in Homer and Hesiod. Robert Graves' *The Greek Myths* offers this analysis, as do books based on the ideas of Erich Neumann's *The Great Mother*, J. J. Bachofen's *Myth, Religion, and Mother Right,* those of Jane Ellen Harrison, Joseph Campbell, Marija Gimbutas, Barbara Walker, Raine Eisler among many others.

For a study of sacred sexual customs in the ancient near East, Cyprus, Greece, and even the Bible, see Merlin Stone's *When God was a Woman*, "The Sacred Sexual Practices.'

In *Serpent Visions,* set in the 13th century BC, the Mycenaean period two generations before the Trojan War, the gods are based on Homer with a strong remnant of Minoan and Great Goddess traditions. This novel imagines a period very different from our own, grounded as it is in Judeo-Christian-Islamic traditions.

Teiresias lives in a period of change. The patriarchal Olympian religion is asserting its power, but Goddess/Mother worship still exists in practice and consciousness. In temples such as the historic one in Corinth and shrines and sanctuaries devoted to goddesses, rituals are based on sex and fertility. Women possess more power as priestesses, healers, and seers than they soon shall have.

Spelling of names is, for the most part, transliterated from the Greek, but when they look particularly unfamiliar, e.g. Oidipous for Oedipus, Korinth for Corinth, Ourania for Urania, I have used the Latinate versions.

Acknowledgements

Many thanks to Catherine Wheale of Cambridge, UK, always my earliest reader. Friends who read pieces of the manuscript over the the years included Erika Lindemann, Diana Sharpe, and Mesa Writers Susan Matsumoto, Betsy Johnson, Sharon Dirlam, Cynthia Martin, Hap Ziegler, Elizabeth Campbell, Donanne Hunter and the late Frederic Hunter.

I'm grateful to the late professors and friends in the Religious Studies and Classics departments at the University of California, Santa Barbara: Richard Comstock, Gerry Larson, Walter Capps, and J.R. Sullivan.

Martha Hoffman offered helpful editorial suggestions on an early draft, and Sandy Starkey and Alyse Steidler read the almost-final version.

Special thanks to Margaret Parakos for a summer writing retreat at the Cyprus College of Art in Lemba village above Paphos, where Aphrodite was born of the seafoam, and to Nikos and Georgia Dimitriou who hosted my retreat in Evia, Greece during a subsequent summer. The atmosphere and archeology in these ancient places enhanced my writing, a fascination begun years before when I spent a year in Cyprus with my family while teaching in Nicosia on a Fulbright grant.

In memory of my mother, Eva Hegglund Webber, literature lover who delighted in the novels of Mary Renault and gave me Edith Hamilton's Mythology when I was a child.